LITTLE MISERIES

ALSO BY KIMBERLY OLSON FAKIH

CHILDREN'S FICTION

High on the Hog
Grandpa Putter & Granny Hoe

CHILDREN'S NONFICTION

Off the Clock: A Lexicon of Time Words

REFERENCE

The Literature of Delight: A Guide to Funny Books for
Kids

LITTLE MISERIES

This is not a story about my childhood

a novel by

KIMBERLY OLSON FAKIH

DELPHINIUM BOOKS

LITTLE MISERIES

Printed in the United States of America

For information, address DELPHINIUM BOOKS, INC.,
16350 Ventura Boulevard, Suite D
PO Box 803
Encino, CA 91436

Library of Congress Cataloguing-in-Publication Data is available on request.
ISBN 978-1-953002-20-4
23 24 25 26 27 LBC 5 4 3 2 1

Jacket and interior design by Colin Dockrill, AIGA

Here's to Iowa, and Minnesota, and Nebraska, and all the well-meaning people who raised us. We love them even as they cast us into the flames.

Contents

The First Horror Story I Ever Heard..........................1

The Castles of Iowa..........................7

How the Grismers Stole Christmas..........................12

Streaking..........................25

It Is Hot..........................30

The Second Horror Story 43

Tackle Box..........................53

Bully in the House..........................89

One Way Home..........................103

The Five Days of Christmas..........................115

Everything You Always Wanted to Know About Sex......139

The Perfect Spread..........................161

Once More to the Lake..........................175

Clippings..........................188

Babysitting..........................202

Bonfire..........................220

THE FIRST HORROR STORY I EVER HEARD

Age: 4

Great-Uncle Thaddeus has a droopy face like a basset hound until he's had enough lightning in him, as he likes to call liquor, and then he'll draw his long chin into a heart-shaped look of mischief, sit up straight in a chair, and drop truths that only the lied-to can appreciate. No child can ignore him.

Uncle Tad is banished by the other relatives to the porch because of his vanilla-scented tobacco. With his pipe, pouch, a silver folding tamp that is as handy as a Swiss Army Knife, and his box of wooden matches, he leans into the white wooden siding and stretches out his long skinny legs in his year-round flannels. We gather closer, and I feel as if I might wet myself, I am so excited. I hook my right thumb firmly behind my front teeth, close my mouth around it, and settle in to listen.

The child's screech got everybody to attention. Rennie, six years old and powered by the force of his own voice and his plump legs moving like pistons, tore into the farmyard and pulled his mother's apron taut, pulled her toward the road with one hand and pointed in the direction of the rail yard with the other.

The 4:20 out of Des Moines had just crossed the horizon, and Clara Castle ticked off the number of children she'd seen in the yard, where the workers were; in God's name what was the roaring in her head—she mentioned it every time she spoke of the accident, in all the years that followed.

It's almost a mile to the rail yard, under rain clouds that are threatening and straight north from the farm, and it almost wasn't going to be a rail yard at all, but for the slaughterhouses that were already there, and the mines that were growing in number and depth, and each one of them offering the blood of any train line, the pure black coal of its heartbeat.

Flew they did, across the road, barely a road, Lord, where was Raleigh, that's who was missing, she hadn't seen Raleigh all morning, that was Clara Castle's last lucid thought as they crossed the stockyards of cattle with the smell of tar and shit and dead things rousing up from the blood-caked soil no longer damp enough to attract even flies, and the sweat streaked down her face, and they, she and Rennie, they come up behind the rail yards and they see Raleigh, and he's sort of stooped over between two trains, but he's standing, and her heart slows a bit, to see him, and know he's still her sun and her moon. The most beautiful boy, just fourteen, and like a god, so strong and so good to his family.

"Ma!" he screams. "Ma, I'm sorry!" She cannot take in what is happening in the gray and fading light. Someone's come up to Raleigh, who is so calm, and still, from the waist down, but his face, that face where she sees her own heart beating, is full of something dreadful.

The doctor has arrived, well, he's the veterinarian, and he says, "Clara, I'm giving him some morphine, for the pain," and she watches as the needle goes into her baby's arm, that sweet supple muscle, so golden from the sunshine that has always poured down on Raleigh.

His pants are soaked with rust, and what is it? What does she see? And Rennie wails with the horror, of seeing two train cars joined, with Raleigh in the middle, the hitch from behind clamped into the hitch in front, through her son's flesh, his ribs, his spine. But he's alive!

She takes it in, while Raleigh babbles about picking up loose coal to bring home, for the fire, just a little extra fuel because everyone is making do, and firewood in Iowa, well, they burn dried cornstalks before they take down wood, which keeps the fierce prairie winds off the crops during the drought.

One train rolled into the other, and Raleigh, right there.

The doctor looks at her with pity, and what the hell is that man doing?

"Save him," she screeches, "pull it out, pull it out!" and she sees that the joined hitches are spattered with blood and bone and skin.

And it's a bolt of understanding and she buries her face in Rennie's little body while it lands on her, that her boy has been half-crushed, and that if the trains are unhitched, just what that means.

She falls to her knees, sobbing, and Raleigh still screaming his apologies for causing her any trouble, and she cannot face it.

Her own mother, Margaret, arrives then, from over Memory Way, the town that was the town before New Market, and Margaret pulls up in a trap and stills the horse, and climbs out into the mud and bloody pool that surrounds Raleigh, and she says, very quietly into the boy's yelps, "Stop."

And Clara stops, too, and so does Rennie.

Margaret, who was five when she helped her father saw the legs off soldiers at Antietam, and who once carried a poxed baby born dead, its mama a Union nurse who wasn't more than Raleigh's age, to a grave for all the smallpox victims and tossed it—tossed the poor thing—in, Margaret is from a century where horrors have been seen and borne and buried. By the thousands.

Raleigh hiccups and goes silent.

Margaret says, "Hank, please do give Raleigh a little more of that," and she points at the syringe, and the doctor does.

Margaret says, "Can someone please go ask the butcher to fry up a chop, and maybe some vegetables and bring them here? Oh, and ask his wife if she's got a nice slab of pie or cake to send along, too, " and a young girl, about ten, stops sobbing and runs in the direction of the main road.

Margaret says, "May we have some laudanum?" and the pharmacist, standing near and knowing no bandage could ever stem that bleeding, dashes back in the direction of home, and his cabinet.

"Whiskey, too," she calls in the direction of his receding form.

Margaret says, "Can someone go down to the Methodist Hall and see if the rector is there? If he's not, check the pool hall. If not there, get the Lutherans."

Margaret says, "Raleigh, my darling. Would you like to try a cigarette?"

Raleigh, who has had many cigarettes behind a neighbor's barn, nods.

Margaret says, "Someone please ring the fire bell to get as many people here as possible who would like to say goodbye to my beloved Raleigh," and a teenage boy who has been picking coal is happy to have a reason to get away.

Clara Castle finds that all her sorrow has been lodged away, for now, and she moves up to her son to cup his cheek.

Margaret says, "Raleigh. Tell me how you are."

Raleigh's arms cover what's left of his torso while he tries to keep his balance. "I'm okay, Grandma," he gasps, out of breath, and the sun breaks through the clouds, shining in otherworldly streaks upon his twisted mass of metal and flesh.

"I believe you are," she says. "I know you will be, you know it, too?" and he agrees.

The food arrives, the whiskey arrives, the choir arrives, the rector, too, and Raleigh? To Raleigh, it's the biggest party he's ever been to, and it's in his honor. If he didn't have two train cars hitched together in his midsection, it would be a pretty good day.

Margaret oversees the scene, and she's the one who sends all the children away when it's time for the train to be unhitched. Using levers and force, and two good horses, the cars are separated. Raleigh's not there when this happens. He has seen the way home, and with Clara's weepy blessing, he goes. Sometimes, a veterinarian is exactly who you want to be in charge when it's time for mercy.

What a row of sorrows, us children, and all of us sobbing, on the porch, facing the fields. Uncle Tad draws off his pipe, his cheeks hollowing and then relaxing as he surveys us through our hiccups and sniffles. In the distance, I hear water running and the chatter of my mother and grandmother and great-grandmother over the clattering of dishes being stacked and washed and dried. If you're of a sort of young and helpless age, the sounds of ordinary things being tended to in a satisfactory way, without fuss or question, can make any bad dream subside a bit.

"Stop your crying," he says to us, lined up like stacked kings on a checkerboard. "There's a lesson in there somewhere. Terrible things happen to good people, and good things happen to awful people, and we shake our heads over both. We're united by this, that we don't understand. It flies in the face of every school lesson we got. If you work, you will succeed. If you practice, you will do well. If you go to church, God will protect you. If you're kind, the kingdom of heaven will be before you, and the angels will open the gates, and all is well."

He stands up and whacks the bowl of his pipe against the porch post. His long legs step easily over us going and coming, and I reach up with both arms. He picks me up as if I'm a sack of potatoes and tucks me in next to him on the bench, next to his tobacco and the tamp.

"It's not like that, though," Uncle Tad says. "I'm not waiting on God, or angels, or my mother or father, the judge and justice of the peace, the police, or the Democrats, or anyone to save me. This is my heaven, right here, with you." He leans over and plants a kiss on the very top of my head and carefully pulls my thumb out of my mouth. "Right here," he says, and taps my nose.

The Castles of Iowa

Age: 11

I am not nauseous. We have just passed through Daven-port, driving home from our annual trip to the summer cabin. I forgot to take Dramamine, and I'm fine. I can sit up and read my books but also watch the trees give way to flat-lands, some hilly farmland, fenced-off forests. I have clari-ty instead of the fog of unwellness or medicine. The fields are golden, heading for September. The roads are dry and empty because we drive home on a weekday. Avoiding traf-fic is one of my father's mantras. In his later years, it will be altered to "avoiding night driving." But he is a young man now, only thirty-nine, and avoiding traffic is a strategy he seems to need to make a ten-hour drive tolerable.

My mother is dozing in the front seat, not needed as navigator, as my father always knows the way home. The way north, re-remembered every year, is straight county roads, to the interstate, dodging construction, then off-the-grid winding dirt roads through the pines to the boxy cabin by the lake. Now my father is making the drive in reverse. Whatever direction we go, though, the scent of new asphalt, pig mucks, and pine trees comes through the open car win-dows as easy as sunlight, laying out faded proof of my fami-ly's former glorious holdings. In Iowa, every cornfield has a line of faded metal Castles Seed signs, which mingle along the Minnesota byways with newer wooden "No Trespassing" notices among the forested patches, warning off hunters.

Grandmother Castle told my mother to call the cabin a compound when she married into the family, even though the rest of the cabins did not belong to our family anymore. One hundred years before, my relatives sold them off to another family, on the way up the economic ladder as our family was sliding down.

My father catches my eye in his rearview mirror and raises both eyebrows.

"You're up?" he asks, and shakes his head, as the answer is obvious. My brother and sister are sleeping, too, so my father's voice is low.

"I feel good," I admit.

"Maybe you grew out of it," he says. "Another sign that you're all getting older."

We pass a field that has already been harvested, with lines of dried stalks like golden stubble after a shave. "Seed corn," he says appreciatively, following my gaze. Windowpane wire fencing, rusty and reddened by the late afternoon sun, is punctuated every tenth of a mile with a tractor-red Castle Seed sign, which says more about how old these fields are than our family's present reach.

He seems nothing but proud of the family past. There is no sign that he feels slighted, or left out, or cheated.

I have my own version of pride. When I was five years old, I took my grandparents to Miss Biddle's kindergarten class for show and tell. The assignment was to bring something I was proud of, and I had them: Two Castles, two Jenkinses, two Kendricks—she used to be a Castle, before she married—and a spare—another Jenkins. These last three were great-grandparents, on my mother's side, and why I thought of them as a personal accomplishment is lost to me. I knew I had great-grandparents when many my age did not.

I did not actually bring them to class. The Kendricks still ran a dairy farm in New Market, Iowa, and the Jenkinses worked at their hardware store. Grandpa Castle worked at the downtown office of his real estate mortgage company, with my father, and his wife had bridge club, which sounded important to me. My presentation therefore was in photographs and words I had written on construction paper. It was my first experience public speaking and it was the one and only time I remember being a show-off and getting praised for it.

"Remember Castle Car Bingo?" my father asks, relaxing into the conversation.

I nod. During long drives to the lake and back, my brother, sister, and I made a hatch mark on paper every time we saw a street sign or seed posting with the Castle name on it. When you hit the fifth one, you drew a line through the marks and started over. We were usually rewarded with ice cream at one of the stops for gas.

"Some stretches all you kids were yelling 'Bingo' every thirty seconds! You drove us crazy, but now I wish you were all little kids again."

"Why?" This is a line of conversation that we never cover. And I am always eager to be older. In kindergarten, I couldn't wait to be in sixth grade. This year I can't wait to be in high school.

My father pauses while he lights a cigarette, a task my mother usually does for him. The county roads are accommodating, all but empty, so he can use one knee to hold the steering wheel while he manages.

"It's all going kind of fast," he says, poking the still-glowing cigarette lighter back into its socket. "I mean, every year we're up at the lake and I get to spend real time with all of you. The rest of the time I'm working with your grandpa to pay for these things."

"I thought you liked work," I say. "I mean, it's your job."

"Kimmy, adults *have to* work," he says. "And my work means talking to people, and I guess I like that."

"What did you want to do when you grew up?"

"A pilot," he says. "I loved planes."

"Wow, really?" I love knowing this about him—and for him to be talking to me. It is a strange and rare experience.

"I couldn't, because of my terrible eyesight," he admits. "*Your* terrible eyesight, too. Sorry about that." My mother stirs in the front seat, then leans her head into the passenger window with a sigh.

He continues. "But Castles go into Castle, my father always said. And it used to be a pretty big company. By the time he took it over, most of it had been sold off after the Depression and the rest was devalued parcels of land. Now he and I work off a different kind of land use. Real estate."

Our last name is so well known across the ninety-nine counties of Iowa that people don't really even notice it anymore. But the fields are only half of it. Even today, I spy Castles on aging water towers, grain silos, street signs, and feed stores.

One of my great-great-grandfathers, made rich when the new railroad purchased all his land around New Market, Iowa, had the foresight to cultivate the Castle seeds, secure ownership of the silos where they were stored, hire the managers to run the silos, and still siphon off enough to sell seed pouches at distant farm stores at a markup. A hundred years later, if farming weren't such a god-awful bust, as my father liked to point out, it would have been a monopoly, but back then it was just a smart piece of horse sense that allowed the Castle name to grow, even after the fields went to seed. Our name is still on grain elevators that are taller than office buildings in downtown Des Moines. The letters spelling our name are two stories tall.

I was about five when I finally heard the word "castle" the right way, meaning a building in a fairy-tale kingdom that had nothing to do with me. That was the day I learned to read, when the letters took shape on the page and I saw for the first time my last name in *all small letters,* and therefore not like the "Castle" I heard whenever anyone read aloud to me.

This unfathomable disorientation followed me around for days, tormenting me like my older brother Paul's tickles.

In a childhood of being bullied, Paul was the first, and Grandmother Castle was the second, and the Castle name itself the third and most enduring. It gave me an insurmountable sense of being apart from everyone else, and a vague feeling of loss. I grew up, then, suffering grief for something that wasn't my fault, which came with all kinds of subtexts and injustices that could not be acknowledged, lest we inflict more pain. I mean, they talked all the time of losing the business, or losing the money. Most of the time, my father and his father told back-slapping stories to each other about what relatives now dead had done. They spoke of a deal as if it were an ancient football game, before their time, when their team lost. But there was some greater loss, too, and I only understood it as rank. We had been mighty. We had fallen. And we all knew, in some way, that there had been others on the land before us.

If no one else notices this, or feels it, there is a very good chance that I have the wrong answers. And there is no one to ask about that. Not even my father, on a day he is feeling a little talkative.

11

How the Grismers Stole Christmas

Age: 8

It's bitterly windy on the front step at the house on the corner of Sixty-Eighth Street and College Avenue, Christmas Eve. The inside of my nose tightens with every cold breath. My father, in his bespoke overcoat and Pendleton wool scarf plumped up in a fat ascot, has rung the doorbell twice, and it's clear that no footsteps are approaching the front door from the inside. I can hear a creepy, Halloween-worthy voice giving a speech of some sort in sarcasm-tinged monotony. The volume of the television is higher than it is at my great-grandmother's nursing home, where all the residents are deaf, dead, or about to be.

Finally, Marvy Grismer, my mother's age but better dressed, opens the door, pressing one finger to her pursed lips and silencing our holiday welcome. She is breathless and glancing over her shoulder nervously, as if she's left something to burn or perhaps a child in danger. She is pulling on the pearls around her throat and not bothering to hide her distress, which is not Des Moines hospitality in 1966, not on Christmas Eve, not on any day.

She is not exclaiming over my mother's new coat, with the festive brooch. She is not slipping icy Coca-Colas into our hands while taking our coats and ushering us into the living room toward piles of her famous green-and-white mint spritz cookies. She leaves us in the hallway (it will be called a foyer in a 1974 real estate ad, when the house goes up for sale) shuffling in our winter boots (Paul) or church shoes (my mother, father, sister Nellie, and me) as we futilely try to not drip melting snow on the marble floor.

Finally, the creepy voice stops talking, and we hear the familiar sounds of an Alka-Seltzer commercial. That's when Mrs. Grismer, instead of helping us with our coats to indicate we're staying, pulls open the pocket doors to the living room, where 364 days of the year plastic covers the furniture and flattens the carpet into plastic runways for our stocking feet. The furniture is covered, still, because it's not yet Christmas Day, but all of it has been rearranged to face the TV console, where the commercial is, miraculously, in color. We had heard of color TVs, somewhere, but it had proved beyond our imaginings, that all those gray tones for the black-and-white set could be translated to the scenes we'd seen in Technicolor movies. Here it is, in a neighbor's house, achingly bright to our wide, adjusting-from-the-dark-hallway eyes.

I've never seen such a beautiful screen, a small painting that moved, with skin tones out of a Crayola box, and clothing in comic strip colors, all accompanied by a fuzzy stereo sound. It's so wonderful that it's unbearable, and I'm not surprised when my sister Nellie's hand slips into my own. She puts her pointer finger on the other hand in her mouth, for comfort. She is only five, but she knows, too, that the night is taking an unexpected turn.

The fizzing of the tablets in a glass, and myriad shades of water, glass, gray, bubbles, are making my legs tingle. My stomach lurches as Mr. Grismer—Kent—welcomes us in, handing everyone mugs of eggnog but never taking his eyes off the screen. He works in advertising, making commercials for the local dairy, Andersen Erickson. To me, he is another man like my father, who goes to an office in a suit. The difference is that he sometimes brings in a crew of people to film us in his backyard, drinking milk. Jumping on their trampoline, then drinking milk. Climbing trees, cue milk. We feel the privilege of being included.

My mother pushes two shopping bags full of gifts—the reason for our visit—toward Mrs. Grismer. "Just dropping these off before church," she says, timid and diminished next to the cherry wood cabinet that houses the television.

"Are we going to see you guys there?" my father asks, gesturing with the glass of eggnog, something like a toast, but aimed toward Amy and Jimmy, sitting cross-legged on the floor, staring raptly at the TV set. She adjusts her dress around her lap to cover her white tights, her eyes never leaving the screen. It reminds me of a fairy's dress, with the crush of light green velvet reflecting light, the seams lined with lace. I'd seen it in the J. C. Penney's catalog. I had stared at that page for hours.

Mr. Grismer shakes his head.

"Promised the kids," he says. "The TV's their present, and this show only airs tonight, you know." My chest constricts, a clench of pain. We'd already missed, I could see by the mantle clock, half of something wonderful. We'd entered their home unaware of any loss, and now I am damaged. All the promise of Christmas Eve is over. That the Grismers are being excused from church *on this night*—this I can hardly take in.

My mother is meekly apologizing to Mrs. Grismer for interrupting their family time. I'm aghast. I want to clutch my throat, which burns with sourness. We are bringing them Christmas presents! How could that be an interruption? Then she repeats my father's question, in her own way.

"Isn't the bell choir performing tonight?"

Mrs. Grismer stares down at the rickrack on her holiday apron, shakes her head once left, once right, tick-tock, no.

This gift run, the one we make every Christmas Eve, first to all our grandparents and other relatives all over Des Moines, where we leave plates of cookies and trails of decorations, always ends at the Grismer home—and then we all go to church together. Then, for we are an orderly family, we will go home to sing a few carols around the piano, open one present each at bedtime, and slip into the twitch-filled sleep of the over-sugared child waiting for Santa Claus.

On this night, everything is altered. The program, starring the green creature with mean, small crooked teeth, the monster-movie narration and a heart to match, resumes after a commercial break, and Marvy, too, watches nervously. She glances once more at my mother, who is automatically shepherding us back through the pocket doors, back to the hallway, out the door, to the car. We leave, into the cold night, gray and white as our TV at home.

This loss is nameless. I want Amy, my age, to giggle with, as we both stare at my older brother and hers from under our eyelashes, fascinated by older boys, older kids. I want my awkward little sister to fall in step with Jimmy Grismer, who is her age and makes her laugh. They always draw on the church bulletin during service, playing grossly exaggerated games of hangman, featuring lolling tongues, bulging eyes, and drops of gray blood, with pledge pencils from the pews. It keeps them quiet.

Instead, my brother climbs into the front seat with my father, which he almost never does. My mother sits between my sister and me, for the long fifteen minutes to church. I am queasy. As a child on ten-hour drives to the lake cabin in northern Minnesota, I down Dramamine with Shasta orange pop, but this is winter. The Viyella dress my mother

15

sewed is tight and itchy against my skin, because my satin slip has ridden up.

I hear my parents not talking. The ride is endless.

"Damn," my father finally says as we glide past the crowded parking lot. "Damn."

"C and E," my brother says, as grave with understanding as he can muster at his age. This is an awful pronouncement of judgment about most of the churchgoers that night. They are the ones, my parents note every holiday and with something I can only call self-satisfaction, who only attend Christmas and Easter services.

My father finally pulls into a spot down the street, and we do not tumble out of the car fighting giggles before entering the narthex. We are sober, careful; our calm is suffocating.

I feel sick in church, with this longing, for wanting something so beyond reason. I don't hear the carols, or love the candlelight, or the reedy old voices rising for hymns. After the service, the sourness rises. I dash outside and vomit into the snow scooped and piled behind the door of the narthex.

"It was the eggnog," my mother says, soothingly, as she holds my fake fur muff out of the way while I wipe my mouth with a Kleenex. She hands me a broken piece of candy cane for my breath. "It wasn't homemade. He got it from his company for free, probably, and the dairy puts in too much sugar and nutmeg."

There is conviction in her voice, and I feel it, too; we would say forever, into all the days of family storytelling in front of us, that I threw up one Christmas Eve from the eggnog from Andersen Erickson. The other truth drifts around the edges of her words, like the scent of White Shoulders laced with Benson & Hedges cigarettes.

When we are home, my mother's cookie plates and the vegetable soup she makes every Christmas fill the house with familiar scents, but I still can't swallow. The present I unwrap is a volume of Nancy Drew, completing my collection. I am listless and, of course, I'd known by feeling the wrapped edges that it was a book before I opened it. My brother and sister are so tightly wound up about the next morning that they go to bed without even being asked, and I get down one of the Childcraft encyclopedias, which always offer a painting, or a how-to, or a fact to comfort me. I browse through it, but the type on the page makes my queasiness worse, so I put it back. I kiss my parents and go to bed, remembering to make my washcloth wet for my mother's inspection when we are asleep.

Sweaty and sad, I am sitting on the bathtub at four thirty Christmas morning, staring at Nancy Drew's titian-colored hair on the cover. This bathroom is just down the hall from where my brother and sister are sleeping, closer to my parents' room. I think I have been quiet, but soon, my mother slips in, pulling a cigarette from the pocket of her bell-shaped housecoat. She also flicks open the slender metal lighter she is never without and takes that first long draw of the cigarette without speaking. The back of her other hand is cool over my hot cheeks.

"It's rough, I know, but you'll feel better in the morning," she says.

Resentment leeches out of me. I want to blame her and my father for useless things—that we have no color TV, that we live near the Grismers, that they have a perfect family and we don't. I cannot speak.

"You will feel better," she repeats. "And you'll be really hungry for sticky rolls." She smiles at me, then catches

17

herself and shakes her head. "Food probably doesn't sound good right now."

"I'm starving," I say, and it's true. I am suddenly so hungry that I could eat toothpaste. She is up and at the door, as if triggered by a gun, and holds out a hand.

"If you promise not to look left nor right when we go down the steps, I can get you a snack," she says. "But if you look, you'll just spoil your own Christmas."

And that's how we leave it. Everything was going to be okay once I started chewing. Lighting up a cigarette and feeding a child—these are the shortest, simplest parenting cure-alls 1966 has to offer.

She is on her third cigarette as I devour a second bowl of cereal, and outside the kitchen window, the sun is casting pink lines across new snow. Overhead, everyone is moving around, getting ready for the annual staircase photograph my father insists on snapping before the unwrapping frenzy begins. The moment is passing, this moment with my mother. She feels it, too.

"They're not happy," she says with finality. And I know this is going to be something about being adults, something that they usually keep from us, but which trickles out every now and then. With so many missing pieces and holes in adult behavior about to be revealed, I feel my bladder tingle with excitement.

"Marvy's making do with that battered station wagon while he gets a new car every spring," she says in a low voice. "The color television—for the kids, he says!—is his idea of making up for how late he stays at the office."

"Like Dad?" I whisper, worried that this was going to be about us, about our family, which has no stories like my classmates'—no missing parents, or second mothers, no nodded understandings about a drunk husband.

"No, no." She smiles. "Not like your dad. He really is at the office, with Grandpa. Mr. Grismer is late at the office in a different way—you'll understand someday."

She stubs the cigarette out in the ashtray and gives me another slow smile. I hear my little sister on the stairs, my father's step. We stand up. I don't mind waiting for someday. Today, we are leaving the kitchen together. My mother lifts one hand to push her hair into place, and I do, too. She follows me down the hall, and we sigh with some kind of contentment about all the things we don't have.

By Christmas night, the Windsor Heights neighborhood where we live starts to glow. Every single house except ours is adorned with necklaces and bracelets of sparkling lights in every color, lining snowy shoveled sidewalks and turning even humble mailboxes into miniature lighthouses for cars turning into invisible winter driveways.

Except at our house. My parents insist that one candle— plastic, taped to the inside sill of every street-facing window, with a white glass "flame"—is more in keeping with the authentic colonial stylings of our home. Last year, I figured out that in something called the "olden days" there wasn't electricity, so they probably used lighted candles, and therefore we weren't that authentic after all.

Moreover, I had learned not to offer my opinion about such things.

At three o'clock, after our cousins and relatives joined us in the annual ritual of eating ourselves into a stupor at midday when we were already full of Christmas cookies and barely recovered from breakfast, my father watches them leave for their next stops, and then turns to us.

"Annual drive!" he says delightedly. A hundred years later, I would know that his enthusiasm was the dinner wine talking. My father wants to take us on a drive out to the country, to see all the Castle family's former glories. I want to curl up with another new book from my gifts, in a new nightgown also from that pile. Instead, I change out of company clothes from Christmas dinner and find my snow boots.

"Move over," Nellie says in the car, bashing my hip with a G.I. Joe she'd received that morning. I scoot myself into the corner behind the driver's side while my mother takes a seat on the other side of Nellie.

"Annual Christmas tour," my father says happily, pulling his great coat in before closing the door. Paul slides into the front passenger seat.

"Annual tour," my mother repeats, her voice muffled from burrowing into Nellie's small form for warmth. "Coldy," she adds. "I wish we were staying home."

"Coldy," I say, "And I agree with staying home." Then I smash into Nellie with a little more force than is necessary. Nellie resists, at first, but then grudgingly snuggles into my mother.

The tour always starts beyond the city limits, to show us a small farmhouse at the end of a quiet lane. It is about a half-hour from our home. "In thirty minutes, an empire rises and falls," my father says. My father *always* says.

To find the first location, he has to drive over a couple of county roads and then turn down a hidden driveway. The snow is mottled from the muddy splashes of passing cars at fairly high speeds. Against the pinkish gray skies of the low sun of Christmas Day, the old Castle farm is just a foundation and some leaning farm buildings, a small barn, and a propped-up last wall of the house, clinging to a brick chimney, or maybe supported by it.

"This is where your great-great-great-grandfather started out, selling seed to his neighbors from the barn," my father says. We know. We all know.

My father is already backing down the path, his right arm across the passenger seat as he cranes his neck to see out the back window, planning his entry back on to the busy road. We hunch down in our seats so he can see over us.

I do not understand his pride. It isn't a farm, but a cemetery with no headstones. Just the grave of the house.

As we drive back in the direction of home, past silvery grain elevators in low moonlight, the countryside of paced but lonely light posts and shadowy telephone wires gradually gives way to straight line suburbia, familiar Des Moines neighborhoods, where the annual tributes to electricity are on display in what I know is the wealthy neighborhood. My dad turns into the enclave of stately homes, planted on hilly ovals of land, so that as the car rounds each turn, a house rises out of the darkness, glimmering with light. Everyone in our family car knows these turns better than we know our own bedrooms.

"Castle Circle," my father says. "Your great-great-grandpa built it, your great-grandpa lived here, your grandpa grew up here, and I played here as a boy." He pulls the car to a full stop before the long driveway on grounds that are enchantment from a story. Small lanterns burn in two straight lines to guide drivers up the hill, while a three-story home with a mansard roof is precisely outlined in thousands of white fairy lights. In the past I felt some sort of vague pride or sense of importance for being connected in any way to this mansion, but this year I feel a longing I don't understand. I want to run up that driveway and sail through the front door to take my place at the family dinner table. But strangers live there now.

My father is smiling as he turns the car back on. For the first time, I wonder why he isn't sobbing. How did our family own that home, and now we do not? Christmas has a crick in it, another broken thing, or at least a dent I don't know what to do with.

Within a few more minutes, we pull into our own driveway. I ignore the cozy chaos of the family room on Christmas night, with all our opened presents still stacked around the room. In the morning, I'll be charged with vacuuming and Nellie with putting all the presents upstairs in our rooms.

Now I change into my new nightgown, and sit down on my bed, piled with pillows I use for reading time. I crack open a book from my father's younger sister, Susie. She always gives me books I haven't read, or even heard of. Last year it was ghost stories by Saki. This year it's something called *The Hobbit*.

My mother knocks softly on the door frame.

She is carrying a wrapped gift.

"What's that?" I ask. I put the book to one side.

"I always find one," she says, with a pursed, lopsided smile. "Something I've hidden and forgotten to put under the tree!" She adds, "It's not a big deal. You were mooning over it in the catalog."

I am excited. The dress like Amy's, in that beautiful mint green.

I could still wear mine for New Year's Eve. We always dress up and go to a restaurant early in the evening, and then stop off at a bookstore.

When I rip off the wrapping paper, though, and open the box, it is not the mint green dress. It is a dark navy color, so dark that I can't make out the princess lines or the pretty gathers on the puffed sleeves, or the dropped waistline that I hoped would look nice on me.

"Thank you," I say carefully. "Were they out of the other color?" I pick at the tag. A small packet with two extra buttons is attached to it.

"Kim," my mother says, sitting down next to me on my bed. "Kimmy, this color is more flattering. And it goes so well with your hair—it's just beautiful with it!"

"More flattering, how?" I ask, although I already know the answer.

"Well, I was worried," she replies. "I just don't think the light green one would be comfortable for you."

I stay silent.

She is rushing over her words. "See, this blue works for church all winter long, and that light green, well, I was afraid it would make you look larger. Dark colors have a way of slenderizing the shape," my mother says. "We girls have to worry about that." She giggled a little, hoping I would join in.

"Mom," I say. "Am I pretty?"

"No, not in the way people mean it on TV. You're *striking*." She's staring at me anxiously.

I didn't have a word in me. Not one word.

"Honey," my mother's voice quavers. "You're what people think of as *cute*. For heaven's sake, what do you want me to say?" Into my silence she puts more explanations. "I want to be honest with you. That's better, isn't it? Honesty? And it's not *me*. It's just how other people think."

I have heard enough. I put the dress on the bed. My mother looks perplexed, and this infuriates me even more. But I know she is right. When people hurl names at me at school, I don't argue. Let them say I am fat. I am bossy. I am a know-it-all. But they aren't my mother.

In the longest silence of my childhood so far, I can almost hear my mother mentally paging through Dr. Spock or whatever expert she's read, looking for the correct thing to say in this moment. She wants me to know what she knows.

But by telling me these things, she is taking the side of all the people who have called me names. I'm supposed to understand them. Instead of saying they are cruel, or wrong, or even just stupid, she's saying this: *They have a point.*

"Kimberly Castle, there are conventions in the world that we all have to abide by," she finally says. There is irritation in her voice, and Christmas, for me, is over. "*I* don't decide what's pretty," she says. "Just remember that." She stands up, exasperated, and leaves me there.

I feel all the losses of the day, then, from what the Castles had years before, and what the Grismers have now, and how my beautiful mother, faced with my questions, has no way to comfort me, and maybe never had.

STREAKING

Age: 9

It is Nellie's war cry that gets our attention before we see that she is naked and running across the just-mowed lawns of the joined backyards, heading right for my mother. She has one hand high in the air as she runs, like the torch bearer in the Olympics, but instead of trailing smoke, her yellow sunsuit flaps behind her.

"Mommmmmmmmmmmm!" she yells, long legs covering the ground so fast we can only stare. As she falls into my mother's arms, I see tears. "I can't get it back on. I tried! I can't get it on."

My mother stubs out her cigarette with her one free hand while Nellie curls herself into her other arm. Paul and I exchange astonished looks from our separate perches, me by the pretzel bowl and him next to Mr. Sorenson, a car magazine between them on the redwood picnic bench they share. No one is looking at Nellie, but it's more like everyone is *not* looking at Nellie.

I want to run away. I only ever see her that way when we take baths, but seeing her outside, in the open, with all the neighbors around, is like watching someone get shot on TV. When I look away, that doesn't move the death one inch. Now, in a setting that is as familiar to me as our own backyard, Nellie is a stranger to me. I am mad at her for putting so much awkwardness on us. It's an intrusion, and more than just her nakedness. It feels like my job to fix it, but I am shut down. My feet are glued to the patio.

We are at the neighbors' patios as often as we are at home. The LaPrads have the best swing set, and a clothesline we can spin. The Sorensons have a tether ball, and smacking it high and away from my brother and sister is one of the few athletic moves I have. "Kimmy's clumsy" is the rumor. "She's just not the athletic sort."

Grandpa and Grandma Jenkins have closed the hardware store for the long weekend, and instead of going to the Kendrick farm, where Grandma's parents live, the Kendricks have come into town and are staying at our house. Sitting in the lawn furniture at the Sorenson patio, they look as out of place as scarecrows at the supper table. Great-Grandma Kendrick without her chickens, compost pile, or kitchen is like an untethered balloon. Great-Grandpa is worse—he's so fidgety that he's accepted a cigarette from my dad, and I've never seen him smoke.

While Nellie holds on to my mother's shoulder for balance, my mother gathers the sunsuit, and helps Nellie step into it, one foot at a time.

"Why did you take it off?" she asks.

"I had to pee," Nellie says, staring at the ground. My mother hoists up the suit over Nellie's stomach. "It got bunchy," she adds, then puts her pointer finger into her mouth like a pacifier and leans into my mother. She hasn't done that in a long time.

My mother smiles at her, so calmly, as she pulls the spaghetti straps out of the stretchy bodice and then turns Nellie a bit to tie them behind her neck in a simple bow. My Grandma Jenkins, right next to her in a lawn chair, pats Nellie on the shoulder, and the rest of the adults on the Sorenson patio unfreeze. While they sip their drinks, Mr. Sorenson demonstrates their new awning, which rolls up and out of the way with a touch of an electric button.

26

"You sure can run," Mr. Sorenson says to Nellie then. I look at his face, trying to measure his meaning, but it seems like a flat-out compliment.

"It's called 'streaking,'" my brother says helpfully. "When someone runs nude." His ears turn bright red when he hears the word "nude" come off his lips, so he picks up the auto magazine, peering more closely at the pages.

"Anyone need another little splash?" Mrs. Sorenson asks, her white-blond hair slicked back in a tight ponytail. She has strong tan arms from gardening, and carries a tray of empty beer cans back through the sliding doors to their patio.

"I'll help you with that, Celia," my mother says, standing up, and in two quick moves consolidating the cigarette ashes from separate ashtrays into one overflowing bowl. She cups a hand over it, against the breeze. Nellie follows them into the house, and I slip into the vacant chair next to Grandma Jenkins.

She pats my leg and gives me a sip of her iced tea. I only ever see her drink on special occasions, like Christmas, when she lets herself have an old-fashioned or a gin and tonic in a glass more ice than liquor—"Light, Milt," she cautions. The iced tea she usually drinks is lemony enough to make my lips pucker.

We have a lot of cousins, because between them, my father and mother have four siblings and they all have children. We have a large backyard beyond a patio, where we have outdoor birthday parties. And our yard, at the lower end of a hill of all the backyards, like the bottom middle square on a tic-tac-toe board, is a gathering place for neighborhood children who can see from their windows when we're outside.

When it snows, though, it is not a steep hill compared to the one behind the Smith home across the street. Our hill is where small children sled, starting up at the Hansen house and ending down in our yard. In the winter, we flood the backyard for a skating rink. In the summer, we climb up trees, roll down the grassy hill, and play hide-and-seek till long after dark. Most of our lives take place in the backyards.

Whenever anyone arrives out front, we hear the crunch and crackle of scattered gravel under the tires, and then the dull thud of the underside of the car scraping at the sudden upward slant of our steep driveway. It requires, my father says constantly, with his hands replacing both car and driveway for a visual, a careful approach at an angle instead of a sharp turn, and a slow speed to give the car a chance to level off. And in fact, anyone who rides a bike knows that. You never approach our driveway head on at high speed or you'll spin out.

Given the number of relatives and friends in my parents' circle and given the number of birthday parties and other celebrations that make our house a year-round meeting place, relatives who have turned into our drive hundreds of times comment at their own inability to navigate the incline. They always come into the house exclaiming in wonder that they never adjust to the driveway's angle.

Now Grandpa Jenkins comes around back from the direction of our front yard, toward the Sorensons' patio already grumbling.

"I just checked under my car, Milt," he says. He's already been in our house; he has a beer in his hand in one of our foam holders. "Fix your goddamned driveway. I can sue you for damages for all the dings it's left me with."

"Frank," my dad replies, grinning broadly, "why don't you do that?"

Grandpa Jenkins stares at me intently, and I scuttle out of the chair next to his wife. We have no spoken agreement about this, but we all do our best to keep him from yelling. He nods, his mouth set in a frown, and settles in the chair by Grandma Jenkins, still grunting.

While my mother uses the terms "Mom" and "Dad" interchangeably no matter which set of parents she's talking to, my father doesn't. He calls her parents Frank and Phyllis. It seems to give him distance from her parents, treating all gruff comments from Grandpa Jenkins as suggestions and mostly ignoring him. Grandpa Jenkins always seems upset when he can't boss my father into a decision. My mother caves at the first sign of his growl.

I rail, quietly, that we are supposed to accommodate this irrationally angry old man. I like being considered polite, but it's hard not to talk back, when he's the one who needs to be corrected, not us.

But the words never come, and I accept it as my duty to help keep the peace.

I do not question why Nellie's sunsuit, which she has been wearing all summer long, is so hard for her to manage today.

It Is Hot

Age: 9

It is hot. Nellie is chatting with my mother by the dishwasher. It's some elaborate story about a new treehouse she is building with her best friend, Stevie Canine. They sit in his treehouse and draw up plans for an extension. They have raided all the garages for lumber and ropes.

I tune her out and fan myself with a limp cloth napkin. The morning newspaper is still splayed across the table. My mother reads the front page and the sports page, with a cigarette and her second cup of coffee, in the bathroom off the hallway, after the breakfast dishes are done. My father reads the front pages, and the financials. He takes the *Wall Street Journal* with him to work, but the *Des Moines Register* usually only merits a quick look-through, and he barely sniffs at the sports pages before he scoots away from the table.

By the time I get to the kitchen, he has been gone for hours and the paper is all mine. The headline is about politics, which is boring. Sweat drips off the tip of my nose, and on to the comics page of the newspaper.

It is hot. My mother is loading the dishwasher on the other side of the pass-through counter, and as she dips up and down, she looks like the colorful glass birds found in gas station souvenir shops off the interstate when we drive to Minnesota every summer. She tips lower and lower as she adjusts dishes and then abruptly, as if she's had her fill, stands up and presses at her lower back.

She is muttering as she works, which is normal. It is very meta-muttering, about muttering, and how no one helps, but if I offer to do so, she will tensely turn me down.

It is so fucking hot. A boy on the playground, a sixth grader, used this sentence on the last day of school. It made my heart pound when I heard it. I've been looking for a way to use it ever since, and this is the right moment. I wish I dared say it out loud.

My father had gotten up early, far earlier than usual, and called the air-conditioning company, and then dressed for the office in his summer-weight wool suit, a crisp pink shirt with collar stays and French cuffs, and highly polished black wingtips with spaghetti laces. He had brushed his wavy red hair back with two hairbrushes and would not look at himself all day, but he would return home looking as neat and tidy and untouched by the heat as he had at dawn.

About the compressor. It is in the attic above my bedroom, and it runs so silently that only a whisper of cool air coming out of floor vents indicates it is on. I never think about the air-conditioning, which so permeates every corner of our home that there is a thick wool afghan on the couch in the family room, and we sleep cozily under sheets and light cotton blankets all summer long. I never hear the compressor, which stopped in the middle of the night without a protest, but the ceasing of slight breezes made the house quieter than usual, and the temperature in my room went up, degree by degree, until I finally kicked the covers to the bottom of the bed.

It was already morning twilight when I opened the windows, which whooshed as they swung out, as if the vacuum on the room had been broken. The only advantage of allowing heavy moist air in was that it felt fresh and brought with it the first stirrings of birdsong. It didn't last long. A

31

few minutes later, and as was his habit on mornings when we didn't have school, my father opened the door to check on me, spotted the windows, and quickly, efficiently, closed them.

"We'll get the repair guy here before the house can heat up," he'd said, seeing I was awake. "The house will stay cooler if we keep everything closed." He'd given me a cheerful wave, a chin-up wave. "Grandpa and Grandma Jenkins are coming over for dinner, don't forget." Then he was gone. That was two hours ago.

Jesus. It is hot. Except for the bathrooms, the kitchen, and the center hall foyer, the floors are all carpeted in nylon and wool blends. The tufts feel sticky underfoot as I pad down the hall into the family room, leaving my mother's bad temper behind. She opened all the windows in the house as soon as my father's car was out of the driveway. Even if the repairman comes, my mother will leave the air conditioner off until an hour before my father is due home.

"Your mother is an orchid," my father likes to say, smiling at her fondly. "The hotter and more humid, the better she likes it."

"And you're a polar bear," my mother answers without humor, accusing as she dons sweaters in July, waiting for October's frosty nights to force him to turn on the heat.

"A polar bear," my father repeats happily, turning the thermostat to 65 degrees on days in January, and to 58 degrees overnight.

I take after him. I long for January. The material of the couch is too warm to my hot legs, so I pull the wooden desk chair around to face the television. The remote is not on the opening in the bookshelf where the television rests, and it is not on the coffee table next to my father's chair—the only two legal spots where the remote is allowed to be parked. I find it tucked into the drawer next to the couch, "closer to the majority of viewers," my mother always says, attempting fairness and neutrality on the subject but implying that my dad is a dictator, hogging the remote.

I skip the remote, listless, twisting the dial, leaving the volume on low as snippets of the broadcast from the only channels cycle by.

"We'll have more on that at noon..."

"They're certainly headed for the courts, Roy."

"Weather at the top of the hour."

"Doctor, you can't be the only one who has noticed the cells are dying!"

Sweat trickles down my back. The television is emitting more heat. I turn it off.

In the kitchen my mother's irritation toward Nellie is ramping up. "Must you prattle on so? Don't you have anything you can do?" Nellie, baby of the family and unaccustomed to criticism, goes quiet and leaves the kitchen to race upstairs to her room. She'll pout behind a closed door for an hour and then forget the comment. I do not understand her ability to pretend certain things have not happened, certain words have not been uttered. I never forget anything like that. I am storing them up, one injustice after another, in a pile of jottings like kindling in campfire.

Last year I had been the one following my mother around, pelting her with one story after another about school, or friends, or enemies, or knowing the difference. One evening, after we had just finished dinner, I was helping clear the dishes.

My father had already left the table and gone around the corner, to the family room. My mother usually loved this half-hour at the table with us, after dinner, before cleaning up.

"You miss all the good stuff," she'd said to my father when he excused himself. But his ritual was to leave the table to us. Except to refill his scotch glass and rustle around in a kitchen cupboard for crackers, he would not stir from the family room till late evening, and sometimes slept in his chair until past midnight.

Paul and Nellie were still at the table, squabbling over the sizes of their respective pieces of chocolate cake, and I could tell from my mother's heavy sighs and long looks in their direction that this time, she was waiting for us to finish the desserts so she could load the dishwasher and start the cycle.

But it was during the school year, and I was telling a story, an important story, about two boys at school and how one of them was doing his science project on Alpha Centauri, and how I'd been the first person to bring up Alpha Centauri and he'd stolen my idea completely. And I wanted to tell my mother alone. I started loading the dishwasher, which brought my mother over, as I knew it would, to correct how I was doing it. My brother and sister scattered. If one of us was working, the others could get pulled in. They knew it. And that had been my plan.

That night, I knew my mother was hitting her most irritated zone, because the usual store of expected responses—"Yes, honey, then what?" and "I know dear, but she is your teacher"—had steadily turned into half-grunts and distracted murmurs of disapproval.

I rushed through the last sentences of the story, sensing the storm was imminent, until my mother whirled around to face me and said angrily, "I hope someday when you have your hands full and a thousand things to do, some little girl follows you around chattering constantly! Then you'll know how it feels."

I didn't miss a beat. She said this to me frequently. But this time it made me mad.

"Me, too! I hope I do! In fact, I can't wait!" I ran out of the kitchen and to the staircase, up to my room, not bothering to slam the door. I could not. My father, who had designed the house and contracted the builders to do the work, had installed slow-closing hydraulic hinges on doors that would never swing shut on an unsuspecting child. Slamming those doors, in other words, was impossible.

I waited a few moments in the middle of my room and, noting that no one had followed me at all, took a minute to be mad, and then quietly opened the bottom desk drawer, where I kept my notebook of broken things.

There were plenty of ordinary entries: "pencil sharpener in family room," "window in garden shed," and "last year's jeans." There were many ways a thing could qualify as broken, and I was keenly aware of them all, including the dream of going to the Olympics ("I should just face it," I'd thought. "I'm too lazy."), my crush on David Traxler ("He walks on his toes."), and my quest to be the best speller in class (Lisa Shimp could hear a word such as "osteoporosis" for the very first time and take it apart in a way that made my legs weak.).

I'd included a mention of Great-Aunt Katherine's breasts, which apparently were not only broken, but gone, because I'd found plastic replacement bosoms cradled in a polished wooden box on the back of the toilet when I had stayed there overnight.

The notebook had started as strictly a list, where I recorded things exactly as they happened, but I had opinions about most things, and so I recorded those, too. I hated Grandpa Jenkins because he insisted on kissing the grandchildren on the lips even when they tried to squirm away.

He yelled on every holiday on which there were televised football games and family dinners.

The most recent entry was, "My mother's maternal attitude." Today, I scribble, "air conditioner." Behind that page is a clipping of a news article—a photograph of the ten class pictures of nurses, captioned with their names and ages. They looked like a row of babysitters. They had been held hostage in a boarding house in Chicago and killed.

In the book of broken things, I never leave updates. It's just a list, no matter what happens. The air conditioner will get fixed. My mother's attitude? Maybe not. These nurses? There is no fixing that. I keep the clipping, but I hadn't added them to the list.

Now, watching my mother's small frame stretching to put away breakfast dishes in the overhead cabinets, I feel sorry for her. They are built high to suit my father's specifications, but too tall for everyone else.

The book of broken things is getting bigger. It will have to include my sister's hurt feelings, my father's cheerful obliviousness to just about everything in the house except the appliances, and my mother's grievances. The notebook, begun out of spite and whimsy, is swelling into a litany of a broken world.

"I'll be upstairs if the repairman comes," my mother says, passing back through the dining area to the center hall. "Come get me, or just show him the ladder to the attic."

"Upstairs" means my mother is going to stretch out on her side of the bed and smoke cigarettes until lunchtime, watching whatever channel the television is on and not really seeing it. She does this in summer and on school days, whether the house is hot or cold, whether anyone is home or not.

I don't know why she does this, or why our house is so spotlessly clean when my mother, other than dishes and cooking, never seems to do anything. From an early age, though, I grasped the need to sit still and let time run on alone. On my birthday, my mother gave me a bright yellow poster showing a child's drawing of a red, ladder-back chair. The caption on the poster said, SOMETIMES I SITS AND THINKS, AND SOMETIMES I JUST SITS.

We had laughed about it when I opened it up, and I was relieved about that laugh, as if my mother did understand me after all.

The doorbell chimes in the center hall while I am standing there. I open the door pieced together from massive panels of oak, painted on the inside and out a simple eggshell white. "Doors should only be one color, on both sides," my father had proclaimed as they scoured the paint shelves and rows of paint chips, seeking the perfect shade.

The door swings open. "Ay-Cee," the repairman bleats, and I figure out his mission from there. Years of training make me point mutely to the doormat and stand back as he wipes his feet and shuffles past. His freckled scalp is sweating through wet, wispy curls of strawberry blond hair, and his dark long-sleeved uniform shows damp continents across his back. "Compressor?" he asks, looking up the steps, and I nod.

"You didn't really let him come in the *front*," my mother says from the top of the stairs. "Really, you know we only use the *side* door." By side door, she means the small space that joins the garage to the main house, off our mud room, and not the formal front door the repairman had used.

My mother can sometimes sound as if we live on some estate where everyone else is staff. Her parents own a hardware store. I think she's learned this tone from my father's mother. Grandmother Castle was born poor, married into the Castle family, and worked her way up to being a full-time snob. Labels are her life, my mother says, without an ounce of awareness that she has adopted some of Grandmother Castle's ways.

Repairmen and the cleaning ladies are never allowed to come through the front door when anyone else in the family answers the doorbell. I don't think it's fair to have different doors for different people. I don't know why I feel this way, except that when Dr. Martin Luther King was on the television, I thought of him as a person who wouldn't approve of two entrances. And because my parents call him the last decent and honest person in America, I want to be someone Dr. King likes.

Now she stares at the repairman, who is busy with his tool belt and doesn't meet her gaze. "This way," she says, sounding more like a stranger with every word. "Thank you, Kim."

It's still so very hot. My thighs are sticking together and my shorts are wrinkling like accordion folds up my crotch. It's impossible to be graceful and sweaty at the same time. I hear my mother talking to the repairman, and their voices fade as he climbs into the attic. I follow the sound of my mother's tread on the hallway carpet back to my parents' bedroom.

How can she lie down with a total stranger in the house? I have read enough of the newspaper daily to glimpse some of the horrors in the world, and one of the lessons from every story, from every news clipping and every ghost story, is to remain vigilant around strangers. Perhaps repairmen are exempt from worrying over. Perhaps if you know the company name, or if there is a patch on the uniform, the repairman is no longer a stranger.

Nellie comes quietly downstairs, then pushes past me impatiently and heads for the family room. I follow her to the television set, which she turns on, rotating the dial three times before it registers with us both that the pictures on all three channels were exactly the same! This has never happened.

We go from channel to channel to channel, and giggle together, hearing a sentence begun on one channel parsed out, at various volumes, over three channels. "Convene," then "the Democratic" and finally, "delegates," before they started over, "to nominate" "our party's" "presidential candidate."

It becomes a game then, to race through the channels fast enough to make the sentence almost flow perfectly, with no pause but a slight gushing click between each phrase. I take my turn, churning out three chunky sentences, before I realize that even though I am clicking the dial around, the television is no longer responding.

It's staying on the same channel, and Nellie stops mid-laugh and stares in horror at the screen. I tug at the dial, just a little, and it comes off easily in my hand. I drop it.

I am dizzy, the idea is so big. The television is such a gigantic item, immutable and omnipresent, that the idea that we can do anything to affect it is unfathomable. It is as if the entire house is broken, and I am the culprit. No one broke the compressor. No one stopped the air conditioner from working.

I broke the TV. I broke the television set, the central player in family evenings together. I gulp air, just gulp it, then look at Nellie.

She is torn between relief that *she* has not broken the television and some deep, terrible compassion for me. She pushes red curls off her sweaty face, and mouths the only word we are both thinking: "Dad."

I try out my voice. "Dad."

Nellie repeats it, slightly louder. She has always been inflicted with empathy for others that often cripples her with dread for the other person. She weeps whenever my brother or I are punished, sweeps up whenever anyone breaks something, cowers in a corner crying if someone else is being bullied.

"Dad," I whisper, picking up the dial, and peering at the back of it. I push it back onto the headless stick right above the "Loudness" dial. The channel dial spins without impediment all the way around. I twist the volume down, until we can't hear the program, then twist further, until the television clicks off.

"Kim," my sister says in a very low voice. "Is it all right?"

"I don't think so," I answer. "I think I'm gonna get it."

Gonna get it. There are no worse words you could string together in our universe. "You're in for it," is enough to make a neighborhood bully back up. "Gonna get it" makes him run home.

"Oh! Oh, no!" cries Nellie. "Oh, no! No!"

"I know. I have to think." In the notebook, I will write, "I broke the TV. Tomorrow, I am breaking the moon." I try to think of all the fixes I have witnessed over my lifetime. None of them have ended well for me.

"Wood glue," I say to Nellie. "Or Elmer's. Do you know where Mom keeps them?"

Nellie flushes with happiness at finding herself included in my plan of action, which sounds practical.

"In the messy drawer," she says, darting away and then back, breathless that we are fixing this, with the glue and with toothpicks, for dabbing glue into the stripped threads of the television knob.

We are silent as I work. Perspiration is dripping off me, but I keep the knob dry, and we hardly breathe as I push it back in place on the television. No glue oozes out and I allow myself a smile.

Nellie purses her lips and squints to read the tiny type on the back of the glue bottle. "We should give it an hour or so."

I am ready for this. "We are going to watch television until it dries," I tell her. "Anyone who comes in, we'll explain that all three channels are showing the same thing."

"I think we should leave," Nellie says. "I don't want to be here at all."

"We have to be here."

"I don't want to watch it," Nellie insists.

The repairman shuffles down the wooden hallway toward the family room. "I'm gonna need a part back at the shop," he says.

I'm the kid, don't talk to me! "My mother's upstairs, " I say quickly. But as the repairman turns back toward the stairway, I nip past him.

"*Stay there!*" I hiss at Nellie over my shoulder.

Taking the steps two at a time made my sticky thighs fiery. "Mom!" I say.

My mother raises herself up on one elbow and runs her fingers through her short-cropped hair. Her face is embossed with blanket lines.

"He wants to talk to you," I tell her, pointing at the repairman, who has arrived after me and stays outside the bedroom door. It is making me queasy, seeing a man near my mother and father's blue-and-white bedroom, and I don't know why. I need Dramamine. I wipe sweat from my upper lip, and shift on one foot.

"It's okay, honey," my mother says. She stands up and brushes off her shorts, puts her palm to the damp, unruly curls at her nape, and goes to meet him.

My mother murmurs something to the repairman, and he ducks his head. Then they go down the steps, and I am so tired.

Downstairs, I hear the drone of the television set, and know Nellie is standing guard. There will be a spanking, later today or whenever the wood glue fails, and who really knows when that will be?

THE SECOND HORROR STORY

Age: 9

Not for the first time, my grandfather calls Nellie over to the door of the basement, saying, "To the workshop, toots?" It's such a privilege, to go downstairs in their new, ranch-style house and see Grandpa Jenkins's collection of tools, many of which he'd acquired when they bought that old hardware store—the kinds with nuts and bolts and two-penny nails in bins for the scooping. He and my grandmother run it six days a week, but it's closed on Sundays.

The workbench is right by the washer and dryer, where I have helped my grandmother with laundry. But my younger sister is the only one my grandfather affords this honor.

"Such a tomboy," all my aunts say affectionately, as if Nellie has been cast for the part. We all have our roles.

I am the overweight middle child, my brother is the doted-on only son, my father is the tailored breadwinner, and my mother feeds us and keeps us clean. She is cheerful but sleepy in the mornings, watching us while she sips her coffee and smokes a morning cigarette, the only time we ever see her without lipstick, and with messy hair. At night, she is always dressed up, for things like Tri-T, bridge club, church, and evenings out with my father. She is easier to hug in the mornings. She is easier to love. Once they are dressed, they are untouchable.

We all used to be cheerful in the morning. But ever since Nellie started first grade, she's been grumpy and quiet. She hates to be teased, and hardly eats, even when my mother makes waffles and pancakes on weekdays.

Bookish and often declared a know-it-all, I have mastered a few facts. One, my older brother is the only grandson, as well as the oldest grandchild, and that is supposed to explain the lavish presents he receives and any special invitations he gets. He never gets into trouble for tickling me till I cannot breathe, till I am gasping and want to die.

When I had half-days for kindergarten, he was the one tasked with bringing me home, where he would have lunch before returning to second grade alone.

One day, we raced home, and I was winning.

He lunged for my legs at the last minute, and I fell. My head hit the corner of the concrete steps, and blood was everywhere. When the doctor stitching me up asked me how it happened, all my mother would say was, "It was an accident."

Another piece of casting, which I accept, is that my younger sister, with her fiery red hair curled into springy ringlets, her pretty freckles-on-ivory complexion and deep-set, velvet brown eyes, is the beloved baby of the family, and always an object of attention, at church, at supper meetings, at school events, and even among the relatives. Thus, she is everyone's darling, and Grandpa's favorite.

My mother, in anticipation of Sunday school and before she goes out with my father, spends most Saturday nights forming those ringlets in my sister's hair, with a wide-tooth comb and a jar of Dippity-Do, while my naturally active sister squirms and yelps over tangles. The next day, though, the blue-haired church organist and the minister will be charmed all over again by the sight of her, and while she pulls angrily at itchy lace collars and has lost too many white gloves, I suspect she likes the attention.

Even though Grandpa Jenkins is my least favorite grandparent, I envy Nellie's status as the chosen one. I am never invited, not once. I am disgruntled, too, that Nellie doesn't seem to appreciate her status, and takes her time joining him at the basement door. She usually skips everywhere but walks toward the basement door with small, shuffling steps. The door closes, and the thunk-thunk of their footsteps fades as they go downstairs.

The reason I know Grandpa Jenkins is my least favorite grandparent is that my other grandparents have been asking us for years to rank them by who we like best. Paul and I have compared conversations, and they have asked both of us separately.

For me, it's simple. I love Grandpa Castle because he is kind, but boring. I love Grandma Jenkins because she is even kinder and bakes pineapple cookies and has never criticized any of us. I *like* Grandma Castle because she has powders and makeup and jewels and clothes and handbags, and she takes me shopping.

She is also the one who puts me on diets she's heard about and wants to try herself. When our parents go out of town, she and Grandpa Castle stay with us—the Jenkinses have the hardware store to run—she brings chocolates for Paul, and slaps my hand if I reach for one. She instructs me constantly, and when I complain to my parents, they exchange looks and laugh.

"Two peas in a pod!" they say.

Grandpa Jenkins, unlike Grandpa Castle, insists on sloppy, long kisses on the lips for hellos and good-byes, and my protests to my mother about this also have been dismissed.

"He's old. He loves you."

I don't care. I always try to be in the car by the time everyone else says farewell. When I ask her why he yells all the time, my mother reminds me that he was supposedly beaten when he was a child by his mother.

His mother. That's Great-Grandma Jenkins, and she is the Scariest Old Woman Ever, living in The Scariest Nursing Home. My mother dutifully takes us to visit her around her birthday and holidays, and we walk through dim, dark hallways that smell of rubbing alcohol and vinegar and pee. The halls are a parking lot for beds, and bed pans, as well as abandoned wheelchairs, which are ten times sadder when no one is in them.

In Great-Grandma Jenkins's room, it smells of menthol and dead roses, but the light streams in the window, alive with dust motes. Usually my mother sits down in the only chair, and Nellie leans into her, watching. I sink down to my knees next to them.

The old lady's earlobes are enormous, long and flapping, and I notice this because she is the only person I have ever known to have pierced ears. A hoop no larger than a baby's pinky fingernail is in each ear, and I stare and stare, trying to figure out if it hurt, if they get tangled in her gray-streaked black hair.

Everything my mother asks has to be repeated three or four times. Every answer my great-grandmother gives is shouted, and garbled, and confused. My mother is trying to be nice, and thanking us for our understanding with her eyes, and I feel sorry for her. Maybe, I think, if this terrible old woman was my mother, I'd be unhappy, too.

But I still run away from Grandpa Jenkins's kisses. Staring at the closed door leading to the basement, I'm trying not to think about my sister's privilege. I am at the dining room table getting ready to fold gum wrappers with my aunt, Sherry, who is the youngest of my mother's four sisters and is still in high school. She only buys Wrigley's gum, so the wrappers are green, yellow, or white. She saves them for when I come over, for something to do after Sunday dinner.

She has a technique for folding the gum wrappers that turns them into stiff paper links. One by one, we feed them into a long chain she's already saved, a flat rope of interlocked chevrons that she rolls up in a ball. It's almost as large as a basketball. We want it to be so big, we can stand next to it. And of course, we chew gum while we work. Every wrapper helps.

Before we start, though, she sets my hair like her own. She wraps pieces of my wavy hair tightly around orange juice cans she has saved and washed after cutting off both ends and smoothing the jagged edges down with a nail file. She uses long bobby pins to secure the hair, then sprays my whole head with setting lotion. When it dries, my hair will be stick straight like Amy Grismer's. We sit there together, working, with the giant rollers pinned to our heads.

The basement door opens and Nellie slips out, closing it quietly behind her.

"You okay?" Sherry asks, and Nellie looks down and smooths her crinkly Sunday dress several times. She doesn't answer but walks over to the dining room table.

"Do you want to help?" I say, trying to see Nellie's eyes, fringed with copper-colored eyelashes. She shakes her head, but pokes at the neat stacks of wrappers with her finger, the ones we haven't folded yet.

"Don't," I say, a little too sharply. She looks up at me, and a tear like a tiny drop of dew pushes over her lower lashes and falls down her cheek. "What a baby!" I add, but Sherry reaches out her arms.

"Come here, Nellie, to my side. I'll show you what we're doing." Nellie stands next to my aunt, but keeps pressing her dress down.

I feel the need to be forgiven. I am anxious for Nellie and me to be okay again. But it doesn't happen. She folds the gum wrappers carefully, using her fingernails to make the creases crisp, like Sherry shows her. I bite my nails, and so my pieces aren't as perfect. But when we are done, the rope of new wrappers is as tall as I am, and Sherry adds it to her ball.

Sherry takes out her rollers, and uses a comb to frizz her hair into a big puff, which she pins into a beehive shape. My Grandma Jenkins, baking pineapple drop cookies that have maraschino cherry frosting slicked across them when they are cool, looks on with a "tsk, tsk, tsk."

"What are you tisking?" I ask.

"Oh, don't mind her," Sherry says, staring into a small mirror. She applies a little frosty pink lipstick from a tube that was in one of her pockets and she looks just like the cover of *Young Miss*, a magazine that comes to the mailbox in her own name. Sherry gives me her copies when she's done. Now she takes out my rollers, too, and I don't want it combed. I like how straight and long it is. I carefully tuck it behind my ear and it stays. I've seen Amy do this when she's reading, to get her hair off her face. It's so shiny and different than my waves, which will return before morning.

"You girls don't need makeup," Grandma Jenkins says. "And Sherry, I think that's the fourth time this week you've seen Gary." Gary is Sherry's boyfriend.

"I like it," I say to Grandma. "She looks pretty." Grandma hands me a cookie, and Sherry takes one from the plate, too, but my sister is too busy stacking the orange juice cans like blocks.

"You grow up fast enough," Grandma says. "I was too young when I got married. You don't have to do that. We have women's lib now, and you can work instead of getting married."

Sherry winks at me. "Women's lib! What if Dad heard you! And you are married but you work at the hardware store."

"I do," Grandma says. "But that's more like working for the family. Like helping out my parents at the farm. I was a very good typist, top of my class at Katherine Gibbs," she adds. "I thought I'd move to the city."

"Mom!" Sherry says. "You mean like running away from the farm?"

"No," she says, sitting down next to us, pressing on cookie crumbs on the plate with her pointer finger, and bringing them up to her tongue. I could eat all the cookies myself, they are so good.

"My parents knew they were selling the dairy side of the business in the next ten years or so, and just keeping a small plot to farm. They didn't want to tie me to that if I didn't want to live there."

This is changing almost everything I know about Grandma Jenkins. I thought she married Grandpa Jenkins to get away from the farm. Now it looks as if she was completely capable of moving away herself.

I glance up at Sherry and tell her what I thought. She gives a little laugh. "Kimmy, didn't you know? She loooooooooved him."

Grandma ducks her head, but I have already seen her blush.

"Grandma, really?" It is so hard to picture Grandpa Jenkins as a young suitor, although I have seen pictures of Grandma as a girl, and she looked just like my mother.

"I did," she says, with a little roughness in her voice. "I really did. Almost every big happiness I've ever known has happened because of your grandpa—marrying him, my four girls, you grandchildren."

To me, he is an overweight bald man with a fringe of gray hair that sometimes looks dyed yellow in the light. His juicy kisses, his shushing of us, his big lounging chair, his loud bark, and his relentless interest in football, all contribute to my liking him the least.

That he was somehow considered lovable, ever, shocks me. It must show on my face because my grandmother starts to explain.

"He was a hard worker," she says first, and then looks down at her simple flat wedding band. "He had a gorgeous car, which he paid for from all the jobs he took while the rest of us were in high school. There was no shame in dropping out; back then, everyone needed money for their family or to help on the farm. And once he had that car, he was something."

Sherry puts down the compact mirror. "Hot shot?" she asks, and it sounds a little mean, you know, considering we are talking about her father.

"Well, I don't know about that," Grandma says, "but he pulled up next to me outside of school, pointed at the passenger seat, and said, 'What about it, dollface?' just like that, and that was it—I was off!"

She stands up and takes the empty plate with her. I cannot even come close to imagining the scene. It is like a radio show, where everything has to stay in your head, but you don't really know how anyone is dressed, or what the setting is. So far all I could imagine was a really old car, like a Model T, and two teenagers who looked like comic book characters, Archie and Veronica, in really old-fashioned clothing, holding their schoolbooks.

Sherry snorts. "Well, I'm sorry, Mom, but I just don't see it." I laugh, and then stop, because Sherry is serious. "I can't wait to be out of here."

"I know." Grandma looks at Sherry, who always says this. She and Gary want to get married after high school, but everyone says they are too young. Grandpa Jenkins says this the loudest.

Grandma is silent for a bit, then turns on the water and starts to swirl soap around in the bowl still streaked with pinkish icing. I can tell from the set of her lips she is distracted.

"No, I don't know," she finally admits. "We have had some pretty terrible times," she says and pauses. "I should not be saying this. Awful." She sighs.

Turning off the water, she comes back over to the table. And in that moment, she isn't a grandmother, or a mother, or even an old woman. I suck in air, knowing something important was going to be announced. From someone I love, down to my toes, my favorite grandparent.

She dries her hands on the dishtowel tucked into her apron. "I play this game in my head," she says. "I think of the worst day of my life, the very worst. No—" She holds up her hand to Sherry. "I'm not going tell you what the worst day was. I think of it, and when I try to trade it away, it's like a fairy tale, right? Or a genie's wish? I get to skip the worst day ever, a day I wanted to die.

"But the trade is, the only trade I can think of that's fair is if I have to give up one of the best days of my life. Just one! Only one of the best days, and there were a few."

Grandma sits down next to me and plays with my long, newly-straight hair as she draws in a long, big breath. Then she smiles so sadly, my eyes start to tingle with tears. "I can't give up one. I'm that selfish."

"But, Mom, for real," Sherry says. "How did you get past the worst day? I mean, what did you do?"

Grandma reaches out her towel-dried hand, and takes Sherry's hand in her own. "He promised me it would never happen again," she replies. "And I believed him."

I am smiling at her when she says this, because her face has cleared up. And I turn to Nellie, to see if she is happier, too. A tear drops straight out of her eye on to her hand, in her lap. I can hear it hit, it is that big. Sherry pushes away from the table, clearing away extra gum wrappers and the chain we made. For her, the conversation is over, but it feels unfinished to me.

Nellie and I sit quietly in the back seat during the drive home. My brother is reading a motorcycle magazine my grandfather gave to him, and now Paul thinks he's a teenager. He's twelve. Nellie and I can usually crack each other up, either playing "I Spy" or just making stupid jokes, but after Grandma's words, she has not said a thing.

In desperation, I say, "Can we play Barbies when we get home?" and she looks at me with such shining eyes and surprise that I feel keenly I am the worst sister ever for not offering more often.

"Can we really?" she whispers, and I nod with relief at her simple happiness.

When we get home, I pull the Barbie case off the high shelf next to my books. For my birthday, my cousins gave me a new evening gown for Barbie and a tweed suit, as if Barbie is going to a meeting. Playing Barbies with my sister is fun, because she looks to me for plots and storylines, and will go along with anything. She is obedient to the point that if we are playing Wizard of Oz with the large family who lives next door, the LaPrads, she will happily take on the role of Toto to my Dorothy.

That night, my mother runs the bathwater and adds Mr. Bubble so that my sister and I can take a bath together. I'm starting to feel as if the tub is too small for both of us. But I tuck my hair up into a shower cap, and we climb out of our clothes and underwear, and play in the bubbles and make foam beards and mustaches and bras for our nonexistent breasts. Sunday night means *Bonanza* is on television, so I finish first and almost step on our dirty clothes getting out of the tub.

"Mom!" I yell, picking up my sister's panties. "Mom," I say again, and I open the door.

"What is it, what's wrong?" she says, rushing to the bathroom from my parents' room down the hall.

I hold up Nellie's underwear. There are streaks of bright blood across the light cotton weave.

Nellie looks down at herself with curiosity and moves away the bubbles.

"Nellie, are you okay?" my mom asks. Nellie nods. She puts her hands behind her on the bottom of the tub, and raises up her core like a little bridge to show us her vagina.

"See?" she says, walking like a crab the length of the tub. She makes us both laugh, and my mother catches my eyes.

"I'll call the doctor tomorrow and see what he says," she tells me.

In the morning, she has already phoned Dr. Hess by the time I get home for lunch.

"He says it's normal for girls to do damage down there when they are roughhousing. Like when you land too hard on your brother's bike," she says, "or go horseback riding."

My mother is cutting sandwiches, smoking a cigarette, and glancing at a recipe next to her shopping list. "But Nellie has her own bike—a girl's bike," I say. "And we don't go horseback riding." I can feel myself annoying my mother, as I do to my whole family with my constant comments and questions.

"Mom?" I say.

"Kimmy, stop," my mother says wearily. "Dr. Hess says it's completely normal for some of the delicate skin to tear a little with tomboys. It happens all the time."

I smile at her and accept her word. *It happens all the time.* As I sit down at the kitchen table to wait for my sandwich, I put away my worries about Nellie's tears and am reassured. This will not be one of my worst days.

TACKLE BOX

Age: 10

The morning we drive to the lake is like Christmas for me. I have hardly slept, packing and repacking the books I want and a blank notebook I can use for writing letters, pulling out one more sweater against the cold northern nights, putting it back. I'd gone to sleep listening to the sounds of my parents loading the car, in angry whispers, below my bedroom and out the garage door. Very late, I'd heard the sound of my father backing his car out of the driveway on some errand. Earlier in the day it was for inner tube patches and glue from the hardware store but this late at night it would be to the 24-hour convenience store a mile away for one last carton of cigarettes, or two.

Running out of cigarettes or liquor is something I've yet to witness. My parents take care to stock up on those. Whether we run out of Flintstone vitamins is beyond comment, but allowing the cupboard where the cigarettes are kept to drop below a certain level always makes their conversations low and fast—something about what she has not taken care of, or her tight-lipped anger that yet another thing is on her list.

My father tips his head into the bedroom.

"Already up, honey?" he says in a gravelly whisper. I am fully dressed, sitting on top of my bed, which I've already made. I'd recently learned the word "rhetorical."

My sister, however, is still sighing deeply with sleep. With his finger, as if stabbing at hot coffee, he jabs the air to signal that I should wake her up. Then he disappears. He has lists of lists to make sure everything will be in the car, and I will soon hear more of my mother's "Yes, Milt," and "No, Milt," to his every query.

On lake mornings, when we leave in the middle of the night, we are allowed to keep our pajamas on in the car. When I wake her, Nellie clambers out of bed, slips on her robe and slippers, and heads down to the kitchen. I am right behind her on the steps, wrapping the book I was reading into my windbreaker. I grab one of the miniature boxes of cereal my mother has set out on the counter, then go out the side door.

Above the outline of trees and houses, the sky on all sides of the driveway is a navy turning pink as my parents finish loading the station wagon. From the back seat, I feel the tension in my father's every grunt and move, as he tightens the ropes holding the car-top carrier, takes one more load of groceries out of my mother's hands, double-checks the glovebox.

They have tucked Nellie in the cargo area with blankets and she's back to sleep. My brother flips through a car magazine next to me in the passenger seat, ignoring my father and mother completely. I have taken Dramamine for motion sickness. We are hardly out of the driveway when the sounds of the car begin to blur. In a drowsy, half-listening state, I hear one of my parents push in the car lighter just below the radio, and wait for its click back that it is "ready," then I smell the first woodsy puff of my father's cigarette. We back down our steep driveway, and make a scraping noise as the bottom of the loaded cargo compartment hits the pavement.

Truncated conversation between my parents comes through as a dream.

"Is the map...?"

"Handy. I have it. We take this to the interstate," my mother says.

"Did you pack—?" asks my father.

"Right here," my mother replies, and pours a splash of something into his coffee mug. I am accustomed to the smell of scotch at all hours of the day, even before sunlight as my father drives north toward the lake, and to our first stop, pancakes 150 miles away at eight o'clock. I think nothing of that scent. I like it.

My father and mother talk in low voices while, next to me, my brother wakes up my sister to devil her, oh, about a large reddish birthmark on her neck, her short curly hair, her boyishness, her sleepiness in the mornings. His teasing is 99 percent good-natured, but that last percent, that was downright mean. Was he teased, too? That's the excuse they all use for Grandpa Jenkins's bullying, but I never actually see Paul teased. I try to keep my distance most of the time.

Paul isn't very interesting, unless he is with friends. Then I am fascinated. How can they like him? And he is funny with them. He gets along with them. There is this other, more compelling person occupying the same body as my brother. Nicer, too.

When I wake up, it is to the sound of my father pulling into a parking spot. We all climb out and stretch while he goes around the car checking the locks. Inside, the family we travel with, Ray and Joyce and their three girls, Victoria, Dee, and Dot, are already sitting down at a large table.

"Been here long?" my father asks, hugging Joyce and giving Ray a hearty handshake.

"Just pulled in," Ray answers, and he and my father wave their watches at each other in victory. Maybe that's why they are friends. My father has a definite problem with anyone, ever, being late.

The scent of maple syrup hangs over the restaurant, along with bacon, coffee, and eggs. With so many travelers heading north to some of Minnesota's 10,000 lakes, the owner keeps the menu small and true to appetites for hearty breakfasts, served fast. I order Texas toast, thick and evenly brown and crisp from being fried in a batter that was mostly Crisco. It sags under the stream of syrup I pour across it. Nellie orders a cheeseburger, as always, and they come through with French fries, too. By the time both families are back in their respective cars, my queasiness has passed, I am no longer tired, and I can't wait to dig into my library books. I have checked out six, put six more on hold, and when my father drives back for work mid-vacation, he'll make the switch for me.

By two o'clock, we are bouncing down the dried, muddy road to the rustic resort where we camp in a cabin every summer. We park to the right of the cabin in a gravel clearing, in full view of the lake; my mother always wants to be able to see children swimming or playing on the beach. I want to run straight down to the water but we are programmed to unload the car and put our suitcases by our beds, for unpacking later.

Ray's family, in a cabin back in the woods a bit, and just to the left of the ridge, has started unloading their car together. I can hear all of them laughing and chattering while they work. Victoria, sixteen, is sweet to both of her younger sisters, Dot, my brother's age, and Dee, my age. I know it can't be true, but every family seems better than mine.

I take in a load of kitchen supplies closest to the surface, and then pause on the screened porch to gaze out at the water. Breaking all established protocols—why was no one yelling at anyone about this?—my brother has walked down to the dock to close in on a large and flashy new boat tied up there. My father—again, no shouting when I expected it—has followed him.

I start down the two steps of the porch to join them, stopping to hold the door open for my mother. Her jaw is clenched and she says, without letting the cigarette fall from her lips, "Nope. No, Kim. Get another load from the car."

"But..." I point to the shore.

She shrugs me off. "I don't want to argue. I could use the help." The screen door slams for the first of a hundred times that summer as she disappears inside, and I move slowly toward the car. There is no reason to hurry. If they aren't helping, I am not going to rush.

Nellie is already in her bathing suit and sneakers, and darting past me toward my father and Paul, her towel flying behind her like a cape. She squats by the boat ramp next to the dock and pokes at minnows in the shallows. I realize that Nellie had been wearing her swimsuit since we left home and probably while she slept last night, under her pajamas. How did she pee all day?

In a rush of self-righteous energy, I decide to be the hero. I will unpack the entire car, alone, leaving my mother inside and making as many trips as it takes to get us settled in the cabin. My mother comes out to the porch just in time to take a box of groceries from my arms.

"I've got it," I say. "You stay inside. I'll bring everything." She nods, grudgingly, in an I'll-believe-it-when-I-see-it way. Still, she turns back to the kitchen, which smells of pine cleaner and floor wax and, in her estimate, doesn't need a thorough going-over before she unpacks.

My anger at the rest of the family fuses me into a focused, deliberate force. I am on automatic, and if something is too heavy to carry, I drag it. I leave most of it at the bottom of the steps and it's gone when I return with more. I grab all the snack wrappers, car bingo, Nellie's pajamas, Paul's car magazine, and more from the cargo area. I locate my lightweight suitcase, and I fly up the homely spiral stairs, fashioned out of pine scraps, to the vaulted open sleeping loft I share with Nellie. Under the loft are three rooms, so that the floor of the loft is their ceiling. My parents always took the large one, then in the center is a bathroom with a shower, and finally, Paul's room. My next trip to the car will be to gather all the snorkeling equipment my parents and Paul use and throw it on his bed. He can sort it later.

Fishing equipment rattles in long metal tubes. A second long metal tube is insulated, and will hold cold cans of beer for the fishermen to take out on the lake. I hang both of these on hooks on the porch.

Back and forth I race, watching my mother as she finishes emptying a box and delivering her another one before she could ask. I use an Adirondack chair from the front porch to climb up to the car-top carrier, lift the lid on its hinges, and find our life jackets, "Castle" written across the pumpkin orange cloth in permanent marker, padding kitchen appliances: electric can opener, carving knife, blender. So there were some things my mother could not leave behind.

I hear splashing, and see that both my brother and my dad have rolled up their pants and taken off their shoes to wade in with Nellie. I virtuously ignore them, keep to my mission, and soon the car is clear of all the stuff we have dragged to our log cabin home.

Inside, though, nothing I'd done has registered with my mother. I want her to notice and say, "Wow, you did that!" or even, "Thank you. Just us working, right?" I'm not even mad. I'm just looking for credit.

"It's done," I say, somewhat invitingly. "Car's all clear. What else can I do?"

As I seldom volunteer this way—we have assigned chores at home—I expect this to have some impact.

It does not.

"See if you can find an extension cord in some of your dad's stuff," she says. "There are never enough outlets."

She is configuring the countertops for maximum efficiency, with catsup and mustard, salt and pepper in a basket she brought from home, and paper plates, knives, and forks forming a centerpiece on the table where we not only eat, but play cards on rainy days or paint our fingernails, and where the adults play bridge all night.

I know all her habits, the whole routine, and it is easy to fall in and take all the soda pops out of their cases and load up the refrigerator that is just outside my parents' bedroom. It's a little outside the kitchen, there, but that spot has the grace and advantage of allowing people to rustle around in it without disrupting the small U-shaped nook where my mother cooks and washes dishes.

The life jackets go on hooks in the porch; I find the 100-watt lightbulbs my father brings every year and replace all the dusty 40-watt bulbs wired into the log rafters and those in the occasional lamps around the room. I take the fly strips—for biting black flies and mosquitoes that find a way in every time the screen door opens—out of their wrappers and hang one in each room, plus another in the loft. I set up my area with the books and a flashlight nearby and go back down the steps to see what else needs to happen.

My mother has opened up a bag of Tootsie Rolls and unwrapped one. We always have candy at the lake, and trail mixes, and doughnuts from local bakeries. With a can of pop to wash it all down, it is a good lunch.

"No dishwasher," she says to herself in disbelief, turning to fill a shallow pink plastic basin with soapy water. "I never really remember that. No dishwasher."

"And no washing machine," I join in.

"God," she says, standing up straight and looking right at me. "Right?"

She fumbles for a cigarette with her one dry hand. I help her, put it in her lips, and light it while she squints at me.

"I wish I were in my own kitchen," she says.

"I wish I smoked," I reply.

Mid-inhale, she sputters, then puts the cigarette in a plaid bean bag ashtray to burn. "What? Oh my God, Kimmy!"

We both crack up then, until she is bending over, wiping one eye where the mascara had smeared.

"Oh, that feels good," she says. "You always make me laugh." She shakes her head. "They really are creeps, aren't they?" I nod. "Okay. Go put on your suit. We are off duty. I'll race you to the water."

From the side, the boat looks like a giant black shark, shiny as obsidian and tapering in the back to a compact trimmed fin for the inboard motor. An eye is painted on either side of the bow, with a wide grin of jagged teeth decorating the front. The speedboat thuds dully against the splintery wooden dock, riding up and down on the waves rolling ashore. It is ugly. It is amazing. I can't stop looking at it, and neither can my brother.

He has mechanical gifts and, even at thirteen, can put together a plastic reproduction of a V-8 engine from a kit, or fix the lawnmower, or be trusted to steer the tiny outboard motor we attach to a small rowboat for fishing.

The look of this newcomer has rendered him silent. No taunts, no teasing.

He shakes his head and takes a deep breath. "She's something, isn't she?" he finally says, still staring at it.

"What are you, a pirate?" I reply. I feel like needling him. He still has not been yelled at for shirking his chores. I am in the right. It is inarguable. "'SHE'?" I repeat mockingly.

He reaches across the distance between us with one arm and tips me off the dock and into the water before I've even finished goading him.

"Mom!" I scream, waist-high in the water. "Paul threw me in!"

My mother, thumbing through a magazine, barely looks up from her lawn chair onshore, where she is enjoying the last rays of the afternoon. Joyce is sitting next to her while Dee pokes around with a stick, looking for duck eggs in a sort of sludge-filled shallow.

"Paul, be nice to your sister," she says automatically. "Play nice, you two." She looks at Joyce and they both shrug and go back to their magazines.

I stick out my tongue, and wade angrily to shore. "I'm wet!" I say to her, milking the moment.

"Welcome to the lake," she answers, peering at me over the top of her sunglasses. "That's why we're here."

I sit down in the grassy sand next to her chair with a thump, not really mad. My brother and I hurl insults at each other dozens of times a day. I reach for her plastic cup, where the melting ice cubes are turning the last of the amber of scotch into a light golden color that promises a beautiful perfume, and to my nose, smelling just as sweet. The condensation on the glass left a series of watery rings on the distressed blue paint of her Adirondack chair.

Even in the shade, she wears her sunglasses and floppy hat. She watches with interest as a woman in a wheelchair is rolled on to the beach area, her lap covered in once-bright towels that have faded to the soft colors of melted ice cream.

Her caretaker is a tall woman with shoulder-length white-gray hair, tan and muscular in a tank top and bathing suit bottoms, her long fingers gripping the handles of the wheelchair. Her sunglasses slip down her narrow nose as she brings the wheelchair to a halt in the sandy grass overlap between lawn and beach and tucks the towels in.

She looks older than my mother, and her charge, the woman in the wheelchair, has the slumped, boneless posture of someone ancient, barely keeping her head up off her chest. She is wearing at least two visible sweaters and a straw hat, held on with a strap tied under her chin. She, too, wears sunglasses but they are not at all stylish, more like light-blocking goggles.

"There you are, Mother," the younger one says. "I'll be back in just a couple of minutes.

She stands up fully, and nods at us with a smile as she pushes her sunglasses back in place. That is just long enough for her mother to sit up slightly in her chair, and screech, "Jaaaaaane. Jaaaaaaane. Where are my cigarettes?" She says it again, even louder.

"Now, Mother, be patient," Jane replies, stooping to search a large straw bag hanging off the wheelchair.

"Jaaaaaane. Cigaretttttes!"

Jane calmly pulls out a pack of cigarettes and puts one in her mother's mouth, then with practiced timing, cups the lighter against the lake breezes, and watches as the older woman inhales with a shudder. Jane pats her shoulder, and puts the lighter back in the bag. She gives us another pleasant grin and walks over to a picnic bench facing the water.

We wait until we are sure Jane is suitably distant, and then my mother turns to me and says, "Just shoot me." She says it simply, firmly, quietly.

"What?" I reply, not seeing the connection at all.

"If that is my state, when I am old, you have my permission to shoot me," she answers. "No jury will convict you. Gads, can you imagine? The patience!"

We laugh together and she pulls a cigarette from a new pack she'd just tamped on the flat wooden arms of the chair. She lights it, and draws a satisfied drag, shaking her head.

"You can shoot me," she says softly, and leans back in the chair.

"When will I get to have scotch?" I ask, inhaling the scent of the liquid, now warm in the summer heat. She is vague—she and my father are often vague in the early afternoons—and murmurs an answer I can't hear, as if forming the words is too much trouble. "When will I get to drink scotch?" I repeat loudly, although I knew she had heard me the first time; she is the one talking too softly.

"I hope never," she answers, turning her head to look at me over the tops of her glasses. "I hope you never ever ever never want to drink scotch. Ever." The moment is over.

The way I feel about scotch is not. I love the scents of my father's aftershave, my mother's Shalimar, and ten-year-old scotch in equal portions. Mingled with the scent of match to cigarette, in that first sulphuric burst, the just-out-of-the-dry-cleaners smell of their evening clothes, and the savory scents of appetizers warming in the oven until their friends came over, that scotch—it stings my eyes, tantalizes me with visions of fun, singing, dancing, life. Not my life now, but some future *me*, a swinging, laughing, wiser me, in fitted bodices and dirndl skirts, open-toed pumps and bouffant bobbed hair. And lipstick. Lipstick that didn't look ridiculous on my plump child's lips, but issued an invitation—here's a fun girl, here's someone to pay attention to, lookee here.

All my yearning has a form. It is my parents' life together, which looks complete and perfect.

After her brief stint at the beach, my mother returns to the cabin, still swearing under her breath about the unfamiliar gas range, sweeping away all the sand we'd tracked in "without a vacuum cleaner," setting up a laundry bag for dirty clothes, and hanging a nylon rope line outside for wet suits and towels.

That night, according to ritual, we eat a casserole my mother made the night before and brought with us in the Styrofoam cooler. In the days to come, there will be fresh fish, and hamburgers, and steaks, but there are traditions that are purely practical, and expecting my mother to cook the first night is not one of them.

Nellie, pushing the casserole around on her paper plate, asks if we can order pizza for dinner.

Still sitting at the table with the rest of us, before she tackles the dishes, my mother reaches into her shorts pocket and pulls out a dime. It is dirty looking, as if she found it on the floor.

"Here you go," she says to my sister. "Go to it. There's a phone booth in town or maybe one at the lodge." She points up the hill, at an even rockier ridge about five hundred feet away. The lodge is about a quarter mile past that. Nellie snatches up the dime, and stomps out of the cabin. The screen door slaps the frame and the walls shake.

My dad says, ever clueless, "That was a little unnecessary, Connie. And this dinner is delicious. Isn't it, guys?" Paul and I just nod. My mother pushes herself away from the table and returns to the kitchen nook. In other years I hardly noticed how difficult the vacation is for her. I don't know why this year I can hear her. I go over to the sink, and swirl the serving spoon and butter knife around in the rinse water, then dry each piece and put it away. She ducks her head to light a cigarette, and puts her other arm around me for a light hug.

"Go find your sister, would you, please?" she says. "I think she probably has a better chance at finding a bear than any pizza out there."

I walk up the ridge. To the left is Ray's cabin, and to the right is the road that winds around toward the lodge. It's so steep that the backs of my calves are burning from the short hike; just as quickly, I am on the other side, trying to slide and walk down the slippery gravel without losing my balance. My sister is sitting on a rock that looks out over the lake through the trees, eating a Butterfinger and swinging her legs.

"Never made it to the phone?" I say. She shakes her head. The lodge stocks a few kinds of candy—Twizzlers, chocolate bars, Chuckles, black licorice.

"So, no pizza?" I ask. She shrugs. I motion to her to move over, then sit down. She points at the chocolate bar, but I don't want any. I always thought of vacations as family time—my excitement overnight was as much about being all together, which only happened on holidays the rest of the year—but today is different. It feels as if all of us want something, and no one can figure out what it is. And none of us know how to talk about it.

By the time Nellie finishes her candy bar, the sun across the lake is about to sink behind the trees on the other side. We stand up and I brush splinters of orange Butterfinger from her T-shirt. We trudge back up the ridge, putting our heads down into the steep climb, but are not at the top when a small wiry figure appears. The slanting sun's rays hit him, a bent older man, like a spotlight. He grins widely when he sees us.

"Hey, there, hello!" he says, doing the same walk-slide down the hill that I'd performed. Then he stops and puts out his right hand for a shake. Curled into his left hand is the bone handle of a battered tackle box.

My training is spot on. I put my right hand out and it's folded into his gnarled one in a firm shake.

"What's your name, little lady? I'm Ernie. Say, is that your family back there in the little cottage facing the lake?"

"I'm Kim, and this is Ellen, um, Nellie," I explain. Up at the lake, there is no such thing as not talking to strangers. Nellie doesn't talk to him, but she has stopped talking to almost everyone except me. I remember when she was a chatterbox. She is never rude, ever. She is just quiet. I am not.

"Kim, nice to meet you!" He glances at Nellie, and then straightens his shoulders a bit against the gravity of the ridge we are halfway up. He lifts up the tackle box with a grin. "Say! I got candy bars! Would either of you like one?"

"No thank you," I say, "We just ate. But thank you." Over the ridge, I hear the screen door slap. If one of my parents rings the iron bell by the door, it means we are already in trouble for not getting back sooner. So I pull Nellie's hand along with me and jabber, "Nice to meet you, too. We have to go. Good-bye!"

"Good-bye, girls!" He turns back down the ridge, and in a little hitched-step, hop-step, he runs down it. "Good night, ladies!" he repeats, but we don't answer. My father, on the porch, waves as we trot down the hill toward him.

"Were you up at the lodge?" he asks pleasantly. "Your mom thought you'd be back sooner."

"Mom?" I call as I went through the door. "Dad said you were looking for me." We all like to play cards in the evening. Or sometimes she paints my nails, my badly bitten nails, as a sort of promise to future me that they would be prettier if I'd let them grow.

I don't mention Ernie, because I am so happy to be missed, or needed, or both. In the light of the cabin, Ernie seems like a gnome we'd met in the forest, and hardly real. Nellie follows me to the table and sinks down with a pile of Legos, instantly absorbed. Paul is in his room, behind a closed door.

My mother comes out of their bedroom with a plastic package of yarn in dozens of colors. She has a sewing room back home, where we find her each evening, but at the lake she likes to work on needlepoint.

"I'm going to sort through these colors," she tells me. "You always like helping me with that, don't you?" We detangle them and put them in order from light to dark on a plastic ruler with notches that keep them separate. I love tasks like that. I forget all about Ernie.

The smell of the kerosene heater wakes me first the next morning. Up in the loft it's cozy under the wool blankets and the freshly laundered sheets that smell like home. Then coffee scents waft up the steps and the sounds of my parents talking in low relaxed tones. I want to snuggle back in; I want to leap out of bed and go down to the lake. Early mornings are perfect—no one else is around to fight over the rocking chair that lives on the end of the dock, and the fishermen that went out at dawn won't be back till lunch.

Pulling on shorts over my bare legs and a sweatshirt over my baby doll pajamas, I shove my feet into sneakers, fly down the steps and out the door, barely waving at my parents as I pass them. I hear the sizzle of butter hit the cast iron pan and see batter for pancakes. I'll be back.

It's a straight line from our porch door across a lawn and down to the nail-snaggled splintery dock that juts out from the gray sand of the small beach. I veer abruptly from my course, though, and sit down with a slump on one of the large boulders that divides the sand from the lawn.

The rocking chair is already taken. Ernie is leaning halfway out of it as he spreads the contents of his tackle box across a dingy pink bath towel on the dock. He crooks his finger in and out of the compartments, plucking out lures, leaving hooks dangling. So busy is he sorting that he doesn't see me, and I wonder if I can rewind, just back up the path and back into the cabin without him, or anyone, noticing.

Too late. "Hey, there, missy!" he calls. His voice is warm and welcoming in the soft sunlight of early morning. He corrals the air with one skinny arm, summoning me over. "Good morning. Would you like to see what I've got here?"

There does not seem to be a single reason I can say no. And the way the shiny lures are sparkling draw me to the dock. As I approach slowly, I realize his lures are not the metal shapes, feathers, and enameled hammered tin of my father's tackle box. There is a ruby surrounded by a wreath of diamonds, with four hooks like the points of a compass. A waterfall of diamonds and small shimmering silver beads hides the teeth of hooks. A spray of emeralds like fireworks is punctuated by tiny pearl seeds. He watches my face with glee.

"My wife's," he says proudly. "Leota used to be from a real fine family, till she married me."

"Are these real?" I ask. "Real jewels?" The tackle box is a treasure chest? I'd never suspected the possibilities.

"Be careful of the hooks," he says as I lean in closer. "I doubt the gems are real, but Leota could look like the queen when she wanted!" He rummages around under a pile of chains and spools of fishing line, and emerges with an Almond Joy.

"Candy?" he asks. I take it from his hand—I am hungry. I ignore the slightly fishy smell of the wrapper as I tear through it. It is dark chocolate, not my favorite, with two half-bars of covered coconut and two almonds on each.

I bite into it while he continues to sort, and then sink down on my knees near the grease-covered towel to survey the loot. Two dangly earrings are wired into a lure, and a bracelet's charms has hooks between each of them. I see a strange swoop of diamonds, small at one end and a sprawling curlicue fan at the other, and point to it as I chew.

"A tiara—or half of one," he answers happily. "She broke it when she was mad at me—oh, she'd get so mad at me!" He chuckles. "She'd come at me with her fists flying and pummel me good!"

He means actual blows. This information is impossible to take in. I have only ever witnessed the bitten-off words of my parents when they are fighting—more of a crackling in the air than sentences, then sniping, then silence. A storm system that threatens, but never makes landfall.

"Did you divorce?" I ask rudely. I'd been taught never to ask such personal questions of anyone, let alone adults. I'd also never heard an adult discuss fighting so openly before.

"No, no, no, never," he says easily. He stops smiling. He stares out at the water. "It was a long time ago," he adds wistfully.

All the fun has gone out of him, and I can hear myself chewing the last of the chocolate bar. Our screen door slams and I see Nellie, who stands on the lawn in this awkward pose—her hands clasped to her chest, one foot stopped midstep, and her eyes showing worry. Ernie waves at her, but she does not wave back.

"Mom wants you," she calls out in a loud voice. "Pancakes."

"Pancakes!" Ernie says. "Don't that beat all! Delicious."

If he were my age, I would invite him over for breakfast. Instead, I just stand up. "Thanks for the Almond Joy," I say. Then I walk off the dock. He goes back to his sorting.

"He's scary," Nellie says under her breath as we enter the cabin.

"He's kind of magical," I reply.

"Who's magical?" my brother asks, still flipping through his *Car & Driver* magazine next to his plate.

My sister slides back into her seat and resumes eating, her eyes wide and staring as I accept a plate of pancakes from my mother. I ignore him. He rises at the sound of a boat engine puttering into the cove, and looks out the window. He cannot help his fascination with motors.

"*That boat* is magical!" he says, tossing the magazine on to the sofa and walking straight out the door. I see through the picture window that it's the shark boat coasting into the shallows, as Ernie helps pull it into the dock.

I know Paul is curious about the owner; we've been coming to the lake for years and know whose boat is whose. The young man who helps out at the lodge hops out, shakes Ernie's hand, and ties up the boat.

My mother swoops past me and picks up Paul's half-empty plate. "He could clear," she says to herself. "You could *clear*," she says loudly to the picture window, and then looks back at me. "They could clear," she says simply. She sits down in Paul's spot and lights a cigarette. She draws deeply, then taps her ashes into a glistening trail of crumbs and syrup.

"They could."

Next to me, Nellie smiles broadly. She loves being included. My mother takes another drag on the cigarette, then picks up a magazine and her coffee mug and moves into the bathroom. It's all so public, compared to our bathrooms at home, which are all spaced out and down hallways or behind discreet pocket doors. At the cabin, the one bathroom is almost always occupied. She closes the door and I quickly clear everything with Nellie's help.

The day is getting warmer, as the sun rises behind the cabin and starts to shine across the still lake water. Up in the loft, I change out of my pajamas and Nellie puts on her swimsuit and terrycloth shorts.

Back outside, my brother and father, Ray, and Dee are deeply absorbed in something Ernie is saying, and I see the old man wave my brother into the large black boat. My brother's face splits into a grin as he leaps off the dock and into the prow. As he runs his hand over the polished wooden interior, the brass choke, the marble-like knob on the throttle, he seems to be giggling to himself. I have a stab of envy that I always feel when he is allowed to do something first. It is an old battle and one I can never win. He will always be the oldest grandchild, the oldest and only boy.

"Is that his boat?" Nellie asks, and she slips her hand into mine.

"I guess so. I think the other guy was just gassing it up for him."

"Are we going on it?"

"I don't know," I say. Ernie is making the men laugh, and Paul is lost in exploring every surface of the boat. Dee stands awkwardly to one side.

"Come here, girls," my dad says. "Meet Ernie—he's going to take you all out for a ride soon." His words seem like the okay that Nellie needs. She lets go of my hand then, and races up the dock, and lets Paul lift her easily over the side of the boat and into it. She sits down in the driver's seat, and, without touching the steering wheel, pretends to drive.

I sit back down near the pink towel with my back to the water; some test has been passed for her. Ernie, before breakfast, made my sister worry. Ernie, after breakfast, is giving us boat rides.

"Do you like *Leota*?" Ernie asks me. He hangs over me in the sunlight, a shadow, and I close one eye against the brightness.

"What?" I asked. "*Le—Leota*?"

"My boat!" he says, pointing to Nellie and Paul and the large black speedboat. He gestures at the stern with his hands like a musical conductor drawing out the note, making a wide smile in the air. "*L-E-O-T-A*. Named after my Leota, the love of my life."

"It's a fine boat," Ray says respectfully. "How long has your wife been gone?"

"Maybe fifteen year," Ernie says, without adding an S to the end of the word. "Fifteen year, sixteen. Seems like yesterday."

"I'm sorry for your loss," my father says. He is a church deacon and knows how to be serious. "It is a fine, fine boat."

"When can we go?" my brother asks, sitting on the polished black shelf that houses the inboard motor. "How fast can she go?"

74

"We can go right now," Ernie says. My father steps back in, though, and puts an end to the trip.

"Ernie, I think you've earned your fishing day. Kids, we'll take that ride another day. Say thank you, and let's go see what your mom is up to. We need to get her down to the beach!"

"You're welcome," Ernie says easily. "You're welcome. Of course. Anytime."

At the cabin, my mother is fixing sandwiches and wrapping them in wax paper for us to grab all day out of the refrigerator. In a floppy hat that we only see during our stays at the lake, and a plaid two-piece swimsuit, she is humming while she sweeps crumbs on the counter into the sink with one hand and hands me her bronzing lotion with the other.

I carefully sever a squeeze of dark orange gel lotion on to my hand and warm it in my palms. Then I rub it across her shoulders and down her back.

"Don't get it on the suit," she warns. "It will stain." I finish up while she bends over to do her legs. She has on white slip-on sandals with black patent leather daisies and polka dot buttons over her big toes. With a cold iced tea in one hand and a large beach bag in the other that includes pattern books for our back-to-school clothes, she will park on the shore next to Joyce and usually Victoria, and will not return to the cabin for hours.

Nellie is in the loft, Paul is in his room, and my dad is hogging the bathroom for the third time that day. I usually know what to do with every hour at the lake, from reading on the couch rain or shine, to sitting still for hours at a time playing endless games of solitaire, to racing over the hill to the lodge's candy counter with squirreled-away allowance money. No one keeps track of us; my mother looks for us at dinner, but even then, if we don't show up for the meal, we don't eat and fix ourselves up. No search parties are sent out.

If I put on my suit, I'll have to get in the water—no one ever wears a swimsuit without actually swimming. Even my mother and the other ladies at the lake get in and dog paddle around, without getting their hair wet. We are not allowed to splash them or dunk any of them the way we do one another. Hairstyles are something they pay for at the salon, and so they are protected. If my mother is careful, sleeps on a silk pillowcase, and uses a bobby pin occasionally for a stray lock, a hairdo up at the lake will last two weeks.

I can row to Blueberry Island. It's hardly an island, more like a scruff of birch trees splaying toward the sky, but because of the spacing of trees, sunlight can reach the blueberry bushes. More, the eastern and northern sides of it are visible to anyone on our shore, so it's the one place on the lake I can row to alone.

So safe are we at the lake that I don't even have to clear my outing with my parents. If they don't see me, another adult will tell them, and I will be visible most of the time—the underbrush and blueberry bushes are thick but only waist high. And I'll be in a rowboat. I can't go that far, even if I want to.

I grab my life jacket from the hook and a small deep colander that my mother keeps handy all summer long for berry picking, then run down to the musty boathouse. The raftered ceiling is so high, my footsteps echo. Two speedboats have prime positions on the spots farthest from the door, in the deepest waters. Four rowboats are tied up on either side of the dock, their oars stored neatly along the ribs and under the prow.

I pick a small three-seater and untie the rope that moors it to the dock. I climb over the hull, pushing off the dock with my foot, and sit down as the rowboat floats back into open water between the boathouse and the dock, where people are still standing around the *Leota*.

With one oar, I steer the boat away from the shore. Rowing the boat comes naturally to me—we were taught to row and to swim before we could talk. I'd never heard of anyone drowning. Still, there is nothing I do the rest of the year that prepares my palms for the steady friction of the wooden oars as I row. By the time I am at the island, both palms feel blistered. There is no shade anywhere, and I wish I'd just gone swimming with everyone else. I also wish I had packed a lunch. Or brought a soda pop.

As I approach the narrow landing spot, I row faster to build up a little speed with my back to the shore. Once I have momentum, I climb over the seat toward the lake, which puts all the weight in the back of the boat so its front tips up as it moves steadily forward and rides up onto the beach. I jump out of the boat and into the shallows, then pull it up farther on the sand to park it. I grab the colander and duck into the dappled shade of the birch trees.

It is instantly cooler, and the bushes are already heavy with blueberries, especially on the lower branches, which are harder for the birds to get to. I quickly fill up the colander and walk across the island in about twenty-five steps, till I come to the beach on the western side. I sit down in the sand, and let the sun warm me after the coolness under the trees.

I doze, and wake up feeling hot and itchy from sweat, with a faint pink sunburn across my legs. It always turns into freckles, but when I run my finger across it, it feels prickly with tiny blisters. Have I been here for hours?

A dark black speedboat turns toward my beach, and the driver, Ernie, kills the engine out several yards in deeper water.

"Ahoy!" he shouts amiably. "Do you need a ride home? We can pick up the rowboat on the way." Confused, I stand up and see the rowboat adrift, headed toward the open part of the lake, away from our little cove.

Without a dock, of course, the *Leota* can't come any closer to shore—it will scrape and even ruin the bottom of the boat. I hold up my hand and I wave. Picking up my berries, I have no choice but to wade out to waist-high water, hand him the colander, and clamber over the low back. I sort of shimmy on my stomach over the side while Ernie uses a long oar lowered to the bottom of the lake to anchor the boat and keep it still.

"How do you think your boat got loose?" the old man asks, chuckling at me. "Do you think you used the correct knots to secure it?"

"I didn't tie it up," I admit. My dad always makes us drag the boats to higher ground and tie the rope to the trunk of any solidly rooted tree. It's a rule, like always wearing a life jacket, or not swimming after lunch, or discarding an egg salad sandwich left in the sun. It's a rule meant to prevent you from dying, or being harmed, or even just humiliated. I have no excuse.

By this time we have pulled up to the rowboat. He steadies us, boat-to-boat, while I climb in.

"I can tow you," Ernie says.

"I can row home," I reply. He starts to protest.

"Thank you so much," I say, in the voice my mother uses for getting people off the phone. "I'd rather just row back, like normal. That's all."

"Well, sister, that's up to you," Ernie says, so kindly that all my defenses about him, being a stranger, a bit odd, too eager, just deflate. "But this didn't count as your boat ride. I can't wait to take all you kids out for a trip. We'll pack a snack."

"I'd like to," I say. "That will be fun." And I mean it.

He pointed to the tackle box. "Almond Joy? Mounds?" I shake my head, and he waits for me to start rowing before he speeds away. I let the boat rock gently over his wake before I put my back to it, and row toward the shore, and home.

My brother loses no time telling me what an idiot I am. I have barely returned the boat to its slip when he scampers into the boat house.

"You're in so much trouble," he crows. "You left without asking, you lost the boat, you got stranded." He is delighted to find me in the wrong—very much in the wrong—when I am always the one toeing the line.

"Paul is the adventurous one," Grandfather Castle said after my brother crashed his new bike. "Kimmy's the one you can count on to be safe at home, reading."

"Kimmy's bossy. Paul is the leader." That's Grandmother Castle, who has encouraged me to embrace cottage cheese over cookies before it's too late.

Paul runs to the cabin without me, probably so he'll have a seat ringside. And he is right. The minute I walk into the cabin, where everyone but my mother is already sitting down to dinner, and despite handing over a colander of blueberries, my parents are so angry, they hardly look at me.

This is what one finger does: My mother motions to the dinner table and tells me to sit down, and sit still—all that, in just one finger. My father starts to talk but she interrupts. She can't keep it in.

79

"If it hadn't been for Ernie," my mother says, "I just don't know."

"Kimmy, if the boat just floated away," my father says, "we'd probably have figured out where you were. But boats are expensive to replace, and there's no guarantee some other boat wouldn't have just towed it away."

"In daylight?" I ask. There has been no rash of stolen rowboats, to my knowledge.

"Kim!" my mother says warningly. "You listen to your father."

My father nods along, but he is calmer than she is. "What if it had floated to the middle of the lake, and some speedboat, at night, didn't see it? Someone could have been hurt. Or property would have been damaged. The lake is so dangerous. I thought I'd made that clear."

The lectures about being up at the lake fall somewhere short of the horrors of ghost stories, but I know them all: poison ivy, illegal hunters in the woods, fish hooks, sharp knives, hatchets and axes for splitting wood, trees falling across electrical lines during storms, electric tools near water, drowning, swimming too soon after lunch, getting a cramp while swimming, dragging someone down with you, bloodsuckers, and broken glass in the sand.

Boats are a special category of danger, with propellers that could slice in half a child swimming too close, a steady exhaust of gas ("No smoking near an outboard engine!"—which no adult complies with, ever), the potential to fall overboard or get whacked by an oar or run out of gas and get stranded. There are also exploding pop cans in the heat and, worst of all, motor explosions.

For me there are also sunburns so severe I take aspirin for the fever, swallowing lake water where people peed, going into the woods without bug spray or extra batteries for my flashlight, bats, leeches, snails, and spiders.

I sit there in silence, considering vacation briefly through my parents' eyes, and wonder how we stumbled across this version of family getaway. I've never wanted to go to Disneyland, as the Grismers do each summer, but maybe they know something we don't.

A knock on the screen door puts a stop to my thoughts. "The lake is just like glass tonight," Ernie calls from outside. "Don't mean to interrupt your supper, but would the kids like to go out?"

The silence this meets lives in a zone that, given my very well-behaved parents, feels almost rude. They both speak at once, over each other, but as I listen, I realize that they are going from no, it's impossible ("until we finish yelling at Kim" is likely the great unspoken thought) to of course, they are so grateful to him, of course we can go.

"We'll talk about this later," my father says as soon as Ernie leaves to go prepare the boat. "I don't want to punish your brother and sister, or even Ernie, who seems so excited. He's like the Pied Piper, for heaven's sake."

"Am I getting spanked?" I ask, dreading the answer but knowing I won't be able to enjoy the boat ride worrying about it.

"I don't think so," my father answers. "But Kimmy, this is so serious to me. You could have gotten hurt. You could have gotten someone else hurt. I think maybe a spanking would be letting you off easy. I have to think."

I take my life jacket off the hook and put it on. My mother, with pursed lips, comes out to the porch with a can of Off! and sprays my arms, legs, and head.

Dot and Dee are already on the *Leota*, tied to the dock. Nellie, who ran down to the beach without finishing her dinner, cheers up when she sees I am not crying. It means, to her, that I haven't been spanked. She waves at a place on one of the upholstered seats next to her. I have whiplash, going from all that disappointment at the dinner table to this happy chattering crew. I climb aboard and don't join in as usual with the rest of the group.

I need to think. I'd been grounded once, and that punishment felt more like a reward. I was sent to my room to do homework right after school, where all my books and toys are. The harder punishment was when I lost my allowance for a month, which had led me to steal butter rum Life Savers from my brother's desk.

One summer, the flu had kept me home from the Iowa State Fair. It was punishment, but no one's fault. My imagination fails me. I have no idea what my parents are going to do to me, but it fills me with dread.

Paul, as always the only boy on board, takes the role of copilot, in the passenger seat to the left of Ernie, in the driver's seat. Dot unties the moorings and looks at all of us to make sure our life jackets are cinched up. Paul follows Ernie's gaze as the old man looks over his shoulder to back away from the dock, and yells, "All clear." Ernie brings the boat about, heading toward open water.

Even though I was in the boat that very afternoon, now I can really pay attention. The interior of the *Leota* is as sharp and tidy as a beautiful leather couch. Every surface is a blood red, right down to the fiberglass sidewalls, flecked with confetti-like glitter. It's the belly of the shark, as Ernie pushes down the throttle and the front of the boat lifts.

The sensation in my stomach as the boat picks up speed feels like a wonderful vibration, and I find myself laughing—we are all laughing from our bellies, helpless with the rush of air, the speed, and the incredible whoosh of being in that boat. The sun sparkles through distant spruce, glinting in its last moments off the water and making everything I see glow, a kaleidoscope of shifting, shimmering colors. I yell my joy. Dee joins in with whoops. We all yell together.

Paul looks back at me with such brotherly affection that tears come to my eyes. In this late hour of a long and waning day, he is loving this, and he loves me, too, and he is glad I am there to share it. We hit open water as dusk comes to the lake, and the sun slips behind the trees to the west.

Now we fly, shooting across the water as the day fades to a blue-gray, and then a deeper shade that with the clouds looks like dark crushed velvet. We settle in, and I close my eyes as the wind rushes over my face, so calm and peaceful despite the engine's roar. We all feel it, and even the younger children, my sister Nellie, and Dee, grin as they sit on the floor of the boat, pulling their knees as close as the life jacket allows. The air grows cooler, giving us goose bumps, but no one minds. My legs are hot and cold at the same time, badly sunburned, but the racing air is like cool water across them, and it's soothing, clearing away the rest of the day.

My brother takes a turn driving for a few minutes and, as the shore grows dimmer and farther away, suggests he turn back in the direction of our cove.

"No, son," Ernie shouts agreeably over the noise, and retaking his place at the wheel. "I got something to show you. Me and Leota found it the year we honeymooned on this lake." He turns on the headlamps, and we can see that the boat is aimed in the direction of a distant cliff-like rock, jutting up out of the water.

He steers wide around it as we get closer, slowing the boat a little, and looks unhappy. "We're too heavy," he pro-

83

nounces. "We need to go faster." He gives the wheel to Paul, who circles the rock as if taking it in.

Ernie moves the little kids away from one of the storage bins. "We've got too much weight," he repeats. He opens up a panel and grunts as he pulls out first one red tank of gas, and then another.

"Too heavy," he says again, and hoists the gas tank over the side of the boat. It hits the water with a heavy splash as we continue on. I see Paul look back but he stays at the wheel.

"Mister—sir! We shouldn't throw the gas overboard!" he calls out. "It's not—it's not good for the lake."

"Wait," I say, emboldened by Paul's concern. Dee begins to cry. "Wait, wait! We might need that." Every child in that boat knows that basic safety tip. Take extra gas. I hear another splash—the second gas tank.

Ernie calmly reclaims the wheel, so happy, and then pushes the throttle all the way down.

"Power!" he cries. "We needed to lose weight so you can see *Leota* really open up!" We feel it. We are going even faster. But it smells, to me, as if something is burning. Not gas.

I pull on Paul's windbreaker. "I smell something burning!"

He takes a sniff and nods, then looks around the lake, peering into the sky. There is white smoke everywhere, against the velvet sky, from hundreds of fires, from people grilling, or having a bonfire, or even just burning wood in a fireplace.

Paul shrugged. "Could be anything!" he shouts. He looks ahead.

Ernie is muttering about going faster, and then brightens up. "This is the way! Now I got it. That's where we're going!" he says excitedly. "We're almost there!" We slice through the water and I peer ahead.

I can't see anything but that rock sticking up out of the water like a ramp. Ernie drives around it once, and then away from it, and I see Paul's shoulders go soft. As if all the tension has run out of him.

It doesn't last. Slowing down to a mere putt-putt, Ernie turns the *Leota* to face the base of the ramp, like a bull ready to face a matador. He looks at me, and he winks.

"Paul!" I shout. "Paul!" I stand up from the back of the boat just as Ernie plunges the throttle forward, and the force of it makes me lose my balance and fall back on to Nellie, who wails.

"Not now," I shriek at her. "Not now! Paul!" He sees it, too, that Ernie is headed, as if on a motorcycle or in a car, toward the ramp. We both know, without ever having heard from an adult or read it in a book, that you cannot drive a boat up a rock. Of all the dangers that I'd listened to over the years, here is one they haven't mentioned: Going for a boat ride with a maniac.

Ernie is locked over the wheel, determined to keep his course. Paul grabs the wheel, which surprises Ernie. The boat jerks to the left before righting its course back toward the rock. It's coming up fast. Ernie grips the wheel harder and shoves at Paul with his elbow.

I push up from Nellie's lap and lean forward into the force of the rushing wind and the slant of the boat. I take two long steps and clamp my hands down over my brother's hand on the steering wheel.

With my entire weight I pull him and his arm toward me, all the way to the left.

The boat tips so sharply as it turns that it almost flips over. I hear part of the bottom—no, I feel part of the bottom scraping rock. Dee, Nellie, and Dot slide to the left of the boat, which only makes it more likely that we'll tip. I brace up against Paul so he can reach over Ernie, bringing his right hand down on the man's gnarled claw gripping the throttle. Paul pulls the throttle back to neutral and turns the ignition key, shutting off the boat abruptly. It's sucked backward into the high waves and the force of its own wake, threatening to flood the cabin.

I don't know whether to laugh or cry. Ernie doesn't move. I still smell burning, like an electrical wire. I look back to see smoke coming out of the engine housing.

Paul sees it, too, and we both look for a fire bucket or anything we can use for water. I grab the tackle box, open it up, and dump everything right into the lake. Paul takes it to scoop up lake water, which he pours across the back of the boat. I stare as the dark shapes of floats, lures, and jewelry sink. Then I find a foam holder for pop cans and begin bailing water, too.

Dot, Dee, and Nellie, who have been told their whole lives never to put their hands outside the boat, dip hands and cans and cups and anything they could find into the lake over the low back rim, and then fling water at the flames.

We smell electrical fires and melting plastic, which is the fiberglass, and we hear the fire hissing at us. We keep going, and it doesn't take long to extinguish.

At some point, Paul looks at the tackle box, and I nod at him. He flings it over the side, and into the lake. We are exhausted.

Ernie still hasn't moved. He sits in the front seat, slumped. He won't even look at us.

There's a moment, when I'm solving a math problem, that I get a piece of it, and know it's right. A little happiness lives there, in that tiny result. But then I have to go to the next line of the problem.

I look at Paul. "I don't think the boat's going to start," I say.

He scoffs, as if it is a joke, maybe because we are so relieved in the sudden stillness. Then his face changes.

"I don't think so either," he says grimly.

There are two oars tucked into the fiberglass sides, which is sort of the law, in boating. No matter how many engines you have, or how much gas, at some point, you are going to need to paddle.

I yank one oar out, and hand it to Paul. I take the other, and Dot turns on her flashlight, aimed off the front of the boat.

There is a sort of calm about us. We're tired, and a mess, but no one is howling. We know for certain our parents will come find us. But it's a big lake. We begin to row.

The sky turns to dawn before my father, Ray, and our mothers, in a borrowed speedboat, come across us. We are miles from home.

When I wake up, it is already the end of the next day. I am disoriented, and still anxious to learn what my punishment is. The sun is low in the sky. I am starving.

Ernie, his car, and the *Leota* are gone. My brother, the hero, up before I am, is eating the last of my favorite cereal for his snack before dinner.

"What is the big deal, Kim? Why do you have to get so dramatic? Just put it on the list," my mother says, and just like that, everything is back to normal. "We'll get it the next time we're in town."

I sit down with toast she made for me, with apricot preserves and butter melting into a puddle around the edges. It is so good. My dad comes in the cabin with a bowl of fish filets from the fish hut. He also brings the scent of the fish hut, and the lake, with him.

His face brightens when he sees me sitting there next to Paul.

"How're you feeling?" he asks, putting the bowl down by the frying pan, and washing his hands under the faucet.

"Okay, I guess," I say. I am worried.

"Paul told us what you did," my dad says.

I put down my toast. I look at Paul, who just shrugs. *Here it comes.*

"You did good, Kim," my dad says. "You kept your head in an emergency. That's all I ever want."

My mother nods from the kitchen nook, where she is breading the fish in egg wash and cornmeal and heating the oil. He comes over, his sweatshirt splattered with blood and little fragments of fish.

"That's something they can't teach you in school," he says. "That's just you." And he goes to shower and dress in clean clothes while my mother fries up the day's catch.

BULLY IN THE HOUSE

Age: 10

The defining characteristic of Mr. Bass, the new gym teacher, is not his gut, which hangs over the top of his navy chinos, an apron of dough under the tight cotton shirt he wears tucked in. It's not his short, black crew cut, a style that looks so cute on Rich Spencer but does nothing for Mr. Bass's meaty, angry face. It's not his expensive white tennis shoes, which are actually made for tennis (whereas we call any shoe made out of cloth that name, or call it a "sneaker"). His shoes are seamed, and white, and the laces are perfectly tied.

On the back of his wide neck, below his hairline and visible above his shirt collar, Mr. Bass has a pink, squishy birthmark that looks like coarsely ground beef. Or a raw, flat cube steak. In thickness and shape it is about the size of a child's outstretched palm.

He does not hide it, but we tacitly understand we are not allowed to ask about it. So whenever he is writing on the chalkboard with his back to us, I stare at it and cannot hear a word he says.

He told us at the beginning of the year that he was forced to teach health class as part of taking the post as gym teacher. I don't think that's any of my business—an unexpressed opinion. And I'm not sure that having a grudging teacher is a good thing, when there are wonderful teachers like Mrs. Schaumburg, who makes me want to do everything right, read every book she suggests, dress just like her, and grow up to become a teacher. When we walk into her classroom, she greets us as if we are the very people she was hoping to see.

Still, Mr. Bass's discontent is like a peephole through which I find out that even adults don't get to do everything the way they want. It's a quiet comfort, sorting through this kind of information. There are rules, and even if you are not a child, you have to follow them.

I have been in the car while my father patiently outwaits a traffic light, red even when there are no cars around, on an early morning before church.

"Lights are to keep us safe," he answers when I ask why we cannot just go.

"From other cars," I remind him, believing I've found a loophole.

"Rules are there to keep us safe even when no one's looking," he says. "Even when there is no reason to follow a rule, we've all agreed to abide by it, by getting our driver's license. If I break the rule, other people will think they can break the rule, and that is like a hole in the social contract. Like a moth in your grandma's knitting. One hole leads to many, and soon the fabric is worthless." The light turns green.

In gym, Mr. Bass is a bully. He is nice to athletic children, and mean to the rest of us. I'm not going to say it's because he is also not athletic. I don't know. We never see him run, or vault, or sprint. He stands with a clipboard and his whistle and shouts horrible things to us as we do laps.

"Andersen! Haul your stinky fanny around those corners! Don't stop!"

"Castle! You're not even trying!"

"Loughlin, you're going to have to get your hair messy! Get going!"

"Decker, good job—if you want to run like a girl. Come on!"

He is also a terrible classroom teacher. His chalk drawings of how a cold virus is spread and why we need to wash our hands after sneezing don't make sense.

At the desk next to mine, John Higgins uses his right arm to shield his meticulous, detailed drawing of a Panzer tank from World War II. Mr. Bass makes fun of John for being left-handed and for how he runs in track, but he needs this boy for drawings. I mean it. The picture shows a stream of bullets blasting out of the large gun, leaving soldiers dead in the tank's oncoming path. The soldiers have pools of blood, in blue Bic ink, around them, but the way I know they are dead is that John has drawn their eyes as two X's.

Last fall, all the boys in the class were sent away to play dodgeball while Mr. Bass showed the girls a black-and-white film about menstruation. In it, a very nicely dressed mother sat on a couch talking to her daughter about where the sanitary pads were stored in their home. In my house, they are under the bathroom sink, next to a large rubber bulb and tube that my mother says is for irrigation. The film shows a cupboard door opening and a hand reaching in.

The mother also talks to the daughter about how to cinch up the pad on a free garter belt that came in the box. Everyone stays dressed. There are no diagrams. They smile and then go get a glass of milk.

I still have questions. I still don't understand how blood can just drop out of your body or why, as the movie says, it is a "different kind of pain." I don't know why my mother calls it a "curse" when she is talking to her sisters, or jokes to a friend on the telephone that she's "falling off a barn roof" or why because it's about becoming a woman, I am supposed to just go along with all of it.

The day Amy Grismer tells me it is also called a "period," I imagine little splashes of blood dotting the end of every sentence I read or write.

I am relieved, though, to read about occasional spotting in the years before our periods start. It helps explain Nellie's bloody underwear, I think.

My mother pours a little shot of crème de menthe, like bright green syrup, into her coffee when she's menstruating. It smells like Christmas morning and the name is so beautiful. My mother thinks I don't see her, but I have developed listening and other sensory tracking capabilities honed to every move anyone makes in our house, and I also have vast, sneaky peripheral vision. I miss little. And what I do miss, I eventually connect.

If you're going to be mysterious, you're just fueling my interest.

The projector is on a wheeled cart in the back of the health classroom, where we meet on Tuesdays and Thursdays instead of going to gym. One day we arrive and only half of the fluorescent lights are on. The white screen is pulled down in front of the chalkboard, and Mr. Bass is pushing his desk to one side so we have a clear view. In the middle of his desk is a large black suitcase, boxy and sleek, but standing on one end. The little suitcase my father calls his mini-bar for traveling has the same hinges. So did my Barbie case. It opens like a book in your lap, and all the things—things like Barbie's dresses on the rack—stay in place.

I am certain there are no dolls in the case on Mr. Bass's desk.

"Siddown!" Mr. Bass yells. "Siddown, now. We got a lot to cover."

He stomps around the room. "I don't have to tell you people, do I?" Mr. Bass says. "The world is a dangerous place. You all know what can happen out there."

For emphasis, he points out beyond the wide, wall-size grid of aluminum windows that keep the classroom full of light. He pulls at the gray strings next to the blinds, and they close. The room is dark.

We scramble for our seats and face the screen. He flicks the switch on the film, which has already been threaded, and scenes of devastation begin immediately.

We watch as an electrical outlet set into wood paneling begins to spark around the cords that are plugged into it. Then it bursts into flame. The entire wall starts to melt and buckle in the blaze. The next scene is an ambulance outside a house; there are gurneys with people coughing and wearing oxygen masks as they are put into the ambulance.

"Didn't make it, huh?" says an ambulance driver as the other one takes the pulse of someone on a third gurney. They solemnly pull a blanket over the face. The scene fades to a single question in large red type: "Did Charlie Smith have to die? NO!"

In the next scene, a father is smoking a cigarette while reading the paper in bed next to his sleeping wife. There's a crib. He dozes off and the cigarette sets the newspaper on fire. Over the fading sounds of a baby crying, the next scene shows their house, crumbling into embers. The exhausted firemen shake their heads as they load up the fire truck and drive away. "They didn't need to die," says one.

The rest of the film is about burn statistics, and some pictures of limbs with third- and fourth-degree burns. Faces with skin grafts. A doctor explaining how skin was taken from a person's stomach, or thigh, and put on the face.

"Even if you survive the fire, your life will never be the same," a narrator intones. I'm physically sick. The skin grafts have made me wonder about Mr. Bass's neck. Was it a burn? I suddenly feel so sorry for him that my brain cracks. I am used to not liking him for being cruel and demanding in gym class, but now I want to know why no one was watching him, how he came to be in danger.

The film ends in white and gray blank flickers, and Mr. Bass shuts off the projector and snaps the lights back on. It's probably the lighting, but we all look a little green, and very uncomfortable.

"Fire safety," he says. "This is a conversation you need to have with your parents."

He pulls at the white screen until it retracts back up into the holder that runs along the top of the chalkboard. Written there is the lesson of the day as a list, which he covers quickly.

"Make an escape plan. Right? Everyone should know two ways to get out any room in the house, in case one is blocked by fire."

"My bedroom only has one door," says Beth Swanson, without raising her hand.

"Can you jump out of the window if you have to?" he asks. We all giggle nervously. She shakes her head no, and her blond curls quiver.

"Then you have to make your parents buy a rope ladder that you keep in your room." He turns back to the list. "Make a towel wet and breathe through it. Crawl under the smoke. Got that?"

I was taking notes. My bedroom is on the second floor, too.

"What if there is no smoke?" John Higgins asks.

"Feel the door, see if it's hot. You can open it if it's not."

The presentation is full of holes. Then Mr. Bass sits down on top of his desk, and opens the suitcase wide so we can all see it.

"What's better than escaping a fire?" he asks us. We are clueless. We are ten-year-olds. Craig Johnson raises his hand. He has been using the same pencil all year, and it's now a nub. He hates sharpening it.

"Preventing a fire?" he offers.

"YES!" Mr. Bass yelps, and we all laugh. I can almost like him when he laughs, because he looks sincere. He points at the felt walls of the suitcase, where four round plastic disks are attached. They have little bull's-eyes on them, like targets. He touches one, on the side, and it shrieks. It's so high-pitched it makes my teeth hurt. After the nausea, it's kind of a relief. Or I'm going to throw up right in front of the entire class.

"Warning! There is a fire in your house. Evacuate," he says over the noise. He turns it off. Tears spring to my eyes in the sudden silence.

"These detect smoke, before it's deadly. You need them in every room in your house, up on the ceiling. Before anyone in your family is hurt—or dies. These fire detectors are now available and they are going to save lives."

He stands up and walks over to Melissa Loughlin. "Will the family it saves be yours?" he asks her, leering, and forcing her to crane her neck to look up at him.

He strolls over to Mary Sylvester. She's really good at dodgeball, and he likes her. She is a gutsy athlete, and is also really fast with answers. "Is your family going to die in a fire, Sylvester?" he says.

"I—I hope not."

"But you can make sure they *don't!*" he yells. "All of you have the power to prevent your family from dying in terrible fires!" He walks up and down the aisles between our desks, and puts a small white card on each one. I take mine from his outstretched hand. BOB BASS, it reads. FIRE SAFETY EXPERT. FREE CONSULTATIONS. Underneath is the same target logo that is on the disks, and a phone number.

"Have your parents give me a call," he says. "Unless they just don't care about dying in a fire." He glances up at the clock.

"Class is over. I hope to hear from your parents soon."

We are all sodden with information and silent with fear as we return to Mrs. Schaumburg's class, where we'll be the rest of the day. She's as welcoming as ever, and I am disappointed. We are shattered, frightened, about to go up in flames. She has no clue.

If even Mrs. Schaumburg can be completely unaware of what we have just been through, it makes the world so frightening. How can someone I think loves us not know the anguished shuffle of Amy Grismer over to her desk? Almost the only security we have is the assumption that even if adults are not accountable to us, they are there to care for us, and at the very least keep us safe from fires. From the explosive tempers of other adults. Someone must be in charge. Someone must be the boss. I simply cannot make sense of my surroundings without this belief.

I am not in charge of my entire family's safety. But if they die, it will be my fault.

Mrs. Schaumburg is talking, sorting papers, smiling at us tenderly. "If you all settle in for math," she says, "we'll have the last half-hour of the school day for reading *Charlotte's Web*."

This is a balm, and I'm not the only one to notice. We settle in. When she reads to us, and we sit in a circle on the floor listening, it's like a movie in my head. The pictures are better than anything in the illustrations. I will look at them later, when the book is back in the library. Floating along with the story, I almost forget Mr. Bass. A short attention span may be the only reason I do not walk around in a constant state of terror. By the time we go home, I've all but forgotten about dying in a blaze. The business card is just a bookmark in my math book.

Mr. Bass's special target is Billy, our fat, smelly kid. We tease him, or ignore him, but he remains cheerful, willing to laugh at himself, and never fights back. His eyes are two raisins in a plump freckled face, and there is a light stain of gray across the back of his neck. It looks almost permanent, but soap and water, more than one teacher has told him, would take care of it.

It's a struggle to put his story together. I am also fat, and teased for being fat, and I don't fight back either. But my mother makes me bathe, and sews clothes that fit me, and puts my hair in curlers on Saturday nights.

I think that anyone, any teacher, would see that he is a good boy, who shows up, but he doesn't have much to work with. I've seen Mr. Bass yell at him. It doesn't make Billy run faster, or jump higher, or try harder—but that doesn't stop Mr. Bass.

His mother doesn't look out for Billy, if he has a mother. Who would let him go to school in a yellowing T-shirt and a winter coat that doesn't zip closed over his stomach—who would not help him wash his neck, the part he cannot see?

Where he lives is a mystery, because it's not on my grid. Beyond the streets where we go back and forth to school on foot, there are neighborhoods we bike to, and neighborhoods we only drive to, but I don't know where Billy belongs. I have read too many books, so I think of him as living in a boxcar, without running water, and with a useless refrigerator, unplugged in the yard.

His temperament, so quiet and self-contained, doesn't match that picture, though, so I also imagine him heroically descending into coal mines overnight, in Wales, of course, after watching *How Green Was My Valley*. All the boys in that movie have rings of dirt on their necks, and it is a badge of hard work, done in service to the family.

For Mr. Bass, the main problem with Billy is Kenny.

Kenny Noyce is the first boy I kissed, cornering him on the playground when we were six years old. It was morning, and the bell had rung, and we were close to the same height in those days.

I loved Kenny Noyce from the time we were in kindergarten together, and through all our elementary years, sharing classrooms and class photos. He is a nice boy, when boys aren't praised for that, and he is kind, when kind is not currency.

He is also athletic, and all heart as he pulls himself on small crutches around the bases in softball after his powerful shoulders hit the ball into the distant field. Other boys run the bases for him, maybe on bad days when he has started to outgrow his custom shoes, one with a four-inch platform that make his legs more of a match in length, or maybe on a day when his crooked hips ache, his left slightly higher in jeans that have been altered to fit the bunched-up curve of his waist. He is always one of the team captains for dodgeball, and everyone wants to be on his team.

He is an encouraging captain, yelling "Great shot, Kim," or "Go, David!" to his team mates. But it's really just safer to be on his team. He plays to win, and he lobs dodgeballs with such force and focus that if he aims at the opposing team, you're not only out, but bruised by flaming red marks where the ball hits.

One spring day, we are outside practicing events for track and field day. There is the standing broad jump, the running broad jump, pole vaulting, and different races. Miss Essington's sixth graders are up the hill from us, having class outside in the spring weather. She is also the assistant principal, and the closest thing we have to an authority whenever Mrs. Lightfoot is not around. She is strict, everyone knows that, but she also has the calm of a teacher who has seen just about everything.

I can hear their murmuring, and she is smiling as she talks to them, sitting with her feet curled up underneath her dirndl skirt in the spring grass. It is long and easy under our feet, not yet mowed, not yet dry and spiky from heat. My brother, Paul, is up there, and Kenny Noyce's brother, Will, and Tommy Grismer, too.

I can tell they are distracted by us, because they have to sit still and talk with the teacher, I think, while we get to run around. In spring, when our lungs fill for the first time with fresh sunny air, it's as if we are about to burst. We hurl ourselves around the track till we drop. We skip instead of walk. Cartwheel instead of skip.

Kenny is practicing hangs on the monkey bars. For the President's Physical Fitness Test, we are required to hang at least a minute. Kenny lasts three. The rest of us take turns swinging across the monkey bars, using the momentum of our bodies to reach up and grasp another bar, pulling ourselves hand-over-hand toward one end. I drop at the midpoint. Kenny turns around on one arm, his shoulder flexing, and starts the way back. When his turn is over, he goes over to the track to walk laps. He doesn't change into sneakers for gym class, the way the rest of us do. He is always in his custom leather shoes.

When it is Billy's turn, he reaches for the first monkey bar with both hands, holds on for a couple of seconds, and then lets go, crumpling to the ground. It doesn't count as a hang. It doesn't count as anything. But Billy's face is red, and sweat is pouring off his head, and he looks as if he is going to vomit, he is breathing so hard.

Mr. Bass comes over with his clipboard.

"What is this?" he screams. "What the hell is this?"

He shoves at Billy with one foot. I hang back, as if I don't notice. No one else is moving, except Kenny, scooting around the track on crutches.

Mr. Bass points at Kenny, and his mouth is open, but he's so mad no words are coming out. His whole face is purple, and the mark on the back of his neck matches. He kicks Billy, on the ground. He is practically slobbering in anger, and he puts it all into kicking Billy.

Up on the hill, Miss Essington stands up and brushes off her skirt before heading toward us.

Mr. Bass takes a great gulping breath. He points at Kenny, in the direction of the track.

"Do you see this kid?" he screams. "He's a goddamned cripple, but he comes out harder and stronger than any of you sissies! You're all an embarrassment, especially you, Andersen!" He kicks Billy again, in the thigh, and the boy whimpers.

I look up the hill, and see all the sixth graders staring at us. My brother looks worried. Tommy Grismer, too. Miss Essington is halfway down the hill, but I, for one, can't move. Kicking a kid is wrong, we all know that, but we don't want that anger directed at us.

Shocked by the swearing and fearing Mr. Bass, none of us can budge. We just watch the way you watch a bull in a field, making sure that when it charges, it's not headed for you.

I don't see Kenny's brother, Will, come down the hill until he is right behind Mr. Bass, and taps him on the shoulder.

He whips around, startled.

"Oh, Christ! What is it, Noyce?"

"What did you call my brother?" Will says quietly. His fists are clenched at his sides.

Mr. Bass could have backed down. He could have checked his temper, his employment manual, his common sense, his gods. Instead, he just makes it worse. We all draw closer. No one is paying any attention to us anyway.

"I said he's a goddamned cripple."

Will draws back his arm as if he is about to punch the man in the face.

Miss Essington, at the bottom of the hill, stops.

I see a crutch, sideways, come up between Mr. Bass's legs from behind, and hear the thud as Kenny delivers an upward blow to the teacher's crotch. Mr. Bass drops with a squeak, first to his knees, and then rolls to his side on the ground, grunting in pain. His face is drained of color.

Miss Essington has already started back up the hill toward school. She has seen what happened, and she has to report it. A teacher has been attacked, after all.

But her pace is slow, and has no urgency. She gathers up all her students, and then turns one last time toward the fourth graders. She catches me staring at her, and she smiles slightly, it seems, as she puts her finger to her lips. *Shhhhh-hh.*

Kenny, a little under four feet tall, stands over Mr. Bass,

101

and looks up at his brother. "I don't want you to worry, Will. You know I can take care of myself," he says.

Then Kenny walks with his jerky gait toward Billy while holding both crutches in one hand. He offers Billy the other, and pulls him right up. We are all so quiet, then, without even a nervous laugh among us. *Shhhhhhh*. We go back up the hill toward our next class, and we never see Mr. Bass again.

ONE WAY HOME

Age: 11

The sky is gray, and it is so early that I have been able to secure my spot on the dock. I am saying good-bye to the lake, which I will not see for another ten months. I don't want to go back home to Des Moines, where there is no swimming, there are no boats, no loons sending us to sleep most nights on the wings of their sorrowful calls.

I cannot bear it, and if I once saw the lake through my mother's eyes, and all its domestic inconveniences, I cannot summon any of that now. I feel so protective of this tiny little sliver of time, and don't have the words for it, because the thought is so big.

I don't want to live in a giant clean house, where there is no sand on the sheets to scratch my sunburn, no scent of the lake in the water we drink, and when you want clean clothes, you open a drawer and that's what you find—not a trip to town with the whole family, and donuts to eat while the dryer runs, or bakeries where ladies hand you a cookie just for coming close to the counter.

My father cannot excuse himself after dinner around the chipped Formica table where we paint our nails, do crossword puzzles, play card games on rainy days, and watch everyone filing in and out of the bathroom all day long. He stays at the table to read his book, or he stands up to prepare to go fishing, but he is always there.

My father, home. No teaching scuba at night, no business dinners. Even when he drives back and forth for weekends, he arrives on Fridays, and for the summer, he and my mother do not dump us on babysitters and sail back into their social lives. He rejoins us in the cabin, in our world, and our schedule. He is ours as he seldom is back home. And my mother, at the table, is ready to chat, not rushing off with instructions for the grandparents, or for the parade of teenagers from the neighborhood who look after us. Not dressing for meetings, or seeing old school friends, or volunteering at the church, or playing bridge. Not up in her sewing room, which is a refuge for her, with her own television set, and a little shelf where she puts her mug of coffee and cigarettes, away from the fabrics and the Singer.

This economy of space and time I come to love over every summer, when I can enter the only door to the cabin, off the front porch, and know who is home and where they are, instantly. Without a phone, there are no sales calls to aggravate my parents, or important people summoning one of them to a gathering, no errands on the way to swim class or choir practice. There's one car, and we're either all in it, traveling someplace together, or it's parked. It's the five of us. No one ringing the doorbells, no school, no mail bringing report cards or catalogs from J. C. Penney's, and its back-to-school sales reminding us that summer is coming to a close.

There are no newspapers, with their mysterious headlines and murdered nurses, and words I don't understand. We don't even have a radio to hum along with the latest songs. I don't find it isolating. It feels like a cocoon.

When we sleep at night, we can hear one another breathing or, when Grandmother Castle comes up, snoring. Then we hear the giggles, too, that sweep through the loft and down to the first floor with every one of her great slobbering exhales.

She's changed by the lake, too, and that makes me love her more. She stops wearing makeup and high heels, and her hair gets straight, almost boyish, when she brushes it behind her ear. Her alarmingly snug pastel-colored pantsuits give way to loose housecoats and soft sweaters, and she's nicer to hug, sort of squishy, because she's not stuffed into a girdle.

She does not come up often. None of them do. They aren't invited, and we see them so often at home, no one really minds. But the Jenkinses drove up a few days ago, and it closed down lake time early. It's a disloyal thought, I know that, but it also feels fair.

The first morning, I just want to read. I want to read on my cot under the skylight. But there is an unsettled energy in the cabin with extra people around. Grandma Jenkins calls up the stairs that she's baked cookies, trying to be useful, and then I look like an ingrate for not immediately sailing down to be with everyone around the table.

Grandpa Jenkins is a mean caged bear and does nothing but pace. My mother is both happy to have her mother around, and nervous that there aren't enough beds—Paul gets a sleeping bag on the sofa—and no television to occupy her father.

Grandpa Jenkins needs to be busy in his workshop, in his hardware store, or in front of the television set, watching football. The lake offers none of these, and he is tense with boredom.

So he picks on us. I have one of Grandma's cookies in one hand and my book in the other.

"What kind of trash is that?" he asks, pointing to the cover, where a boy and a girl are holding hands.

Here's the thing about caged bears: you can walk away from the cage. I know he won't follow me—he isn't that comfortable walking on the rocky, tree-root-laced trails back and forth to the beach unless he is holding someone's arm. So I leave the cabin.

Conversation still drifts out the screen door. I hear him ask Paul if he wants to go fishing. Nellie isn't far behind me when I take my place at the end of the dock. She stares off in the direction of Blueberry Island.

"He wants to go to town for ice cream," she says in a low voice, and I know whom she means. She sits down and draws her knees up to her chest.

"There's ice cream at the lodge," I say.

"Mom told him that," she says in a low voice. "He told her he wanted to take a little drive into town."

"Great," I say. "Let him."

"He wants me to go with him," Nellie says.

I hear the sounds of the rowboats in the boathouse thudding dully against the dock. I hear the waves lapping the shore behind us.

"I don't want to go with him," she whispers into her knees. "I don't want to."

I stare, unseeing, at the page. I just want to read. And I do what adults do when they want to do what they want to do. I don't look up. I harden myself.

"He's your grandfather. He loves you," I force myself to say. When I feel her leave, I look up from the book and she is back on the path to the cabin, her red curls lifting slightly in the wind off the lake.

By the time the Jenkinses leave the next day, I can't talk. Swallowing food suffocates me, my throat is so closed up with a sob, or an ache that I can't explain. This is hilarious to my brother—"She's going to die of starvation!"—because I am the last person anyone would think would starve.

When I force myself back to the cabin on the day we leave, my father is slamming all the car doors, locking the car-top carrier, going into every room on the main floor and even up to the loft to look under the beds, for a sock, a note, a paperback book, a shoe.

My mother mutters at the pile of dirty rags she's taking home, and about the piles of laundry she will face, and wipes down the counters and shelves with ferocious swipes.

"My stomach hurts," my sister says, "it really, really does," and we all ignore her.

"Go check your bed," my mother says. "Make sure you have all your toys. We're not coming back for them."

Nellie and I climb the steps of the spiral staircase, where I grab my car bag. It has the library book I saved for the drive home, an open package of Doublemint Gum, and a postcard of a loon on the lake: WELCOME TO COOK COUNTY, MINNESOTA!

"It really hurts," Nellie says again, and I am thinking the same thing: It always really hurts to leave. And then I remember her stomachache, and I feel a little sorry for her, because getting into the car when you're queasy is just a long version of wanting to vomit so you'll feel better.

Take the Dramamine, nap till lunchtime, and the lake begins to fade. It helps that there is a pool at the motel where we are staying tonight. Paul pretends he left my library books in the cabin for the past half-hour of the drive, teasing me about the cost of replacing books and library fines. And Nellie's moaning over her stomachache has made the drive feel twice as long as usual. I am happy to get out of the car and get away from them at the restaurant.

Of course, when we stop for lunch at Little Falls, Ray's family stops, too. They live in St. Paul now, and their drive will be over in three more hours. Perfect family, perfect distance. I envy Ray's family, where both older sisters tend to the youngest, as if they are friends. That would be a small puncture in my cocoon, if it hadn't already been destroyed by just leaving the lake. I feel alone. I never feel alone at the lake. It's like I've already gone home.

We are eight hours from Des Moines, but right on schedule, because of the overnight at the motel. My parents joke about it as we get out of the car for lunch.

"Postpone getting home, okay?" my dad asks.

"Postpone laundry!" my mother answers. "A pool for them."

"A nightcap for us," he adds.

"Perfect."

The restaurant is crowded and we wait before we can get a table for ten in the center. Once we are seated, I order a cheeseburger with American cheese, as always, and Paul orders a Reuben, like my mother.

Nellie is mewling that she's not hungry, and when the waitress puts a little cup of chicken soup with some saltines in front of her, my sister throws up.

My father is next to Nellie, and puts down his roast beef au jus sandwich to help her wipe her mouth. Then he feels her forehead.

His eyes. I have never seen such eyes. A dad should never ever let his kids see that look. Not when he's supposed to be in charge and know everything.

My mother has seen his face, too, and stands up with such force that she knocks the table violently. Most of the water glasses splash over.

"She's burning up!" he shouts, and picks her up in his arms like a Raggedy Ann. She seems to weigh nothing. And he doesn't seem to mind the vomit all over his sweatshirt, as he carries her out to the lobby.

My mother grabs her purse and looks at Ray and Joyce. They say, almost at the same time, "We've got them," and that's just about the only reference to Paul and me for the next few hours. Nellie is about to die. But no one is saying anything about her either.

Dot, Victoria, and Dee look punished. They act as if this is the worst thing that could have happened to them, even as their mother orders ice cream for all of us, and Ray pays the bill.

"When are we goooooing?" Dee, the littlest sister, moans, and her mother hushes her. I want to slap her. When we were four, and met for the first time, we threw sand at each other on the beach until Joyce pulled us apart. I still remember swallowing sand, and how it hurt my throat.

Victoria has a driver's license, and offers to drive the rest of the family home, and this worries me.

"You can't," Ray says. "Milt took our car to the emergency room. We have their car, and their boat."

Emergency room. A hospital. My brother is still chewing the rest of his sandwich in silence, and when he swallows, I hear it. The smell of vomit is in my nose, even though the busboy has tried to clean it up. I cannot find a place for my thoughts to land. The lake is gone, home is too far away, all our stuff is in a car that strangers are going to drive to their house? What is happening?

Dee, oddly, delivers me. She opens the tote bag that she carries everywhere and starts handing comic books around the table. *Richie Rich* for Paul, and *Millie the Model* for me, and her sisters split up the *Archie* comic books that are left.

I'm not really following the stories, but time passes while I look at the clothes and the dots of color across the pages. We keep reading as Joyce herds us out to the front lobby, freeing up our table for the cleaning staff.

An hour or so later, as I stare down at a page, my dad leans over me, and kisses the top of my head. Ray's family is watching my father closely, looking for clues.

"Hey," he says, and it's a tone he almost never uses, so gentle and inquiring. Just that, one small word, and I start sobbing. The comic book slides out of my lap. He has left his sweatshirt somewhere. I hug him close.

"Is she okay?" Paul asks, and his voice is trembling, too.

"She was *not* okay," he answers. "Her appendix almost burst. But they got it. She is in the operating room and your mom's with her." He looks at me.

I thought she was just faking. *Oh, God. Don't let her die.*

"Kimmy, I have to go back to be with your mom. Nellie will be fine, I think. But she has to stay in the hospital for two or three days."

Ray steps in. "Milt, we'll take them back to our house."

I don't want to be at someone's house.

I'm not the only one working out the logistics. Dee, Dot, and Victoria look ready to kill me. Their car is a sedan, not a station wagon. Two more passengers means one in the front with Ray and Joyce, and four almost-teenagers in the back.

My dad and Ray stand to one side, talking quietly, in almost identical bleached khakis, polo shirts, and dock shoes. It's the uniform of the lake, although my father's is pressed and crisp, and Ray's is rumpled and worn. He is also wearing the bucket hat he is never without. He uses the ribbon around the crown to hold fishing lures, or unlit cigarettes, or once, a shopping list from Joyce.

The lobby is empty. All the other vacationers have finished lunch and are back on the road. The smell of food, of burgers and chicken soup and pancakes, has faded and the scent of Pine-Sol fills the air as the staff prepares for the supper shift. But the men have a plan.

"Okay," my father says. "Let's get the Antrims back on the road. They're going to take our boat to their house. Then I'll drop you both at the hotel, and go back to the hospital. Your mom can see you tonight."

In the parking lot, while the rest of us stand around, my father and Ray do an elaborate switching of the two cars, unhitching the boat from the station wagon and hitching it up to their car. They make sure all the wiring is correct, the left turn signal and the right turn signal and the brake lights. My father finds the small packed bag in our car that my mother had put together for the overnight motel stop. It has swimsuits, pajamas, and clean underwear—for all three of us. I try not to think that one of us is missing.

I am so jealous that their family just gets to go home, that their vacation will come to a normal close.

Joyce hugs Paul and me and gets in the car. The girls are bickering quietly as they settle, three across, in the back seat. I imagine that they are thrilled to be out of it. As the car starts, they try to wave at us out the back window, but the boat, raised up by the trailer, mostly obscures our view of them.

My father has made reservations at a hotel near the hospital. We'll stay there until Nellie gets better. He checks us in at the front desk, gives Paul a key to the hotel room, and walks us there. We put on our swimsuits, and at the indoor pool, he sits in a plastic chair and watches us.

We always look forward to the novelty of a hotel after the lake; for me, it makes it a little easier to leave summer behind. And my dad is going out of his way to be cheerful. But it feels

111

so wrong. I don't want to swim while Nellie is having an operation.

I lower myself into the water, and I see Paul is just as tentative. We just sort of walk around in the shallow end. We are not splashing one another, or swimming.

"Hey, kids?" my dad calls. He glances at his watch. "I'm going to use the pay phone over there." He points to a spot just outside the humid auditorium that houses the pool. We nod, of course, and he leaves, but he returns a little too quickly. They have no new information on Nellie, he says, as he summons us over to the side of the pool and squats to talk to us.

"I have to go check on your mom and sister," he says. "You two stick together. Be safe here, and go back to the room where you're ready. I left you change for the candy machines in the room—but you should go together, and take a room key. Just—take care of each other."

We are both in the water, so he cannot hug us good-bye. He awkwardly pats Paul's head, squeezes my shoulder. He walks away, and gets almost all the way to the pay phone. Paul and I, like automatons trained to follow a light, watch him as he turns and sprints back toward us.

"Get out of the pool," he says anxiously. "Just come up here so I can talk to you."

We obey. Everything is so weird. We'll do anything he says. We pull hotel towels around our dripping shoulders and listen.

"You guys don't always get along so well," he begins. "You don't. I wish you did. I didn't have a sister till I was fourteen years old, and by the time she could talk and walk and be in any way interesting, I was in college.

"Today. Just today, you please have to get along and take care of each other. You see, your mom and I love each other, but we aren't related. Not the way you kids are. You have both our blood in you. You belong to each other in a way your mom and I never can."

He is so desperate to be clear with us. "When your mom and I are gone—I'm sorry, Kimmy, I know this makes you sad. Your grandmother says you were born with a worry line across your forehead."

My dad swallows hard, and his eyes are red behind his glasses. "You kids." His voice is gruff with tears. "I have to tell you both this."

I am frightened—beyond my usual worry—because he never talks to us like this. I realize that he never had a chance to have lunch, so he probably hasn't had a drink.

In fact, I understand about the alcohol right this minute. When everything is just too hard, and no one can figure it out, it just—the pressure to know what to do is killing. It is killing my dad right now. The alcohol isn't the end game. Drinking isn't the point. Getting away from that pressure is the only thing that matters. If I could, I would have poured him a drink right there.

Because he is way too excited right now, and I am uncomfortable. I also know he is about to tell us the truth. He doesn't want to tell us, and we don't want to hear it, but we have to pass this way. The three of us. And I am ready, eager, to know this one truth about our family.

"When we are gone, the way your grandparents will also be gone, you will only have one another. You two, and Nellie. That's it. No one else will know anything about your family, or your childhood, or your adventures, or good days, like Christmas, or today, this terrible day, but you three. Not the real way."

He runs his fingers through his curly red hair, almost the only time I've ever seen him do that. He uses those two brushes every morning but never touches it again the rest of the day.

"Please?" he says. "Just don't tease. Just don't fight. Just today, be nice to each other."

Paul sort of steps up, then. He takes my hand, still clammy from swimming, and from the humidity in the room. "We will."

I join in. My dad's eyes are absolutely haunted. "We will," I repeat.

He smiles, but just barely. "You have the key?" he says to Paul.

Paul nods.

"Okay, then," my father says. "I'm trusting you both. If everything is okay, I'll be back for dinner, and I'll try to bring your mom. Wait in the room. And use the chain on the door."

The minute he's gone, my brother drops my hand. I tense up, thinking he's about to push me in the pool.

"You know," he says, "I thought Nellie was just making it up."

My relief at this is inexpressible. But he has just said it out loud. Like, it's okay to say it. It was okay to think it.

"I thought she was faking it," I admitted. "Because she always does."

"I guess not this time," Paul replies.

If everything is okay, my father said, he'll be back for dinner. This is a hook to hang a thought on.

Paul is on to the next thing, and shrugs. "I kind of don't want to swim," he says. "Do you want to go watch TV?"

Do I? I breathe. Really deeply.

At last, my brain can land. Television, a cartoon, maybe a familiar show, even just some nice static across an old Western. My brother found a path back to some kind of normal— candy bars and TV and waiting for news of our sister.

THE FIVE DAYS OF CHRISTMAS

Age: 10

Day 1

I start counting the days of Christmas on the first day we
have off from school. On Monday morning, December
23, I wake up so excited that I know I won't be able to sit
still to read. The doorbell rings all day, my mother flips the
holiday records at half-hour intervals, and the Christmas
soup—bubbling away on the stove but not for eating till
tomorrow—makes the house smell good, and my father is
home—the office is closed.

My mother pulls my father into little projects all day
long, and they bicker amiably about every decision, but I
like them this way, both home and near. I assume the whole
world has the week off.

Nellie is excited, too, scrambling out of bed almost the
moment I have opened my eyes. "Can we eat cereal on the
bed?" she asks, and I know what she wants. It's the perfect
thing to do on a day off—we bring snacks to the room, or
cereal boxes in the flavors we like, and we read and scare ourselves with stories about "the boy under the bed."

It's so early and everyone else is sleeping in. We tiptoe
downstairs where I grab Cap'n Crunch, and she chooses
Sugar Pops. Then we go back to our room and scour our
shelves for books we want to read or magazines—*Highlights*
for her, and *Reader's Digest* for me—we've brought up from

downstairs. We start reading, our backs against the head-board, but there are two sides, the foot of the bed and one length, where we could be surprised by the boy's long arm, reaching up from under the bed. He is the reason we turn off the light across the room at night and take a running jump into bed from some distance. We know we cannot have our feet too close to his home in the dark.

I don't know when we decided he lives there. But if, while we were shifting around, a sheet starts to fall over the side, we must grab it so the boy can't get it. Or if Nellie's foot is hanging off the end, I stare at her meaningfully until her eyes grow wide with fright. And she can't just jerk her foot away. She has to do it quietly so the boy won't notice. She pulls the corners of her mouth down in concentration, and little whimpers come out of her that only I can hear.

She is happy, next to me, munching along with the Sugar Pops, and living inside this self-induced threat to ourselves. The boy, who never comes out, is modeled after real neigh-borhood bullies, Kirby Wolf and Keevin Meese, and he will be ruthless if he catches us and delivers his (and their re-al-life) worst punishment, which is being spit into a corner.

On the playground, Kirby and Keevin will pick you out, like a weak member of some herd you didn't know you were a part of, and they jointly spit at you, while you back up, try-ing to get away from glob after glob of spit. And when you cannot back up any farther, because of the schoolyard fence, which is just chicken wire between steel posts, or because of the jungle gym or because of the rough red brick of the school building itself, they just keep spitting until they are tired, or their mouths are dry, or a teacher calls them away.

Whoever you are, you have to figure out what to do next. The terror of being spit into a corner is real, it's hap-pened to all of us, and we all know that if we tattle, Kirby and Keevin will just do it to you again. I don't understand their power, and yet I never challenge it knowingly.

Teachers do not recognize them as bullies. They are well behaved in class, and sharp with facts. So only we know, and we don't talk about it among ourselves. We lose every fight to them, but without blood and bruises, and because they never want anything, like money or lunch, there is almost no evidence of what they've done. Even if you don't have a hanky or tissue, you can use a long sleeve or flowing skirt, or the napkin from your lunchbox. There's always a way to just wipe off your face and go back to class. Their crimes are invisible to adults, and Kirby and Keevin are never detected.

When it comes to the boy under the bed, he's just as invisible, but Nellie and I know he's there, and we know how to keep him at bay. We don't let anything hang over the edge of the bed, and we occasionally throw a couple pieces of cereal under the bed, just for good measure. It makes my sister laugh, this ritual. I love making her laugh.

As for the cereal we leave there, the cleaning lady, Juanita, says nothing, and one time when my mother vacuumed and asked about it, I just shrugged.

The lesson of Kirby and Keevin is that things happen outside of adults' awareness and control. It's a thought too big to take in, that adults don't know everything, that bullying and even danger are possible because of this.

Day 2

On Christmas Eve, we wake up to a blizzard, and you would think none of us has ever seen snow. My mother and father are either phoning everyone they know to make counterplans to anything that might be canceled because of the weather, or the phone is ringing so often that my parents, in exasperation, have demanded that the three of us answer for them.

I can hear the rattle of wrapping paper behind the closed door to the sewing room. The long screech of tape snaps off the roll of the dispenser before my mother taps it into place on a package. I'm happy to be of service so that more packages can get wrapped.

"Castle residence, this is Kim," I say a dozen times, and it's Marvy Grismer asking if we're going to church that night, if Jimmy can ride with us, or it's my aunt Deo wondering what time we're dropping off cookies and if we can pick up Grandma Jenkins on the way, because they don't want to shovel out two lanes of their driveway. But I call my mother to the phone so many times that she gets annoyed and sends us outside.

Right after this, right before we go, I see her do something no one in my family has ever done. She takes the phone off the hook.

Even my father, at the dinner hour, when phone calls are treated like alien invasions to our "family time," never takes the phone off the hook. As if he has a contract with the phone company, that they have installed a phone and we will always answer. It's up to him, therefore, to educate unwitting callers. "No, she can't come to the phone, you'll have to try later. No, I can't take a message. We're having dinner."

With my mother's act, anyone who calls us will get a busy signal. And keep trying, maybe even worrying about not being able to get through.

The upside is that the incessant ringing stops.

But come on. Getting thrown out of the house is exactly what we were hoping for. It's blizzarding, and we want to go sledding. We take Nellie's plastic disk saucer and our Radio Flyer from the garage and kick the soft, almost sandy snow out of the way to cross the street. We can hear the snowplows somewhere in the neighborhood, but our street hasn't been touched. There are no car tracks, even though the day before Christmas is a busy day for deliveries. The florist brought poinsettias from one of my father's business associates that morning, but the heavy snowfall has covered his tracks in the driveway, as if he were never there.

We cross the street, and go down the Smith driveway. David Smith's mother is a nurse and a single mother, and all I can think whenever I hear that is "no father." David has a key to his house. He wears it on a lanyard he made at day camp last summer. When we are enrolled in day camp, it's so we get sunshine and learn crafts. When David goes, it's so he won't be "shut up in that dark house all day alone," a pronouncement my mother makes every day when the school bus takes him off to day camp.

The rest of us do not have keys to our houses. One of our parents is always there, or the cleaning lady, or babysitters, or grandparents. My mother is David's emergency contact, and I cannot imagine what will happen if he actually needs something, because my mother is seldom home.

This gives us something like higher perch in the hierarchy than David, who is my brother's age, and who once, while building a workbench, was hammering the top surface while Paul worked on the lower shelf, and accidentally smashed a nail down into his head. It grazed Paul's forehead, but the way the blood was gushing over his face was thrilling and terrible.

David's mother is always at work. Nights, weekends, days—she is never there. The tacit law is that no child can be inside anyone else's house unless a parent is there, so at David's, we are only allowed to play outside. In the summer and spring, "outside" includes his garage, where behind a closed garage door and subsequently very smoky area, he grills bananas basted in butter that we eat with cinnamon sugar, and he always has marshmallows for roasting, and bread for toasting. He is very matter-of-fact about cooking. I don't know what he eats the rest of the time.

David's yard, in snow, is the bottom of the most perfect staging ground for sled run after sled run. We trudge up the hill so many times our legs ache, but the rush of coming down pays for each effort. Opposite the hill, the yard slopes up slightly toward an empty lot, so we not only sled down the hill, but ride up the other side of the bowl to a gentle stop in deep snow.

We are hot, sweaty, and icy by the time the sun sets, and the snow has stopped falling. When the three of us cross back to our house, we have to climb over two chunky walls of snow, rocks, and ice where the snowplows have gone by. My father is shoveling a path down our driveway so we can go to church that night. He sees our flushed faces and waves us inside, reminding us to stomp the snow off our boots before we get into the kitchen.

The scent of Christmas soup, which is long-simmered beef and chunks of root vegetables, greets us and fogs up my glasses. We strip down to our long underwear while my mother mops around us and sorts the outer clothing on to hangers to dry.

While she is busy, I pick up the kitchen phone and it sounds normal. The dial tone restores a piece of myself I did not know was missing. I did not like being unreachable, and disconnected. I did not know I felt this way, until I heard that steady sound.

Day 3

On Christmas Day morning, the newspaper slaps the front porch. Except for the crunch of the paperboy's boots on the snowy front yards, the streets are dark and empty; the sun won't rise for another two hours, at seven twenty-nine. I am awake early with the first Nancy Drew book, *The Secret of the Old Clock* by Carolyn Keene, which is soothing because I know what's going to happen, and worth reading again because it's good plotting.

Every night, after bedtime, my father makes his rounds, checking for plugged-in cords and lights left burning. He is obsessed with wasting electricity. Correction: He hates wasting money on electricity. Sometimes he stands by the electric meter in the garage, with a flashlight, certain that all the fuses are off, and that all the lights are out, and he's fuming.

"What is still running?" he says, watching the meter go around and around. "What's still on?"

He doesn't show a fraction of that passion for, say, my report card, or my brother's intricate model cars, constructed painstakingly from tiny plastic pieces he breaks off from a long rod. The fit of a suit—yes. A thread hanging off my dress—yes. He carries a slender silver charm on his keychain, the size of a matchbook, that has tiny foldable scissors, a sharp little blade, a flat nail file, and a silver toothpick. He uses all of these at least once a day.

Because reading by flashlight is going to further "ruin" my eyes, my parents put a nightstand next to my bed, equipped with a lamp, and a boxy electric clock.

Pointing at the clock when she first gave it to me, my mother had said, "As long as you're never late for school—

121

and that means time for breakfast, too—you can stay up as late as you'd like to read. Try not to disturb Nellie."

She had leaned in a little then, and spoke in a whisper. "If anyone asks—and no one had better ask—I have given up on trying to make you go to bed." She put her finger to her lips.

I felt the privilege, and the excitement, of knowing I'd never have to lie awake in the night again, wondering what had happened next in a book.

Next door, the Lindstroms' chocolate poodle is barking. The paperboy is working his way up the street. I turn off the light and stare at the clock, where the numerals and the hands glow a soft green.

If I am quiet, I can get the newspaper and read it at the kitchen table until everyone else wakes up. I keep my eyes straight on the front door, looking neither left, toward the living room tree, blinking with holiday lights amid a peninsula of stacked gifts, nor right toward the family room hearth, where there are stockings full of candy and small presents. Opening it soundlessly—there are no squeaky doors or floors in the entire house, thanks to my father's attention to such worrying details—I nab the paper, dodging the cold that darts through the open door, and take it around the corner to the kitchen table.

Except for a coffee cake wrapped in green cellophane on the counter, there are almost no signs of Christmas in there. I turn on the Depression-glass lamp that hangs over the round oak table, which is perfect for reading or doing homework. My father hates to eat or read in dim lighting. In fact, my father is something of a fussbudget. I had learned this by listening to other adults discuss one another. It was such a relief to have a name and category for any of their behavior.

Being the first person to read the paper comes with privileges. First, I love slipping off the red rubber band, and adding it to the kitchen's messy drawer. Second, the paper feels cool, almost damp, with an inky smell as I unfold it, and spread the front page out. And if I read a story that is continued, I am certain to find that page right where it is supposed to be.

I almost never read the front page. I usually only read the weather in one corner, and small announcements set in a small type that appear across the bottom of the columns.

But the picture of a blond, smiling girl gazes out at me from a school photo. She is wearing the same dress that my arch-nemesis, fellow-reader Melissa Loughlin, owns, with a jewel neck collar folded over with a large button closure to one side. I stare at her. There are never children on the front page unless they are at an event the paper is covering, like a store opening, or a concert.

GIRL, 10, GOES MISSING ON CHRISTMAS EVE, the page announces in big bold letters. Her name is Pamela Powers. She is my age. She'd gone to her brother's wrestling match at the YMCA, and then went to wash her hands.

"Honey, what are you doing up?" my father asks, entering the kitchen. He's in a red plaid Pendleton wool robe he only wears on Christmas. He plugs in the coffeepot and sits down next to me while waiting for it to brew.

"I couldn't sleep," I say to him. He puts his hand out, and I am so grateful I reach for it, to squeeze it. My heart is racing about Pamela. He squeezes back, but then points, with the jut of his chin, at the newspaper. I slide the front page over to him and watch as he scans it.

His brow, below a hairline of graying red hair, furrows while his eyebrows twitch up in surprise a couple of times, before he holds the paper up in front of his face, blocking my view.

"Anything interesting in here?" he says from behind the paper. He and I don't really talk much, not the way my mother and I do.

I pull the section with the comics toward me. In one corner of the page is the big round scene I always read first: *The Family Circus.* It's blurring, because my eyes are stinging, then filling up with tears. What did it mean, that she'd gone to wash her hands, and disappeared?

I wonder about her parents, if they are still at the Y, waiting for her to come back. I think about my mother, at the grocery store, once when we were separated, and how she'd charged around the corner and found me in front of the toys and grabbed me by the shoulders.

"Don't you *ever* walk away from me again!" she'd cried. "You scared the living daylights out of me, do you understand?" She was so angry at me, she didn't even speak to me after that. I didn't even get spanked, and that was even more terrifying; I had done something so wrong that not even a good spanking answered it.

Is Pamela's mother mad? Worried? Is she awake right now, on Christmas morning? I am aware of every sound: the coffee percolating behind me, my dad turning a page, the steps of someone else coming down the stairs.

A tear slips down my cheek and lands on the comics page with a damp slap, so the classified ads on the page behind it show through. Wet newsprint has such a distinct scent I associate with my dad's rage at the paperboy, for leaving the paper in the rain, or accidentally throwing it in a puddle, or even just leaving it too near other wet papers, instead of in a dry plastic bag. *Fussbudget with anger issues.*

My mother comes in, then, in her robe and slippers, but also with lipstick and combed hair, because she knows my father will be taking photographs all morning long. She squeezes my shoulder as she passes me, and says, "Merry Christmas!" in a very sunny voice, instead of asking me if I'd snooped around and ruined my holiday.

The rules for my older brother, little sister, and me, about bedtimes, and staying close when we are in stores, and doing our homework before dinner, had always seemed like obstacles, to be ignored, or cheated, or pushed through despite protests. I could stay up late as long as I wasn't caught, or my brother could do his homework on the way to school, as long as he actually got it done.

The rules had always been the problem, and I chafed at all of them, at least until my mother bent a little, and gave me the lamp, and told me I could read at night, or let me have a bowl of cereal in the middle of the night instead of making me wait for a hot breakfast.

My mother yawns a bit, and stretches, then pours fresh coffee for my father and one for herself. They smile at each other when she brings it to the table, and she clinks her mug with his, and asks me if I want hot chocolate now or when the others wake up. She tips my face up toward hers with one finger, under my chin, and looks at me with concern.

"I'll wait for the others," I say in a very normal voice.

It works. It gives her the smile back, so she can be happy it's Christmas, and all the shopping is done, and all the packages are wrapped, and we are at the beginning of the good part, after all those preparations.

Any lingering resentment I have for all the rules in my family, at school, in church, at the lake, all of it falls away for me then. Like uncooked spaghetti before it softens in the boiling water, I see the rules as rigid only until someone lets go. Without the rules, a child will ruin her eyes reading with a flashlight, or by staying up too late to be able to do well in school the next day. A girl can disappear on Christmas Eve, in an ordinary YMCA, wearing orange stretch pants and bobby socks under her snow boots. Without the rules, her presents will stay under the tree, unopened, perhaps through the day.

In mere moments later, my brother and sister rattle down the steps, and want to skip the annual sibling photo on the staircase and go right into unwrapping. My father protests, and with great good nature and, I'd seen, a little vodka in his tomato juice, herds them back. I rush to take my place, uncomplaining.

"It's the tradition!" he reminds the other two as he puts Paul in front, me in the middle, and my sister at the top of the steps, where she looks, unusually, the tallest.

Tradition is a nicer name for rules, and that day, I want to keep all the traditions we have. We take turns opening packages, have a break for hot chocolate and coffee cake, and refold wrapping paper to my mother's satisfaction. I move between tears and contentment all day long, and when I go to find the front page of the morning paper to finish reading the article, the newspaper is gone.

I don't mind. In the afternoon, I take my seat at the piano and bang out all the usual Christmas carols while everyone sings along. I set the table for dinner, and welcome my grandparents, and I am all day long the very most perfect Kim I can be. I do all this in the name of protecting us, of protecting Pamela, to keep my family safe, and to keep hers safe, too.

I don't remember the presents I receive. I don't know what I eat that day. We travel out to the Castle farm, then to the mansion, all our rituals intact, unbroken, even by the snow-filled streets. We drive home in the waning light and there are more relatives stopping by, and carols on the record player, and clattering of side dishes for the roast in the kitchen and all the condiments my mother brings out once a year. I listen very hard, for any movement outside our home, and I'm at the door in the wintry evening darkness to take *The Des Moines Tribune* right out of the paperboy's hands.

His name is Ted, and he knows better than to throw it at our porch, because if he misses, my father will report him to the newspaper. Even if it's close enough to grab, one or two steps down, my father will still dial the number of the circulation desk.

"It's the principle of the thing," he'll say, to everyone who is near, although no one has asked. "We pay for delivery to the front door. That's not the front door."

I sit on the landing of our stairs, where we took photos that morning, but now I need to be away from Christmas. Away from all of them. It's almost the same story as the morning edition, and no one knows anything more about where Pamela is.

SHE JUST WENT TO WASH HER HANDS, was the headline. She wanted a Clark Bar, but her hands were dirty because the family had stopped off at a pet store on the way to the YMCA. Pamela was asking for a dime so she could go to the vending machine, which I've only done every single time we're at the downtown YMCA. I know the hallway she walked down, and the bathroom door she pushed open, and the Lysol scent of the stalls.

I wear glasses. I've been wearing them since third grade, when I noticed that I couldn't get the words and numbers in the arithmetic book to come into focus. Last year, swimming at the Y, I noticed that when I brought my head up out of the water, the world was temporarily but perfectly clear.

127

The chlorine water in my eye just till I blinked it away was like a contact lens, I thought, and that glimpse of what sight could be without the heavy glasses that slid down my nose was fleeting and crisp.

I have that crisp vision now, looking at the front page of the evening paper. I can see Pamela skipping down that hall, and even dancing a bit, because the floors are so polished and smooth. And with everyone at the wrestling match, those hallways are empty. Or almost empty.

Nellie finds me sitting there, and looks at me worriedly. She nestles in next to me and puts her hand on my leg, in red tights that match the print of my quilted A-line skirt.

She puts her finger in her mouth and then snuggles a bit more into my shoulder while I read. The story is too short for me. And there is a word I do not understand, "vagrant." I lean forward and peek into the family room, where my father and his father smoke pipes of vanilla-scented tobacco by the fireplace. I won't be able to get to the dictionary without their noticing.

And in no time at all, we are called over to eat Christmas cookies, and cut up the fudge Grandmother Castle made us, and talk about the dinner we just ate and how full we all are. And there are new books to read, but I just leave them on my lap, staring at the covers.

Day 4

Thursday morning, I hear the paperboy's approach, and then see him through the windows on either side of our front door. When my father finds me at the kitchen table for the second morning in a row, he looks puzzled. "You do know you have the week off?" he asks. "You do know you're allowed to sleep late? Your reading light was on pretty near midnight."

I have my elbows on the table, and my head over the newspaper, so he can't see my face as I read this line: *The suspect was seen carrying a rolled-up carpet. When asked what was in it, he said it was a mannequin.* I cannot even imagine this scene.

"I know," I say, keeping my voice even. "I'm excited. We're going sledding later."

And that's enough of an explanation for him, a reason that I'm at the kitchen table and it's not even sunrise and it's definitely not Christmas anymore. If I occasionally feel wounded by his lack of interest in me, or in us, I feel its grace now.

I hand him the front page before he asks. They no longer suspect a "vagrant," but a temporary resident of the YMCA, of taking Pamela away. I do not raise my eyes when I slide the paper across the oak table. I'm afraid to show how stiff and still I have gone from the headline, and the story.

I'm too tired to move when my mother comes bustling in. Her hair is messy from sleep, and she's not wearing lipstick, so things are getting back to normal. She has on her old quilted robe that zips up to her neck and which she says is "warm as toast." She tousles my hair as she goes by, then rustles around in the messy drawer. Handing me a rubber band, she says, "Ponytail?"

It's just enough of what goes on around here every day to get me past the sort of stunned feeling I have. She starts to unload the dishwasher that ran overnight, and I go to help. It's always easier to talk to my mother when our hands are busy. It's a big load, too, with all the platters and glasses that were used for Christmas dinner.

She has a cigarette lit, but it's mostly going to ash while we work.

"What are you plans, honey?" she asks when I use a step stool to put away the wineglasses in the dining room break-front.

"I was thinking we'd go sledding, but maybe it's too warm," I reply, looking at the drips of snow starting to stream off the roof, melted by the morning sun.

"Oh, it's supposed to drop today again," she says. "They are warning holiday travelers of icy roads." She slips right back into the work of putting dishes away.

With candy machines, a swimming pool, and a giant gymnasium, the YMCA looks like a nice place to live to me. My grandparents live in an apartment building and it doesn't have a pool, or a playground, or anything. I want to ask my mother about people living at the YMCA, but there isn't any way I can think to bring it up. So we work silently, and soon my brother and sister are at the breakfast table and the moment has passed. Time is now marked for me by newspaper delivery. And the afternoon edition makes me feel ill.

A 12-year-old boy who helped the suspect with the door saw an open bundle and glimpsed a pair of legs.

In the night, my legs twitch from fatigue and exertion but I cannot go to sleep. Nancy Drew seems like a big phony to me. I don't understand how the neighbors can come over for homemade eggnog and cheese platters my mother has carefully laid across our kitchen table and joke and laugh. I don't understand how my brother can tease my little sister for wanting to play with his G.I. Joes.

In the half-light of my reading lamp, I open my book and feel sick at the dialogue of George and Bess, Nancy's very best friends. I usually love them. I usually wish for friends like George and Bess. But nothing about their world lines up with how I feel about Pamela, and how she is ten, and how she is gone. Once, Nancy Drew herself was kidnapped. I had read enough of the other books to know that she would be fine. Everything always turns out okay. What is stolen will be found. What is hidden will be uncovered. Bad people have reasons for misbehaving, and Nancy Drew's father, a lawyer, makes sure that justice will be done.

The newspapers have robbed me of all my reservoirs of reassurance. The next morning, it is Friday. Christmas week is fleeting, and I mourn the holidays as I turn out the lamp and pull the quilt over my shoulder. They are not over, but they should be. I want a do-over, for Pamela's sake. I fall asleep thinking about candy vending machines.

Day 5

At dawn, there it is, the slap of the newspaper, and I wake up, electrified, but it's a jolt that leaves me limp. So I stay in bed. I fall back into a deep sleep again, and it barely registers when Nellie gets up. Sometime after that, my father looks in while he's still in his pajamas, holding his mug of coffee with one hand while he puts the palm of the other on my forehead.

This is so unlike him that I almost panic, not knowing what to think. He is not the one who takes care of me. He's not the one who notices anything.

"Missed you at breakfast," he says, "but it is your week off. Sleeping in or sick?"

"I'm fine," I say, because really, nothing is wrong. "I'm fine, but tired."

"I'm taking your mother out tonight for our anniversary," he says. "But we can stay in if you don't feel good." My mother comes in just then, and she takes her usual place on the foot of the bed, bringing her legs up to her chest, and cozily curling her arms around her knees.

"We're having a double dinner with the Castles," she explains. "Their anniversary was yesterday but, I don't know, it just got lost in the shuffle."

Lost in the shuffle is something that never happens in my family, especially not with Grandfather and Grandmother Castle. Anniversaries tick off like a clock you know is going to chime. My mother shops and lays presents aside. Those are wrapped in paper that is not meant for holiday gifts, prints that are not green or red. I always sort of hate those packages. They are marked by silver or white paper as not for us. They are held out from the rest. They are like a chorus of "Happy Birthday" in the middle of carols.

She usually has us draw cards, or at least sign them, from her to my dad, or from them both to my grandparents. I realize that none of that has happened this week.

Also, they are both still in their pajamas! This is the headline. I don't need newspapers. My parents, except on Christmas, are never in their pajamas after nine in the morning. People might stop by. The house may be on fire. Cows need to be milked. When the aliens arrive, or the Communists, they will need to see us in our natural habitat, and that does not include pajamas this late in the morning.

There has been some great relaxing of standards this week and I am anxious to correct it. How can I finally understand the need for rules, only to have the adults go off the playbook?

"No," I say, and sit up a little bit in bed and swing my legs over the side. "I'm not sick. You should go. Who's coming over?" In the fall, when my brother turned thirteen, my parents had talked about not needing babysitters anymore.

I'd been excited. The thought of being home on our own was thrilling. It hadn't happened yet.

Now my mother says, "Cathy," who is our piano teacher's daughter, and I am relieved. I can hardly name why. When she comes over, we do crafts and she makes popcorn that is better than anyone else's.

My father leaves the room at these details, free to go back to his day. My mother seems to wait a minute, I think, for him to be out of earshot. She scooches off the end of the bed so that her feet dangle next to mine, and she stares at the carpet. I see a tear streak down her cheek. She blinks.

"Ask me anything," she says. "About anything, anytime."

"Anything?" I ask softly, suddenly teary, too. She grips my hand in both of hers tightly.

"Anything. Everything. Nothing," she replies.

I sniffle, but her three words land on my ear and makes me giggle. That clears the room.

"Okay."

She hugs me. "I have to get dressed!" she says, and stands up fast. "What if someone drops in?"

It is too warm for sledding. I'm glad. I want to stay inside. I read for a while, then feel the day passing, and get out of bed.

The bright sun outside the window has warmed the glass, so that when I breathe on it, it hardly fogs at all. When I dress, I choose play clothes for inside. Not stretch pants with a strap for the bottom of my foot, to wear inside snow boots. I put my clothes in the hamper in the bathroom, and go downstairs.

The newspaper is stacked neatly on the table in the kitchen, and it's clear everyone else has read it. The front page is full of stories about the Apollo 8 mission, but when I flip it over, so the fold is on top, there's a picture of unopened packages around a Christmas tree. I can see the wires in the branches, but the lights are not on. It is a sad picture, even without the words to the article.

The family of Pamela Powers will not open their presents until Pamela is found safe, they say. The police have taken their manhunt to other parts of the state, and are said to be closing in on the suspect. No charges have been filed. Lieutenant Leaming reports, "We're just going to talk to the man. See what he saw."

Nellie comes in from the family room, dressed in her snow pants. She has slipped the suspenders off her shoulders so the buckles clank a bit when she moves. "Are we going sledding?" she asks me, her brown eyes wide.

"I don't think so," I say. I want to read inside, and drink cocoa, and eat fudge and Christmas cookies. She nods, and slips into the chair next to me, her pants making a swoosh across the nubby cloth of the seat.

"Can I have the comics?" she asks, and I finger down through the stack and slide that section across to her. "Can you tell me about that girl?" she whispers, her eyes on the comics page. My body locks up at her words.

I look over at her. My parents are almost as far away from the kitchen as they can be and still be in the same house as we are. They are getting dressed, and talking. The TV is on in the family room, a Western from the sounds of shouts and shooting, which means Paul is in there, too.

"What do you already know?" I say in a low voice.

"I know that nobody wants to talk about her," Nellie says. "But they can't help it."

This is what it's like to be my mother, I think. Nellie wanders silently from room to room in our lives, following us around, and I never thought about all she sees and notices, the way I do.

"What do you think happened to her?" Nellie asks. She has put her finger on Li'l Abner's big foot as he runs away from Daisy Mae. I don't really understand that comic. Why would Daisy Mae chase someone who doesn't want her?

"Happened how?" I say.

"Do you think someone hurt her?"

This is what is feels like, I think, to sort of know an answer but not to want to share it because it's just too big to put into words, where it has the chance of becoming real. But trying to lie about it would feel worse. It feels like a Camp Fire Girl code-of-honor sort of moment for me. I don't want my parents to lie to me, so I cannot be dishonest with Nellie.

"Yes." I say it plain. I don't even whisper. "Yes, I do."

"And do you think she'll die of it?"

The horror of her words stumps me. I, too, was worried about Pammy being hurt. Of her being in pain, and being alone. I realize now it was like a cartoon version of her I had in my head, like Nell tied to the train tracks in *Dudley Do-Right* episodes, and screaming, "Help! Help!" while the engine rushes closer.

When Nellie asks that question, though, a fog lifts, like in the swimming pool, where I can see everything so clearly. Part of me wonders why Nellie would connect Pamela's disappearance to her being hurt. What does a six-year-old know about that? Even I cannot think about it—I don't have words, or pictures, to help me see it and understand it.

Even though she didn't mean to, Nellie has put a word in my head: "Death."

And what does she know about that?

135

"Yes." She looks at me with trust, and I nod, stripped of any need to shield her, or me, from this news. "I don't want her to, but it just sounds so final," I say. "I don't think anyone expects to find her."

Nellie pushes back on the chair, hard, straight back from the table, and leaps out of it.

"Boo-boo?" I ask, using the name I called her when she was a baby. I rush after her up the steps to our room. She closes the door, softly, before I get there, and I can hear her crying on the other side.

I open the door. "Nellie? Nellie?" I start to come in.

She marches over to the door and pushes me in the stomach. "Leave me alone!" she cries, unexpectedly fierce. I back away, and I am shaking.

"Okay." I have to go past my parents' room, where their door has just opened.

"Are you girls fighting?" my dad says, heading down the steps without waiting for an answer.

"I hope not," says my mother, looking back at the tidy room she's leaving, and smoothing her hair, and in all ways back to her singsong self. "It's the holidays, and the holidays are not for fighting!"

I hear her in the kitchen, and I hear my father outside, whacking melting icicles off the gutters with a broom. Paul is in the family room, and I am at the top of the steps. I take a few steps back toward our room, where my sister is sobbing as I've never heard.

"Oh, help," I hear her say, though her voice is muffled. I leave her there.

Cathy, the sitter, arrives by four, and she's brought cloth binding tape and asks for scraps from my mother's sewing room. She's asked all of us to grab our loose-leaf notebooks and to take the pages out.

We need a place to work safely, so Paul runs out to the garage for old newspapers that Cathy spreads out on our kitchen table. We brush the outside of the notebooks with Elmer's Glue, and affix panels of fabric to them, folding the edges of the scraps to the inside, with an extra dab. When the glue has dried enough, Cathy helps us decorate, so I use the binding tape to spell out "KIM" because my name has straight lines. Paul has covered his notebook with black Naugahyde, like a fake leather, and Nellie's is messy, but cute, in polka dots. She is quiet, but works at following instructions from Cathy, and tries to use a Popsicle stick to smooth out air bubbles in her cover. After the anger and tears I saw this afternoon, her face is still, and calm.

We sit at the table, where I can watch Cathy pop the corn, and melt the butter, and get out the big bowl. Then she opens the cupboard and finds an amber bottle of Lawry's Seasoned Salt. She sprinkles it over the popcorn and then locates the sugar bowl that my mother leaves with the coffee mugs in the cupboard by the sink. She tilts the sugar bowl till sugar cascades over the popcorn, a dusting of sweet. Then she tosses all of it with big wooden spoons.

We sit around and wait for the notebooks to dry, and eat popcorn by the handfuls, and it tastes so good, and it's just us kids, and Nellie seems okay, and I'm as hungry as if we didn't have TV dinners an hour ago. I wash my buttery hands, then help Cathy clear up our workspace.

I fold the glue-streaked newspapers in on themselves and roll them up so no scraps fall to the floor. And that's when I see it, because my eyes always read everything they land on, from shampoo bottles when I'm showering to cereal boxes when I'm eating, to mailboxes we pass when I'm in the car with my mother, or poison labels on the insecticides when I'm in the garage. If there are words in front of me, I will read them.

The half-dressed, frozen body of Pamela Powers was found this morning, dumped in a ditch.

I throw the newspapers, all of them, away, and join the others in the family room. They are laughing at an episode of *Get Smart*. Nellie, too. I cannot join in. I thought knowing what happened to Pamela would help me. But it hasn't. I don't know how to help anyone, anywhere. I'm carrying around a secret, but I don't know what it is. It belongs to Pamela, a girl I don't even know, who has been dead since Christmas Eve.

Everything You Always Wanted to Know About Sex* (but your parents hid this book from you)

Age: 11

My mother and I are in Younkers, the department store where we always go school shopping. I have gotten taller over the summer, and—and we don't discuss this—have breasts. I need a bra. I also need blouses that fit my new shape and have sleeves that are long enough for my arms. The blouses must also be opaque. I have witnessed the bra-snapping that girls get when boys can see through their clothing.

While my mother still sews my dresses and skirts, she says blouses are too detailed. She goes through the racks, holding up one shirt and then another, putting each back with a small, pursed mouth.

Finding little that satisfies her, she turns away from me, and away from the life-sized mannequin who is perfectly turned out in back-to-school clothes, from the tam-o'-shanter atop her red bob to the small red satchel that crosses her navy cardigan with mother-of-pearl buttons, Black Watch pleated skirt, and crisp white shirt with Peter Pan collar. Her hand is permanently raised to her lips, a C of her thumb and forefinger at the side of her mouth, as if she is calling to her perfect older brother to wait up. He will.

He will touch her shoulder with one mannequin hand and then walk her to school in their perfect mannequin world.

"We'll find something for you in the Big Girls section," my mother calls out from one rack of blouses over. "You've outgrown normal sizes."

She stops to light a cigarette, flicking the lighter closed with a practiced hand and squinting through the smoke to stare at a line of clearance clothes.

"The prices on these A-line skirts are not bad. The fabric would cost me more. No pleats, I think, because they'll just make you look larger."

"Can you not hear yourself?" I shriek. "Can you kindly not defile me in public?" She moves blithely down the aisle and I see what's happened. The words have stayed in my head.

A saleslady hurries over to help, then. "Ma'am?" she calls to my mother. "I think you're finding that this young lady is growing up, that's all. May I send you to the ladies blouses over by the elevator?"

"She's eleven," my mother answers. "I don't think I need to pay grown-up prices for her just yet."

"Well, there's a nice clearance rack over there, too. Pop by. See if there is something." She pats my shoulder. "Nothing wrong with growing up, is there?"

I am comforted. And we find two perfect white blouses, one with a Peter Pan collar, the other with eyelet. My mother is cheerful by the time we leave, and I'm looking forward, again, to starting at a new school.

From the first day of fifth grade at Windsor Elementary, though, I am an outsider. First, a dozen students arrive that morning from another school, taking over the classroom as if they have always been there. I feel like I've moved to a new town, not just a new school where I'll be taking accelerated classes. I was thinking "new pool of friends." I did not consider "new people to exclude me." They all grew up together, and went from kindergarten to fourth grade knowing who was funny, athletic, good at math, great at handwriting.

Mrs. Lightfoot is the reason I transferred.

"She's not being pushed enough by the classes she's in," she told my parents last spring.

"Well, Kim gets the A's," my father said proudly. "But Paul is the one with common sense." He says this often. I never feel good when he says it. I believe it is meant to prevent Paul from feeling bad about his grades. Anyway, "smart" is something that happened to me, not something I did.

My father has never been as protective of my weaknesses as he is of Paul's. Paul is allowed to tease me for my weight, my temper, my clumsiness. I could probably get away with calling him "dummy," but he's not, really, plus I know it's not nice.

"Yes," Miss Lightfoot said and, for the first time, made eye contact with me. "I know Paul, of course, and we're hoping that junior high will provide him with a better test of his mettle." She smiled at me. Maybe she didn't like my father's comparison either.

Last time Miss Lightfoot paid any attention to me was for wearing culottes instead of a proper skirt to school. She'd sent me home. My mother was mortified, because she had made the culottes and reassured me when I was worried about them that I would be okay. She even sewed a panel over the front, believing it would hide that they were essentially shorts. I had never been sent home from school in my life and I have thought ever since that Miss Lightfoot hates me.

Among my new classmates, there's a funny girl with wavy light brown hair, Mary McCracken, who is just as good at sports as she is at math problems, and tall, willowy Carolyn Waters, who has handwriting as flowing and elegant as my mother's. There is Martin Schweigal, small and demure, who raises his hand before anyone else and never gets anything wrong. If Ken dolls were once boys, they would look like Martin Schweigal.

At this school, there is a sense, in classes, that arguing with teachers is okay. Answering once is good, and following up to debate a point is not "back talk." I cannot do it. I have not been trained that way.

Rachel Adelman has also transferred from Cowles, and we are enemies from the beginning. We have been, off and on, best friends since we were in kindergarten. We'd hug at the lockers. She'd call me "Kimmy!" when no one else my age did, and I called her "Rachel Baby!" after watching too many Elvis Presley movies in reruns on Saturday.

It's almost chemical now, our dislike of one another. We are like repelling magnets. When I raise my hand to ask a question, she gives a little "tsk" under her breath before getting busy with her pencil box, which has a roll-up lid. When she corrects Mrs. Cowen, the fifth grade teacher, about her first name, during attendance, I roll my eyes.

Perhaps she has decided, as I have, to have a whole new personality at Windsor and is worried I'll blow her cover. I come up with this theory after I hear her introduce herself as "Rah-SHELL." For my part, I have decided to spell my name with a "y" instead of "i" for a change.

On the day we have to line up to get our annual tuberculosis screening test, I am behind Rachel, with a dry throat, and I cough. She whirls around, and says, "What are you doing, trying to give me TB?"

I do not answer, and when it's my turn, I silently offer the nurse my forearm: Swab of alcohol, wave of her hand to dry it, stamp me with a tack that has four prongs of medicine, slap, the Band-Aid.

The next day, when everyone's Band-Aids have fallen off, the four little dots on their skin are hardly noticeable as they file past the nurse. I have protected my Band-Aid through bath time and washing up, but I peel it off and find an angry wound. Each spot on my arm is raised and red, and when the nurse feels it, it's warm to the touch. She puts an assistant principal in charge and takes me to her office.

"That's not good," she says, looking at her list of instructions. "Sometimes that's caused when you scratch it—in your sleep," she adds, seeing me shake my head no. "But this looks positive to me."

I feel light-headed and have trouble standing. She sees me wobble, and makes me sit down.

"Do I—I have TB?" I ask and think of Beth, in *Little Women*. Beth dies.

"I really, really doubt it," says the school nurse. "But we'll just send a note home for your parents, and you'll check in with your regular doctor."

I hate Dr. Hess. I hate his cat clock. I hate the way he dismisses everything, like why my little sister's underwear was bloody. I hate notes home, which have to be signed to prove I have shown them to my mother.

"Don't worry!" the nurse says into the silence. "You'll be fine. You're probably perfectly healthy. Although," she adds, as if remembering her nursing manual, "you could stand to take off some weight."

I tell no one I might have TB. The word "infectious" is making me nervous. I want to forge my mother's name on the note from the nurse. She has, however, spectacular pen-

143

manship, and mine is more of a crabbed version of linked letters. It would be too obvious.

The next day when I get to class, there is a folded note on my desk. I look around the room, to see if anyone is watching me, and I'm so happy to see it that I open it up at once.

"You are dying of TB," it says. "You should stay home and die and leave the rest of us alone." I am quaking. I recognize Rachel's writing. She's also read *Little Women*. I crumple up the note and stuff it into my book bag.

That day, we start reading *Animal Farm*, and I am transfixed. It's funny, and while Mrs. Cowen explains communism to us and why George Orwell wrote the book, I feel stretched. I understand the language and ideas. I read the book while walking home and after dinner, finishing it by bedtime.

The next morning, I'm packing the book up and find the mean note. The dots on my arm have faded. I get out a piece of loose-leaf paper, and a purple marker from my desk. I think for a moment about the meanest thing I can say. Recently, Rachel has been hit with acne.

"You are a walking zit," I say, picking a word I have never before used in public or written down. "If you get squeezed, you'll pop. Bye-bye."

I fold up the note and toss hers into the wastebasket in my room. I'll have to figure out how to get the note about TB signed over the weekend.

I rush to Windsor so I have time to leave the note on Rachel's desk. We're learning algebra, solving for *x*, and I sort of understand it. Ms. Anacek, who told us on the first day that she was neither a "Missus" or a "Miss," and was not wearing a wedding band as my mother did, told us to always show our work. I always knew the answer but never knew why. Without the line-by-line equation to prove it, though, it was the same as being wrong.

Later that day, the students from all classes are gathered in the auditorium, for a public service announcement. The sociology teacher, Mrs. DeWitt, takes the stage. I haven't had her for class yet, but I like the way she takes charge. She has a low, loud voice, and short straight white hair.

"Good afternoon, people," she says, her hands on her hips.

We answer her faintly.

"I can't hear you, people!" she shouts, leaning into the microphone.

"*Good afternoon!*" we yell back. And giggle self-consciously.

"We're not going to waste time sitting here," she says, and we all groan. "We've got a short film that we want you all to see."

The lights dim and we watch, on the televisions set around the room, a film that opens with a picture of a child's red tennis shoe, a Keds, floating down a creek. It bobs, and gets stuck near a rock, but is pushed along by the flow of the water.

The narrator then begins. "How can YOU stay safe? It's simple. Don't play with matches," he says, and I think, *Here we go again.* Mr. Bass.

"Don't drink or eat anything with this sign on it." The film shows a bottle with a skull and bones on it, like a pirate ship.

And then, we see a picture of a girl in a party dress, waiting outside a building that looks like a school, or even the library. She is wearing red sneakers and holding a birthday present.

"And don't ever, ever talk to strangers or go with them, even if they tell you they were sent by your parents, or anyone you know." A large car, like a Buick, pulls up next to her, and she leans closer to the window. A man is talking to her with enthusiasm, and she is smiling. She gets in the car.

The film returns to the creek, where the birthday present is still wrapped, but muddy. There is a red shoe on the bank, and the one that floated down the river in the distance.

"Remember, don't talk to strangers. And never go with them. Stay safe." Teachers watch our faces carefully. The terror of what happened to Pamela Powers has never really left me, but this public service announcement makes it real. Some students are talking quietly, but the girl in front of me is sobbing. I hear something like a soft drizzle, and there is a stream of urine puddling around her foot. A teacher sees it, too, and helps the girl out of her seat. A couple of people point at her, but mostly we watch in silence as she leaves the auditorium. Other people are crying, too.

A janitor comes with a mop and strong, pine-scented cleaner, while Mrs. DeWitt returns to the stage.

"Hello, people," she says. No one answers. She clasps her hands and shrugs. "That's okay. It's a lot to think about, right?"

"Does anyone have any questions?"

Martin, from my class, raises his hand.

"Was that film staged?" he asks.

"Sure," Mrs. DeWitt replies. "That is not a real girl, and it's not a real car, and that man is not a stranger. Anyone else?"

Martin is not finished. "Was there a reason it's staged to look like a fairy tale, starring the Big Bad Wolf?" He holds his fingers in front of him like he's saying a prayer.

Mrs. DeWitt looks at him carefully. "What's your name? More, what's your point?"

Martin looks as prim as he did that morning when he told me that the longest word in the English language not counting scientific compounds is "antiestablishmentarian."

"I'm Martin Schweigal," he says. "And I am simply making the point that strangers aren't the only problem. Sometimes danger is much closer than we think."

The pine scent, the public service announcement, and the warmth of the crowded room are getting to me. Whatever it is that Martin knows, I am not yet ready to grasp.

Mrs. Cowen starts herding everyone back to her classroom. Mrs. DeWitt taps me on the shoulder as I pass.

"Hey, you." She pulls out the note I wrote Rachel and puts it in front of my face. "Look familiar?"

"Yes."

"Well, I found the person you gave it to crying in the bathroom this morning. Does that make you proud? Making someone cry?"

"She—I wrote that to answer something—no," I say. I'm not proud.

"Well, I run detention this week, and guess what? You've got detention with me every single night."

"I can't," I say. "I have choir on Wednesday, and Camp Fire Girls, and—"

"Yeah," says Mrs. DeWitt. "You should have thought of that when you wrote the note."

"But she wrote a mean note to me first," I protest.

"Great. Bring me the note she wrote, and she'll get detention, too." Mrs. DeWitt lets go of my shoulder and tips her head toward the door. "You're free to go."

"I threw it away," I say, standing still.

"Sure ya did. See you after school."

I find a dime in my book bag and call my mother to tell her I'll be late. A year or so before, when I was walking back and forth to Cowles, she'd never minded if I stopped at Amy's for a pop, or stayed after school in the library. This year, she needs to know every detail. Things have changed.

"Why are you going to be late?" she asks once I have her on the phone.

"I have detention."

"Why?"

"I'll explain later," I say.

"I'm picking you up," she says. "It's fall. It's getting dark earlier."

After the film about the red shoe, I am shocked at my relief. Something inside me gives. I start crying.

"Kim. Oh, honey, what's wrong?"

"I just don't know. I wrote a mean note. I feel bad."

My mother listens to me crying for another minute. We both know a pay phone call cannot last very long.

"We'll talk later," she says. "But come on. You shouldn't have done it, I'm willing to bet, but it's not the worst thing that could have happened." The words hang there. She knows. The recognition that she knows me well enough to say that alters me. It changes everything, just for a moment.

"No," I say, sniffling. "It's not. I could have been sent home for wearing culottes."

Her laughter over the line is loud and gratifying. "I love you. I'm coming for you. I'll see you soon." And I forgive myself, and I forgive Rachel, and Mrs. DeWitt, who may never know that I'm not really like that.

A week before the first sleepover I have ever been invited to, my mother puts a new pair of baby doll pajamas on my bed, with the tags still on. I am at my desk, working on homework about Norway, a country I've never visited.

"I thought you might want something new for Amy's," she says. "They're so crisp and pretty just out of the package, but if you want me to wash them first, just put them in the laundry."

And so I have one more decision to make, because I don't know whether having obviously new pajamas, or washed ones—"I always wear these at home"—is the better look.

Why I am plagued by these worries and choices is itself a problem I worry about. I've read so many books, and watched all the movies and TV shows I can find, and read the newspapers willingly for three years, but I cannot find anyone like me. I don't understand why everyone else seems to know what to do, all the time. I want to be like everyone else.

A combination of fear and excitement drives me to consider and pack and repack my small overnight bag very carefully in the days before the party. Will we change in front of each other? Is my underwear going to be like everyone else's? Is my bag? It's not like packing for an overnight at my grandparents' homes. They have toothpaste, and washcloths, and soda pop, and snacks. How can I entrust an entire evening to strangers, including bedtime and waking up in the middle of the night? What's for breakfast?

I reassure myself with facts about what is known. It is at Amy Grismer's house, and her sister Jenny, who is in high school, is supervising. Mr. and Mrs. Grismer will welcome us, and then go out for the night. Many of the girls from my old class at Cowles will be there; more will not and this news is not lost on me—I'm included, even though I no longer go to school with them.

Actually, I'm frantic when I open the invitation. Being included has always been elusive for me, and it's the reason I can't stay mad at anyone else. I don't want the circle of available friends to diminish, even by one. My parents are interested in justice, and will call the parents of the girl who takes my pencil. I am interested in being a member of the group, and have stopped telling my parents when anything gets stolen.

In packing, despite my care, my first disappointment is mighty. After years of coveting the pink and pastel girls' sleeping bags shown in the Penney's catalog, I learn from my mother I'll be borrowing Paul's.

He goes on camping trips with the Boy Scouts. The sleeping bag is used. Worse, it smells musty because, my mother says, he never airs it out and he puts it away wet. Worst of all, Paul has smelly feet. All of him smells. In fact, the steeper his fall into adolescence, the stinkier he is. He has started wearing Frye leather boots like all the other junior high school boys; in a not entirely unrelated aside, he has also started using Brut.

If boys mature later than girls, he and I are probably moving through puberty together. But I already have pimples and he never does; I bathe every night and he's ripe enough that he should, too (but doesn't).

A few days before the slumber party, my mother unzips two sides of the sleeping bag and hangs it flat over a clothesline in the basement to air it out. It is army green on the outside and lined with a dark green flannel printed with creepily realistic flying geese.

"Can I hang it on the patio?" I ask.

"I don't like the look of that," my mother says. Her voice is tight and certain.

We live next door to the LaPrads, who have nine children, allegedly because they are Catholics. In the fuzzy logic of a barely menstrual Presbyterian, this means that since nuns and priests don't get married and have families, it's up to the worshippers to make up the difference.

The LaPrads live in a split-level ranch-style home, with three children to a bedroom, and like Mrs. Smith across the street, their mother works outside the home. We are in and out of their house whenever we are playing, for drinks of water, or snacks. We never sit down, though, because there are no places to sit. There are piles of laundry in every available room we visit. It is clean laundry, but it is everywhere.

My parents always exchange glances when we come home from the LaPrads. There is disapproval tainting their questions about what we ate, where we played, who was home watching us.

To keep our house visitor-ready, a house cleaner, Juanita, comes once a week; my mother runs a mop over the kitchen floor once a day; my father gets out the vacuum whenever he sees mess. If a car pulls into the driveway, even if it's one of the relatives, my mother has drilled us all thoroughly: Wipe the counter in the powder room sink, put out a guest towel from the cupboard and fresh soap from the drawer, and remove all toys to our rooms, *immediately.*

By the time a visitor gets out of the car and comes to the door, there will be fresh coffee brewing, the scent of snacks heating in the oven, and my mother wearing lipstick.

Mrs. LaPrad probably sees more of her children than my mother does. Even though she is the secretary at her children's Catholic school, her schedule cannot stack up to my mother's many clubs, dates, and PTA obligations, all of which keep us in the care of teenaged babysitters, our grandparents, and Juanita, who occasionally stays overnight with us when no one else can. I know she has children, but I do not know anything about who looks after them when she's with us.

I mostly know about clotheslines from movies, or drawings in books, and from the LaPrads, who have one that we treat as a Maypole, by skipping around it as if we're holding ribbons. That's not often, because in warm weather they use it all the time, for sheets, and baby clothes, diapers, and the many white blouses the LaPrads get to wear as part of their school uniform. Even more exotic to me is that a school bus takes them to class every morning and drops them off in the late afternoon.

In a way, we know the LaPrads and don't know them at all. We are neighbors but we don't share schools and after-school events. Our parents don't socialize with the neighbors unless it's an impromptu backyard gathering. The exception is the Grismers, because we see them at church.

I already know a lot about being a snob. My four grandparents, from vastly different economic backgrounds, have by osmosis and bickering taught me to not very consciously sniff out indicators of status, via street names and dress labels, car make and model, house size, and religion, and neighborhood. We don't live in Des Moines—we live in Windsor Heights. This is a better location than where my mother grew up, in West Des Moines, but I am certain no one has ever said that out loud.

My mother tells me that she learned everything about antiques and good living from her mother-in-law, Grandmother Castle, who has fur coats while Grandma Jenkins has none; Grandmother Castle wears glittering rings, and bangles on bangles, and roasts capons for Thanksgiving. Grandma Jenkins wears a simple gold band, and cooks turkey.

The turn of Grandmother Castle's head and the sniff of her powdered nose tells me so much about the people we encounter at church and school, or when she takes us shopping or to the movies. And I am just as snotty about our standing, which I have had no part in earning, with neighborhood children and with cousins; my mother has three sisters she loves, but I am aware that we have the largest house and that this somehow sets us apart. Still, we are not as well off as the Grismers. And as a bonus, they love each other.

Jenny adores Amy, and Amy adores little Jimmy, and Tommy, my brother's age, walks Amy home from Cowles sometimes and they are simply walking, and talking, and he carries her library book. All of this is different from my family, where my brother ignores me or regularly tickles me until I can't breathe and I, in turn, torture my small sister with horrible tales of child kidnappings and car crashes that leave limbs strewn like party streamers across the bushes of our front yards.

Mrs. Grismer is more slender than my mother. Mrs. Grismer sews, my mother's forte, and once she won a sewing contest which no one but I knew my mother had also entered. When she entertains, she serves canapés, never snacks. As Camp Fire Girl leader, her craft projects for earning merit badges were better than the ones my mother had offered the year before. All my classmates knew it and I tried not to show how ashamed I was or even that I cared.

Even this year, when I am at Windsor and she is at Cowles, Amy and I walk to choir together, and when we visit the tiny candy store that is on the way to church, she always selects better candy; she makes it last, and then I spend choir practice watching her enjoy taffy, one nibble at a time, while mine is long gone.

I develop a theory, then, about naming children. I know two Amys, and they are both small, and cute. I know three Kimberlys, two in choir with me, and we are all large for our age, even overweight. It is a relief to know that it is all my mother's fault I am fat.

As a friend, though, Amy is generous with the information Jenny gives her about growing up, so we all use rubbing alcohol and cotton balls for our new pimples, and steal our father's silver razors for shaving our suddenly bristly legs.

There is a rumor we are going to have facials at the slumber party, something I have only read about in magazines.

After a soaking rain, I don't want to take the shortcut through the spongy grass of the backyards up to the Grismers' with my overnight bag and sleeping bag. I walk up the street, and even though there are no sidewalks, I stick close to the curb and cars can see me in the early evening light. In no time I am around the corner and in the driveway of Amy's brick Federal home. I enter through the kitchen door to give Mrs. Grismer cocktail napkins my mother has wrapped as a hostess gift, and she sends me through to the living room, to the party.

Chaos greets me. All the furniture has been pushed back to the walls, some chairs akimbo, and there are presents stacked on the upright piano. We have a baby grand, which is better, but Marvy Grismer is a better pianist than my mother, which evens things up again. Towering bouquets of pink and white balloons are anchored to the floor by flowerpots full of white gravel, so they don't float away.

These balloons float. And I realize with a pit in my stomach that these are helium balloons from a fancy store. In our house, they are usually attached to the wall with cellophane tape, which is really hard to scrape off once the balloons have shriveled. I feel again the little stabs of just going over to the Grismers' house. I always think I'm ready, but I never am.

This is just a better home for a better family to live in. After all these years, I still do not know what to do with this envy.

Amy is a nice girl, though, and we are friends. She waves an excited hello when she sees me. She is squatting over the pile of sleeping bags making a mountain, which are, as I worried they would be, mostly bright pastels. I am self-conscious as I hand over Paul's dark green sleeping bag to add to the pile.

Beth helps her, and I walk over to Melissa and Mary, near a bowl of popcorn. Only when Jimmy Grismer enters the party room and hurls himself at the pile the way we jump into raked leaves in fall, I see that my sleeping bag has been hidden away at the bottom. I hope it doesn't smell. I hope the pink blanket I brought to layer on top masks the look of it.

Melissa and Mary say hello quietly. They are still in school clothes—meaning skirts, because girls are not allowed to wear pants—while I am in a chocolate-colored striped shirt and matching slacks. It's the privilege of living near the Grismer family that I could change after school. The atmosphere is charged with these minute comparisons, which all of us are just learning—the ups and downs of socializing in our neighborhood. I wish I could turn off my brain. My heart aches constantly, like it's in a hold, or a vise.

We play games, and for one of them, we are supposed to find partners. Melissa has Mary, and Amy has Beth. Susan finds Jean Hornby, and because Elizabeth Craig is home sick, there is an odd number at the party. I have no one.

Mrs. Grismer calls in Jenny to even it up, but then everyone wants to be her partner. She has shiny, straight hair, with a bobby pin holding it out of her face, and blue eyes rimmed in glittery blue eye shadow. Jenny very democratically chooses Susan, who was already mad at not being picked by Amy, and so I get Jean.

Jean and I like each other. Like Amy, she has an older sister, Tess, who seems more like a friend to Jean than a sibling. Tess babysits us sometimes and is good at coloring. By not pressing down on the crayon and moving it in small circles, she manages to create one evenly hued field of color. She uses darker colors to shade the edges, and white in spots that make it look shiny, as if we can touch it. Whenever Tess colors with us, I save her work in my desk drawer.

Whenever a lot of us play at Jean's house, she tells us to tiptoe around because her mother gets migraines. The curtains are always closed, keeping the rooms dim. Light hurts her mother's eyes, Jean says. We never question this.

Jean likes me because I have been in her house two or three times when her mother was asleep on the couch with an empty vodka bottle next to her and I never told anyone. Once, Jean wrapped the bottle in a brown grocery bag and threw it away in the Craigs' garbage, and it didn't even clink. Her faint smile, in that moment, told me she had meant to silence it, and I smiled back.

Now we play a game, which is tossing a bean bag to each other until one of us drops it, and everyone gets a little set of sparkly earrings to clip on, whether they have won or lost.

"Unroll your sleeping bags," Jenny says then, "so we can have facials." As we put our sleeping bags flat around the room, the other girls jostle each other for proximity to Amy. Finally, it's arranged, with four bags boxing hers in. Susan is top of the box, near Amy's head, while Melissa and Beth are on either side of her. Jean starts out at Amy's feet, but looks uncomfortable. All the conversation will be up by Amy's head.

Jenny, seeing that I am paralyzed in place—I just don't know where to go—helps Mary, Melissa, Jean, and me put our bags in an X, so all our pillows sort of meet in the middle, and we can all talk to each other. When Amy's group sees this arrangement, they immediately move everyone's bags into a similar shape.

This makes me feel privileged, and I fall in love with Jenny all over again. I tuck the pink blanket around the edges of my bag, and it sort of blends with everyone else's.

Jenny says, "Okay, go change into your pajamas!" and reminds everyone where the bathrooms and bedrooms we can use are. It's more chaos as girls call dibs on the downstairs powder room or dash into the kitchen.

When we return, Mrs. Grismer is in the living room wearing a long light blue gown that flows to her ankles. Kent Grismer is in a tuxedo with a bright red bow tie. While we are telling them how nice they look, he reaches into his pocket and his bow tie twirls. We laugh, far harder than the joke deserves. They leave for their evening and we promise to mind Jenny. And we will.

Amy has on baby doll pajamas, too, a smock-like top and bloomer pants that ride high on the leg. Beth is in her older brother's gigantic football jersey, which is worn and soft. Jean and the others are in long Lanz gowns or pajamas that are tops and bottoms. I am relieved that I match Amy, after being so worried.

Jenny walks around with hot, colorful washcloths, and a basket of nail polish so we can each choose a color. I pick a clear polish to be safe, and watch as Beth chooses a frosty white and Amy a pearly pink.

We lay down with the washcloths across our faces, and Melissa instantly develops the giggles. The warm washcloth tickles, but makes it hard to breathe. Melissa's laughter is contagious and then we're all giggling, the cloths slip from our faces, and we start throwing our washcloths at each other.

Jenny quietly sits down next to Susan, lays her back down with a hand on her shoulder, and with a brush, paints a layer of warmed Noxzema on her cheeks, forehead, and down her nose to her chin, skipping her mouth. We all quiet down as Jenny moves from girl to girl, and then, after giving us all masks, circles the room again with a nail file. Soon we're all sitting stiffly with our nails lacquered and airing out, while the mentholated Noxzema dries out, cracking into flakes if we talk.

Amy, hardly able to move her lips, says, "Can you bring out the book?"

Jenny hesitates.

"It's amazing," Amy says.

"What book?" Jean asks

Jenny goes back and forth between the kitchen and living room, bringing in bowls of buttered popcorn with flecks of salt, and cans of soda pop, and red Twizzlers in a mug. There are vanilla cupcakes with marshmallow frosting and fudgy brownies with a gooey glaze. It's torture to wait till our nails are dry. After what seems like hours, Jenny tells us we can go wash our faces and hands without marking up the new polish.

When I come back, everyone is clustered around Amy, who has an open book in her lap. She holds it up so we can see the mustard yellow book jacket, the longest title I've ever seen: *Everything you always wanted to know about sex** (*but were afraid to ask). The word "sex" is in red type.

Jenny retreats, and Amy reads out the pages, while a quiet settles over the group. At first we squirm a little bit, especially when Amy holds up the pages, like Mrs. Schaumburg did in fourth grade, to show us the illustrations. Everyone is naked. We see a drawing of a woman straddling a man's hips while he lies on his back with closed eyes. In another, a woman is on all fours while the man kneels behind her, his hips pressed to her bottom.

Amy intones the words "Oral sex," so solemnly that I cannot help it. I giggle. She looks up at me, bright pink, and giggles, too.

Emboldened, Amy reads, "Anal sex," but barely gets the words out before the room erupts in laughter. "Lubrication!" she shouts, and collapses.

"Ew!" Beth says, coming in closer to see the drawing.

"He puts his thing? Up the—up the?" Melissa asks, and tightens her lips into a grimace, a mask of worry.

We share a love of reading series books, like Laura Ingalls Wilder, and Maud Hart Lovelace, and Lenore Mattingly Weber. It is almost our only bond. I can see that she, too, is totally unprepared for the information in this book. It's a little betrayal, this book, to know that there is so much of adult life kept secret from us. But it's also deeply thrilling, like a door opening over a cliff. I can glimpse it. I'm not ready to jump.

I'm on my back on my ugly, smelly sleeping bag, with its pink blanket, laughing so hard I cannot speak. For the next thirty minutes, the book gets passed around, and I know I'll be back to Amy's house another day to read it cover to cover. It's talking about sex the way people talk about the weather, and the strange field of twitches, urges, and monthly flows points toward a connection two people share. Curiosity replaces fear. I do want to know more, someday.

For now, barriers dissolve, worries abate, and Mary Sylvester saves the last Twizzler for me, as if we are best friends. And when I look at these new and old friends, I don't see Pamela Powers's grainy image or a red shoe floating down a creek. We are all fully alive with what we do not and cannot yet know.

The Perfect Spread

Age: 12

My mother's chair at her sewing table faces a bulletin board where she pins pieces of pattern or scraps of fabric she's working with. Next to the table is a bureau, and if I sit on the floor with my back to it, I can keep an eye on the door in case someone else comes up the steps or down the hallway from our bedrooms. It's strategic.

It's also the perfect way to talk to her, because she's got her head over sewing and I can stare out the door, beyond, to the hallway, and our eyes never have to meet. I know I am the one who asks difficult questions, I do. I can read the exasperation in her eyes that I'm interrupting her with a subject not on her list: groceries, vacuum, pick up someone from practice, make dinner, oh, God, Kimmy. Her eyes cannot say this, but there is a great unspoken, "Now what?"

When I was younger, and read something in the newspaper that did not make sense to me, or when I spied a new word, I'd ask her without thinking.

She'd either explain, or she'd say, "What a good question! I don't know that either." And then she'd add, "Let's look it up," and we'd go to the dictionary, or the encyclopedia, or sometimes the Childcrafts, and we'd read it together. And so from her I learned that not knowing was okay, that looking up things was okay, that finding the answers was okay.

At least, unless the question I asked made her slump in dismay or something like disbelief that her child was expecting her to have answers that even adults, I learned, did not know. I have made a folder of newspaper clippings with words circled, to find out about someday.

At dinner, though, if a question comes up over homework, my mother is likely to say, "Ask your father." And then she'll get busy with clearing the table, or offering seconds, or a dozen other little tasks. So I know she does not like not knowing something in front of him.

Now that I'm older, questions for my mother come in two parts. The question itself, that's pretty tidy. And the burden of knowing I'm about to make her uncomfortable.

So what I need to determine, before I ever ask anything, is if the answer is going to be worth what I put her through.

She's finishing up a swing dress for me, made of a gauzy stripe that looked so cool and comfortable on the bolt of fabric in the store, but when I put it on, my bra showed through.

"It's sheer," I said. "It's too sheer."

This is how my mother is about sewing. "I'll line it," she said, and now it's today, and it's lined and flowy, and just needs a snap above the back zipper to hold a little collar closed.

And so the dress is in my lap, and I'm sorting notions looking for the most suitable size snap in a mess of cardboards, thread, and buttons.

As I sift through everything, I find a snap I want to use. The instructions printed on the packaging tell me that here is a "male" snap, which has a hard little nip of metal, to fit into the "female" snap, which has an indent. I love this new dress, and can't wait to wear it to my father's fortieth birthday party, but at that wording, I toss the snaps back in with everything else, and choose a hook and eye.

Since the sleepover, the world has changed for me, the way new eyeglasses always make anything crisp, on the first day. The illustrations, more than the writing, in *Everything you always wanted to know about sex** (**BUT WERE AFRAID TO ASK*) have made it impossible for me to look anyone in the eyes.

I assess every single adult, even my grandparents and mother and father and the milkman with his stupid cartons of A&E milk, and the Avon lady and the Fuller Brush man, and the Jehovah's Witnesses who ring our doorbell during dinner hour, making my father swear as he pushes away from the table to answer the door so he can yell at them, and I think, "They do that."

My teachers—oh my God, all my teachers—the choir director at church, the ministers. My piano teacher, Mrs. Grismer and Mr. Grismer, and he probably does it with people he's not married to. I see couples on TV, Mrs. and Mr. Brady, Ozzie and Harriet, and Andy Griffith did it once with a woman TV viewers never met, to get Opie, as far as I can tell, as absurd as that seems.

Old black-and-white Westerns are suddenly way more menacing, and I'll be damned if I can figure out *Gunsmoke* and what's happening with Miss Kitty. She's a "Miss" so no marriage. But her outfits and the tone she takes with Marshall Dillon scream sex. To me.

That completely normal human beings engage in these positions, of straddling, of squatting, and standing, and leaning, all part of sex, is something I really cannot resolve. From all the crimes I've read about, from missing nurses in Chicago to Pammy Powers, almost the only thing I know about sex is that someone decides to have it and gets it, no matter the cost.

That book blurred everything I always was afraid of about sex, and was afraid to put into words. Sex has always been part of an unknown violence that no one will explain.

Now, sex is on some spectrum, where two people like it and do it, and then, and I don't know how, it falls off the range completely, to be replaced with something like brute force.

I cannot understand how something that was so wrong to do to Pamela Powers can be the same thing our parents and grandparents do to each other, apparently, according to that book, all the time. I don't understand this coupling, I don't understand the word. Two years ago, right before I started menstruating, my mother attempted, blushing, to explain that a husband puts his thing in a wife—and it *only* happens if people are married, and that because it will help a baby come, it's good.

I have been to the weddings of aunts, met babysitters' new boyfriends, so I know all about love and new couples. And I thought I knew about sex, too, and it was always the opposite of love.

But this new world, it's almost a *Before* and *After.* How do I process this? I try to think of any other category of force against someone else that is okay sometimes. Robbing a bank? Murder? Cheating at cards?

"Milt, you're such a flirt—your father's such a flirt, Kimmy, did you know?" Lane Kovac, one of my mother's best friends, has a perfect helmet of platinum bouffant hair curling around her cat's-eye glasses and frosty pink lipstick that coordinates with her green-and-hot-pink sheath.

Polite. I am so fucking polite.

My brother has a rock band, and they practice in our basement. They use that word all the time, and they are so fucking cool. The drummer, Jerry, is in sixth grade, like me. Inside my math notebook are several pencil drawings of Jerry's face, each one a meditation on his beauty.

I don't know how to draw, at all, but I feel close to him when I try to put down the shape of his eye, or the wisps of sideburns he cannot grow. He is quite a few inches shorter than I am, but when he is playing the drums, no one is thinking of his height. His eyes close, his rosy lips press into a thin line of concentration, he gives himself over to the beat, and I am so glad he cannot see me staring at him. Words in my head, words I never thought I'd care about—"boyfriend," and "love," and "couple"—fly across my brain when I see him.

My teacher that year, Miss Essington, looks like Lane Kovac's twin sister—the one who was denied access to hair color, beauty products, and salons. She and Lane have the same birdlike features, but Miss Essington's face is usually creased with disapproval as she levels a B or B+ at me. I have returned to Cowles, following the failed Windsor experiment, but I am not doing any better socially here than there.

Miss Essington is as strict as she is sour-looking, and our whole class is well behaved. No one acts up around her. They don't dare.

Once, I took a paper I thought I'd done well on back up to her desk. "I think this should have been an A?" I said, timidly, uncertain of my territory. Even last year, I was an A student. My grades were fine. Only my social life had resulted in awkwardness that was paralyzing.

"Or perhaps an A-plus?" she asked drolly. She hardly looks up from her work, but one glance over her glasses told me she was fully at attention. It's impossible to picture her slouching, or sleeping, or smiling. She's too much of a well-run machine, and those things would be a waste of her time. A clock doesn't slouch, or sleep, or smile. It ticks.

"Yes!" I replied, abruptly pleased it was going so well. "I think it's one of the best things I've written."

"Well, Kim," Miss Essington said, "When you decide to attempt to live up to your full potential, I will gladly give you A's."

"My potential?"

"Yes, Kim. Your full potential. You don't push yourself. And if you don't learn to push yourself, if you do not step up when you are called, you will not have a happy life."

She was not angry that I'd asked. She sounded—disappointed? Resigned?

This was a surprise. Miss Essington turned back to her grading, while with her free hand she smoothed her chignon, in salt-and-pepper gray. She seldom has a hair loose, and wears suits, unlike other teachers in blouses and skirts, or dresses. In this, she is very fashionable, and her trim little pumps and bag always match. I know she is not married, because she told us to call her "Miss."

I want Miss Essington to think well of me. From her assessment of me, she thinks I'm hardly trying. Am I?

Suddenly, grading–and Miss Essington–becomes more complicated. She doesn't want me to try harder because teachers always want us to try harder. She thinks I should push myself to do more with what I have, whatever that is. And that I'll learn more that way. And that may make me— happy?

"Kimmy?" Mrs. Kovac says again. "Isn't he a flirt?" She kisses her husband, Brad, as he passes, by bending his forehead toward her lips. It's very automatic, and hardly registers with Brad, in a loose golf shirt and khaki slacks. He puts up with it, then moves with athletic ease toward Mr. and Mrs. Grismer.

"Yes, Mrs. Kovac, I guess he is," I say, and take her empty glass dangling from her hand. My father has just delivered a fresh drink to her. We're in the newly finished basement, done in a stucco-and-beam style he calls "Tudor" and complete with plastic stained-glass windows with lighting behind them to make us forget we're in the basement. I never do.

He has just turned forty. As a nod to the fashion of the times, his sideburns are an inch longer than they were in the sixties, and his wavy hair curls slightly at his shirt collar. He raises his own glass to Lane, and looks down appreciatively at her hips as she passes by on her way to the bathroom. She, too, gives him a little smile, just a barely turned-up lip, but it makes me feel as if they share a secret.

My mother always asks us to help at parties, so I do, but it's like being in a bad television show with no one to turn to, to ask, "What's happening now?" My father is *not* looking at Lane's hips, but at her bottom. He watches her until the crowd closes the path, and he turns to Jay Hytone, his best friend from scuba class, where he teaches at night. They clink glasses.

"I'm an ass-man, Jay," he says, and I know he doesn't realize I am near. "I am."

Jay smiles and shakes his head in a sympathetic gesture. Nothing in books or in movies—other than Robert Redford unbuttoning Katherine Paul's corset in *Butch Cassidy and the Sundance Kid*—has prepared me for this conversation, this part of being an adult. My parents took me to that movie, which was rated M, for mature audiences only. My mother, sitting next to me, stopped breathing while he undressed her.

167

I push through the crowd of women in polyester wrap dresses and men in wide-lapel sport coats in ice cream colors. In one corner is the rocking chair from the family room, which I festooned in black crepe paper while my dad drove over to the YMCA—the haunted YMCA, in my opinion—to pick up Paul from swim practice. Yes. No one else seems as afraid of the YMCA as I am. No one seems to associate the entire building with what we know happened there two years ago.

I wonder, then, if there are landmarks where terrible things have happened, and I just don't know about them. Maybe every street corner is the site of murder, maybe every suburban basement is a place where small children are molested. In every garage, a small boy has had his head bashed in by a neighbor boy whose mother is away at work. Sometimes people die, and other times, they just go on.

The party started two hours ago, when my father went to get Paul. Friends from the neighborhood and family from all over Des Moines parked their cars on the next block and walked on high heels or men's dress shoes to our house. It's Valentine's Day, too, so my mother put black hearts everywhere. Apparently when you get older, you don't celebrate your age anymore, but dread it. My mother also invited people from my father's office to the party, and I don't recognize everyone.

By the time Paul and my father return, we're hidden in the stained-glass room of the basement, stifling giggles and listening to their steps overhead. Paul is supposed to lure my father downstairs to show him a new move he learned in Ping-Pong. We hear their voices upstairs, and I know from my father's steps that he's making himself a drink. There's a pause at the cupboard where we keep glasses, and another one by the icemaker on the refrigerator, and a third by the stove as he reaches into the liquor cabinet.

Everyone in the basement is getting noisier with each moment, but they hush as soon the basement door opens. They come galloping down the steps, and Paul says, a little too loudly, "Maybe we can play one set?"

I roll my eyes at Nellie, who's next to me, staying close. As if my father ever plays with us. That should give away the whole surprise right there. He comes around the corner from the steps, and the crowd shouts chaotic birthday greetings.

"Oh, well, thank you all!" he says in a bright voice, when the room has quieted down. He hands his scotch to my mother, who kisses him on the cheek. "Thank you, Connie. Yes, I'm forty—tomorrow," he says, shaking hands with everyone. "I'm old now!" He doesn't look unhappy.

Even more people arrive. In the crush, Mrs. Kovac glides past me on the way to the bar, and I'm suddenly up close to the creamiest bosom I've ever seen, captured and displayed by the seaming of the low-cut bodice. Her breasts jiggle like milky white gelatin every step she takes, and while she waits for my brother, now bartending, to make a drink, she leans over her handbag to fetch a cigarette. He is staring at her, too, but he's watching the way she snaps her lighter open and closes her eyes with a little moan before drawing a breath. He waits till she opens her eyes, then hands her the drink.

"Thank you, Paulie," she says sweetly, turning away. He catches my stare, and flushes. It's the way she said his name. *Paulie.*

I am embarrassed by all breasts, all the time. If we're watching television in the family room, and someone's dress is cut a little low, I stand up to go get cookies, or a soda pop, or to take a bath—I just cannot stay there, watching and not-watching. I cannot hear what the actors are saying, I don't know where to look. I just leave.

Upstairs in the kitchen, I work next to my mother, placing cheese straws on glass platters.

Late arrivals, Don and Lori Thacker, push open the kitchen door, bringing with them a gust of cold air. They are laughing and breathless.

"Okay to park in the driveway?" he asks, a tall man with chestnut hair as trimmed and tight to his head as spray paint. "Nobody else is here?"

"Did we miss the surprise?" Lori asks, with all her S's starting near the back of her teeth. "Sorry we're late!" She takes off her gloves and checks her lipstick in a compact mirror. With the tip of her finger, she cleans up the lines.

My mother helps Lori shake off her winter coat, and unwrap the scarf that covers most of her face, except for her sunglasses. She is wrapped like this, summer and winter, in long sleeves and gloves on the hottest day. Once she peels away all the layers, though, her dress is more like a long camisole, or a slip. I would wear it under another dress. Or a sweater. She's not wearing a bra.

"Lori takes care of her skin," my mother says. "Keeps her young," she adds, looking at her own tan. My parents went back to Florida right after Christmas for two weeks. Grandpa and Grandma Jenkins came to live with us. My mother returned looking bronzed and happy.

"You're not late," she says to Lori and Don. "Milt's downstairs. Grab a drink in the family room."

As Don passes me, I catch the smell of whiskey. He's tucking in his shirt, and hitching up his pants, as if he got dressed in the car.

Lori passes me, and the back of her slip dress is partially caught inside her panty hose, which has been pulled up over it. I help her, and she smooths the rest of her outfit with a giggle, then takes the platter of cheese straws from my mother. She tips her head toward the dining room with a question on her face, and we follow her in. I make room on the table by removing an empty plate to replenish with Swedish meatballs in the kitchen.

"Are they *treyf?*" Jay asks me, holding up a toothpick with a meatball on the end. He is the only person I know with a beard. He is large, and always laughing, and my father's very best friend.

"Not kosher, honey," says his wife, Mary Rose. "Pork?"

I actually know the answer to this. "No. She made them with beef this year."

They are the only couple I ever met who were on their second marriages. He came with two sons, and she has four daughters. It's weird to see them without their children around. My father once said, "Mary Rose Grace is Catholic, so they have all those kids. Jay's Jewish, so they're all going to be doctors."

"They're all going to heaven," Jay had answered. "I let Mary baptize them so they won't rot in the ground like me."

Against a backdrop of black-and-white flocked toile wallpaper is my mother's dining room table, with three extensions making it over twelve feet long. It is arrayed with hotplates and toothpicks, sweet-and-sour meatballs, water chestnuts broiled in bacon wraps, cheeseballs with olive centers, and always, always ten kinds of cookies. The other sixth grade teacher, considered the "nice" teacher compared to Miss Essington, Mrs. Zook, is helping herself to the appetizers, and looks at me approvingly. She and my mother are in the same bridge club.

"I can tell you had a hand in all this," she says. "You have such an artist's eye."

I am pleased, because Mrs. Zook is our art teacher at school. We're learning about typography, and I am designing an alphabet. I am fascinated by the idea that people, ordinary humans, created typefaces. And I feel silly for feeling this way. Where did I think they came from? I will find out more. I will test my resolve to do more, try harder, learn new things. I don't want to waste my potential, however much or little I have.

Mr. Zook comes up to take his wife's arm and hand her a drink. He has a pencil-thin moustache, in a rusty shade of brown that matches his eyebrows. He is otherwise bald. Mrs. Zook turns to him so fondly, and kisses him on the cheek as she takes the glass. It's something, is it tender? I realize I don't see that kind of look between my parents, or grandparents, or aunts, and uncles.

My mother calls this spread of food, this menu, a "tea," but I mostly see my father slipping highballs and cocktails into the hands of our guests. One step down from the dining room is the living room, or where we keep the baby grand piano. We're only allowed in there for piano practice and sing-alongs, or during parties.

Lori Thacker is sitting on the bench, ready to pound out the chords to "Happy Birthday." Later the party will end on a sing-along, as all my parents' parties do. My father is already standing near the piano. He loves to sing. Even a song to himself. I know he will join in as loud as anyone.

Once everyone's there, my mother gets the cake ready, and ice cream, and I go about shepherding people from all over the house into the living room for "Happy Birthday." I go back down to the basement, and then see the closed door to the Ping-Pong room. I can hear someone in there, so I open the door and switch on the lights automatically.

"Cake is upstairs," I say and stop, because I glimpse a man's back, his hairy legs bent and naked under his peach-colored sport coat, and his pants around his ankles, while he seems to grind himself into a woman in a green-and-hot-pink dress hitched up around her hips, her back pressed into the wall.

I back out, almost tripping, and shut the door. Still polite, so fucking polite. "I'm sorry," I whisper, and take the steps two at a time. "I'm sorry," I say, storming through people filing into the living room to sing. "I'm sorry," I say hoarsely as I climb the steps to the second floor and the bathroom I share with Paul and Nellie. I hear them all singing "Happy Birthday, dear Milt," while I vomit, then press my forehead into the toilet's cool rim.

There's a soft tap on the door, and I have to say, "Who is it?" because I haven't locked the door.

I don't want anyone to find me there. Nellie opens it a crack, and says, "Are you okay?"

My first answer is some version of "no" but I don't say that out loud. She's so small in her jumper, which has large pockets in the shape of hearts. G.I. Joe is sticking out of one of them, his arms outside the pocket, resembling a hostage who has given up all hope of rescue.

We need protection from the adults. That's it. In that beige-and-rust bathroom, my sister is asking me if I need her, when she is so small, and unprotected, and exposed to all of them. Her eyes are huge, and I realize that parties must be overwhelming for her. She's like a kitten underfoot, and there is nowhere to go.

I rinse out my mouth and wash my hands, and run a comb through my hair. I offer her my hand.

"They're cutting the cake," she whispers, bringing her small body close to mine as we go down the steps to the living room. I understand this part. Cake is safe.

Mrs. Kovac emerges from the basement and passes us, tugging at her dress, patting her bouffant as she rushes into the living room. "Happy Birthday, Milt!" she carols, and someone puts a plate with cake into her hand.

I find I'm angry at all adults. At men for doing this, but I'm just as angry at women for accepting this coupling and all its horrible variations as normal. I'm adrift in thoughts, and don't notice Mr. Grismer backing up to better frame a photograph he's snapping of my mother and father by the buffet.

Nellie drops my hand to get out of the way, but he shoves into me, without even knowing it, and I flail and fall into Jay's lap. He is so good-natured, and laughing at me, everyone is, while my parents are busy with the cake and ice cream. He helps me scramble out of his lap, and I try to rejoin the party. Sex was once outside, somewhere out there, part of assaults and thefts and things that were not part of my world, except in the morning and afternoon edition of the newspapers.

Now it's in my house, or maybe it always was, and it makes me afraid, suddenly, of all adults, everywhere.

ONCE MORE TO THE LAKE

Age: 12

I am up to my chest in water, slipping my feet into the rubbery heel and toe brackets of the water skis. I have been skiing for years, and this is how we've always done it. One of the fathers, this time Ray Antrim, holds my shoulders lightly in the water from behind as I bob and try to keep my crouched sitting position, with the long wood of the skis half-submerged in the lake and the front tips cutting up through the water and facing me. My brother hurls the ski rope toward us from the boat, which is hovering well away from the swimming area. Ray swims out and retrieves it, my personal coach and guide. I hold the Y-shaped handle with both hands, my arms straight out from my shoulders.

"Sit on your skis," Ray says, as he always does, as all the fathers always have. "And if you need to, lean into me." He pounds his skinny chest twice, holds both my elbows just enough to keep me from tipping over sideways in the water, and the boat slowly put-puts away. "Say when you're ready."

"HIT IT!" I yell, and my father, driving the boat, opens it up while the ski rope goes from slack to straight. I hold my breath as the wake of the skis foams up around my face, but in seconds, I snap straight up, pulled by the boat. By keeping the skis strictly parallel, I coast in and out of the churning lines behind the boat, and lift one leg high, just to see if I can keep my balance. When we make one lap past the shore near our cabin, I slip my left foot out of the ski and kick it free.

Someone closer to shore will swim out and bring it in. Then I neatly slip that foot in behind my right one and I am doing what all the teenagers do—slalom.

I try to look casual, even just in front of my brother and father, but I'm not very practiced. I want to hold on with only one hand, but I don't have the courage, or maybe the strength in my shoulders. When the boat comes near our shore a second time, I drop the rope and ski safely into the shallows before sinking into the water.

Next to me, Victoria, wearing frosty white lipstick and mascara, is putting on a marshmallow white flotation belt around her tiny waist. These look so cool, especially compared to bright orange pillow vests, but they are considered dangerous by my parents, because if you are knocked out, a belt doesn't know if you are up or down in the water. At least, that's the theory. The rest of us have to wear the life vests that keep us upright. They are so bulky that I think they might be bulletproof.

"Is Victoria going next?" my dad calls from the boat. "I could use a break from driving."

Paul takes over driving, and slowly approaches the dock so my dad can hop out. Dee, my age, climbs on board to handle the ropes for the skiers.

Ray wades ashore, calling out to his wife, Joyce, for a cigarette. Everyone will get a turn.

I sit on the dock and dangle my legs while Victoria adjusts her bikini bottoms. Victoria, who has the cool blond looks of a Barbie doll, complete with a ponytail high on the back of her head, sees me watching, and smiles. She's seventeen, and old enough to be our babysitter, but now that I'm twelve, we're all pretty much left on our own. Teenagers and younger kids travel in packs, mostly, because board games and card games don't exclude anyone on the basis of size or age. Sometimes we walk through the woods to a lodge on the lake that has ice cream, a jukebox, pinball machines, and Ping-Pong tables. It's not the way it is at home, where fifth graders hang out with fifth graders, and sophomores with other sophomores. It's nice. My brother can't exclude me. I can't leave our little sister behind. And most of the time, I don't mind having her along.

My dad, on shore, takes a long draw on a can of beer he's just opened.

"Vicky," he calls. "You need a hand?" He doesn't wait for her answer, but wades into the water and crouches behind her, holding her shoulders in the water while she puts on a ski.

"Uncle Miltie!" she says, and turns pink under her tan. "You'd better behave." It's a joke, that they all call him "Uncle Miltie," after a comedian that used to be on television. But the way she says it today, it's not joking. She sounds annoyed at him. I don't completely understand her tone, but it's not the way teenagers talk to adults. It's new.

My dad squats in the water behind her, and I can't see where his hands are. She's pressed up against his chest, a gray-and-red coat of curly hair, and she is still pink, and uncomfortable. Her breasts in her bikini top are magnified underwater.

Dot, the middle sister, is pacing up and down the dock and watching.

"I'm going to ski off the dock," she says suddenly. "When it's my turn, I'm going to sit on the end of the dock and start from there."

"Splinter butt!" I say, which I think will make her laugh.

"I don't care!" Dot says, and she sounds *mad*. She's a sort of tough but loving teenager, and will pick up small kids out of the sand when they are fighting and shake them like

177

puppies until they are friends. And she never sounds angry, even when she's doing it.

"Victoria!" she says from the dock, and it startles both Victoria and my dad. The boat is coming in so Dee can throw the rope toward her; my brother is very careful not to get too close. Dot signals to him. "She's going off the dock!"

Victoria flushes, and slips her feet out of the skis, then wades toward the dock. Dot hauls her up by one hand, right out of the water, and Victoria gives her bikini bottom another tug.

My brother smiles. He likes trying new things. Dee tosses the ski rope directly to Dot, and she pulls the boat in with it, like reeling in a fish. My dad is still crouched in the water, sort of dog-paddling, even though he's in water that would only come up to his waist. He's watching Victoria's body move easily down toward the end of the dock, and then he looks at me.

"Honey? Would you mind getting me another beer?" I jump up, glad to have a normal request to focus on.

Before I dash up to the cabin, I pause for a moment to watch Victoria. She's sitting on a towel, and her legs bob up and down in the skis as waves roll into the shore.

Victoria yells, "HIT IT!" and is yanked off the dock by the force of the boat pulling away. Her skis sink a little into the water with her weight until the boat picks up speed, and as she is pulled past the swimming area, she leans hard on her right leg. An arc of water sprays the swimmers, the shore, and some waders.

Dot throws back her head and laughs, and I am relieved. All is well. She turns back to stare at my dad, then catches my eye and looks away. I want to ask Dot something, a question I just can't find words for. I don't understand why she and Vicky are so annoyed with my dad, but I am annoyed, too, for a reason I can't name.

When I bring the beer back to the beach, my father is sitting in the sand next to my mother's lounge chair. He takes it from me wordlessly, and I am about to remind him of his manners, but I see my mother's face, red under her tan. He looks like a shamed dog, brought to heel.

"What's wrong?" I ask. They are silent, together, and yet something is hanging there, unsaid. "What are you guys talking about?"

"I'm in the doghouse," my dad answers, grinning.

"Milt," she says warningly. He ducks his head. She looks at me, and I see the shift in her eyes, from angry wife to concerned mother.

"Your father can be—" she starts to say, but she does not finish.

"An idiot," my dad says. He takes a long sip of beer, then tries to catch her eye, willing her to soften her tone with his bemused gaze.

"Worse than an idiot," my mother replies, not giving an inch. Her lips are pursed, and the corner of her mouth turns up in a grimace. He sags a little, and lowers his eyes, all teasing gone.

"Oh, I knew that," I toss off casually, dangerously, and I leave them there. Silence follows me back to the dock.

That day, all afternoon, we learn to ski off the end of the dock. Dot teaches us. I am still worried about splinter butt, but Dot makes sure there is always something—a towel or a boat cushion—to protect us. And we ski that way for the rest of the season.

The lake always goes glassy, right before sunset. There are fewer speedboats that time of night churning up the waters;

everyone is at supper. The wind dies down, and the air is cooling, and it's time for sweaters or sweatshirts, not swimming. It can be so hot during the day that even a bathing suit feels oppressive, but by nightfall, I am hoping for a bonfire and s'mores, ghost stories, and then hot chocolate and a wool blanket at bedtime. This is a good night at the lake.

My parents and other adults, all the teenagers and children gather around the fire with our long forks in the flames. Bodies in a circle, backs to the darkness, and I can hear the crickets in the grass, the snap and crackle of twigs as someone approaches, and distantly, the loons' evening dirge. Faces are lit like human jack-o'-lanterns, and the conversation is sometimes quiet talk among two or three people and sometimes one person tells a story to the whole group.

When Nellie complains of a stomachache, I sit up, worried.

"Too many marshmallows maybe," my mother says, but she gathers her cigarettes and matches and stands up to go back to the cabin.

"Too many hot dogs," Ray says kindly, watching my father stand up, too. My father leans down, just a little, to take Nellie's hand. As they head up the path, Nellie holds my dad's hand a little tighter.

My brother picks that moment to slip into the darkness with one of the teenage housekeepers who lives in town. They help at the lodge and, once a week, turn us out of our cabins to clean.

Her name is Valerie, and she has, behind thick glasses, the most beautiful green eyes, rimmed with black lashes. Her brown hair is a mop of sun-streaked curls that covers most of her face. One hot day, after cleaning our cabin, she walked down to the lake, threw off her shoes, sweatshirt, and shorts, tossed her glasses on top of her sneakers, and swam out to Blueberry Island and back.

Paul watched the whole thing from the porch and I watched him. His face was full of wonder, as if he was seeing Santa Claus and the reindeer land on the roof. He could not look away.

When Valerie stood up in shallow water and walked up the beach to her clothes, I saw what he saw. With her glistening hair swept off her face, she was shiny golden perfection, a womanly statue in a dripping wet swimsuit. Until then, I had no idea that she was anything but a slightly older kid who had to clean on weekends.

Paul had a crush on Valerie ever since. I wonder if they are kissing.

At the bonfire, most all the ghost stories I hear are familiar. I love knowing what's going to happen even though I have heard them a dozen times. We all scream obligingly.

Dot says, "Do you remember last year, when those people killed Sharon Tate?"

Her parents look at her aghast. Victoria says, "Helter Skelter—the Mansons," and because I always read the newspaper, I know what she is talking about.

"Drugs and hippies," Ray says.

"And sex," Victoria adds, and there's a silence around the bonfire.

Joyce is knitting quietly, hardly looking at her work, but she gazes around the circle. "Anyone else have a story?" she asks.

I want to say I do. But I hold back. We are a collective up at the lake. We are the Castle family, and they are the Antrims, and I'm just one of the daughters. The older Castle girl. I am never really on my own as I am right now, at the bonfire.

At piano recitals, there is always someone to applaud, to tell me I've done well. My parents. It's their duty.

One of my father's business friends came over a few years earlier, driving a Model T. This is an old car, from his grandfather's time, but Mel had bought it, and restored it, and used it to visit on Sundays. If it broke down, he knew how to fix it, and he was never in a hurry to get anywhere. He had no wife. He had no children. And he was just "Mel," not "Mr. Somebody."

The car had room for only one passenger, and it had no roof. It was all open, and when he rolled into the driveway, that sunny day, it sounded like my mother's sewing machine, or typewriter keys in rhythm, the nicest clackety-clack. A toy car would have been noisier. One by one, he took the three of us children for a drive. When it was my turn, I closed my eyes against the air coming over the very short windscreen. It was the same size, that windshield, as the one on a speedboat. I'd seen this sort of car in a movie, *Chitty Chitty Bang Bang*, and while I expected no magic, I loved how we swayed along in our springy wooden seats with every bump and turn.

Mel leaned over to me, and asked, "Do you know why I never smile when I am driving?"

I shook my head.

"I don't want to get bugs in my teeth!"

I laughed so loud it startled me, especially because he was smiling so broadly when he said it.

Beth Swanson was in her front yard, getting the mail out of the box at the end of her driveway, and she waved. I was so happy. I felt so special. It was a perfect drive, and Mel made it even better by pulling in for ice cream at the Dairy Queen.

I had a vanilla cone, dipped in sprinkles, but he didn't have anything. "I had one when Nellie and I drove this way," he said, and I thought how nice he was, to stop for ice cream every single time he had a new passenger.

Because the Model-T went only about 15 miles per hour, it took us a little while to get home, and my ice cream was gone when we pulled in. Paul was waiting in the driveway. He had wanted to go last, I think, hoping Mel would let him drive.

I hopped off the running board, shouted, "Thank you, Mel!" as I dashed inside the kitchen door and straight for the table.

My parents were smiling at me, expectantly, and my father said, "Kimmy, did you have fun?"

The words just fell out of me. That we'd had ice cream, the sound of the motor, Mel's joke about bugs in his teeth. I tried to tell them all how wonderful it was, and maybe I talked too long.

When I took a breath, at last, my father said loudly, "Kim, yes or no. Did you have fun?" He and my mother burst out laughing.

"Yes," I said, and they both laughed again.

"Sometimes," my dad said, "it's just a simple yes or no."

I nodded, moved away, dented.

I am alone at the bonfire, and there will be no one to applaud, but there is also no one to shoot me down.

"I have a story," I say shakily. "A story. It's not a ghost story. It's true."

And just like that, I have them. They want a true story, not something made up. Not about newlyweds, or teenaged girls left in the house alone. They have heard all those.

Without my family at the bonfire, I am free to say almost anything and no one (my brother) can say, "Kim always exaggerates."

I feel the power. No one will kill my story with a "Don't be so dramatic."

I lower my voice.

"We live next door to the Lindstroms," I begin. "They have a chocolate-colored poodle. Mr. Lindstrom has a tool-shed and sometimes the neighborhood kids go in there to play doctor. They have a daughter. They once had two daughters."

It's gratifying that Dee Antrim stops rustling in the bag for another marshmallow. Mrs. Antrim stops knitting.

"Kathy Lindstrom babysits sometimes, but she has—she *had*—an older sister, Donna. When we first moved to that neighborhood, all the houses were still under construction. The sod wasn't laid in any yard but the Lindstrom house, next door but up a hill. They were there the longest. The yards were so muddy, after even a little rain, that my sneakers would come off and sink. I lost so many shoes. And no one had driveways yet. It had been too rainy for the cement trucks. My parents just parked the car any old place."

"It's not scary enough," Dee says dismissively.

"It's not a scary story," I say. "It's just something I'm telling you. And I can stop."

Dot is kind, but also curious. "Keep going, Kim? Please?"

"Well, Donna used to let us play dolls in the toolshed. That's why I mention it. She was nice to us when we first moved in."

"What happened to Donna?" Ray asks, drawing from his pipe. He smokes a musky tobacco, and it mingles with the smell of the bonfire, and of melting chocolate. He then looks at each of his daughters and smiles, and I feel envious of them all. I've never heard Ray get impatient with anyone.

"That's what's sad," I say, and I shrug. "Donna and her boyfriend were just out driving. He was drinking. And it was raining, and everyone said it had never rained like that. And the lights on his Chevy were mud splattered from the new roads, so the light was dim. He was going so fast," I whisper.

"He was trying to get Donna home before curfew because Mr. Lindstrom was so strict. So her boyfriend is driving up this slick street in the torrential rain with dim lights and takes the corner too fast."

I've never had so many people staring at me with so much longing in their eyes. Part of me cannot believe this is happening. They want me to keep going. My heart hurts. Victoria has even stopped filing her nails and is watching me with wide eyes.

"They skid past the Lindstrom house and shoot off the top of the hill, and the wheels leave the ground. The car goes into a pitch, nose first, into our yard. And the car, from the speed, and the force, hits the muddy pit of our yard with a boom, and crumples like an accordion, and they are pinned in there, with the rain coming down in buckets, and the wind howling, and porch lights going on and everyone coming out of their homes to see what the noise was."

Dot whispers, "Are they dead?"

I nod. "Dead. It rains for another whole day, like a monsoon, and with ambulances, tow trucks, and police cars, our yard was like a swamp. My mother wouldn't let us go out back for weeks."

"I told you it wasn't scary," Dee said. She was toasting more marshmallows.

"I'll tell you what's scary," I reply. My voice is thick with tears. Or maybe I'm pretending. I can't tell anymore. "The force of the car when it crumpled, the hood of the car crashed through the windshield, and sheared off . . . *decapitated* Donna. All the way. And honestly, no one ever said out loud, but they could not find Donna's head in all that mud. Ever."

This made me sick just to say it.

"Kim?" Joyce says warningly.

I rush on, almost crying, "My dad put in the sod, and had people lay down sod, the lawn, and for years, no grass would grow where they crashed."

Ray looks at me then, and winks. My tears clear up, I think, because of that.

"I remember that," he says. He draws on his pipe slowly, then lets out the smoke. "Milt told me about that."

His daughters look at him, horrified. It made the whole story so much better, just those few words.

"Not ever?" Dee asks meekly.

"Oh, it finally came in, but sparse." I wait a couple of beats. I hear my heart, and now that I'm no longer weepy, I am afraid of the giggles. I think the tears and giggles must come from the same place in me, so I tamp that down, get very serious, and keep my eyes on the flames. All that's left is to bring the story home.

"My father put down a circle of white gravel, and planted a crabapple tree in the middle. We waited forever for it to grow fruit. Nellie was almost four by the time it finally had blossoms, and because Paul and I were at school, she was the one who found the first crabapple, the first one that was large enough to notice."

One. Two. Three. Four. "And every crabapple that ever grows on that tree is in the shape of a tiny shrunken head, with the mouth shaped like an O."

By this time, I am rasping the words more than whispering them. Everyone leans in to hear me. In the distance,

186

I hear the slap of our screen door. They'll be back and ruin the story, so I bring it to a close.

"Is that really true?" Dee asks, her voice barely audible. I take a deep, deep breath.

I lean in. They lean in. The fire.

Snap, crackle, pop. A simple yes or no.

"The mouth is shaped like an O," I say again softly. "Like a silent—" and I scream. The very biggest scream I can muster. Everyone roars, and jumps from where they are sitting, glory, like frogs off a lily pad. And then they are laughing, looking at each other and at me, shaking their heads at all of it.

My dad comes into the circle, then. "Well, that must have been a good one," he says.

He looks at me to clue him in.

But I don't. Instead, I stand up to go check on Nellie.

He looks at me with puzzled eyes. I am usually so eager to please.

"Good one, Kimmy!" Ray says, wiping his eyes. "Milt, you should have heard that!"

Dot pats me on the back.

"Can I borrow that one?" she whispers in my ear as I pass. I glance over at my father.

"Yes," I say, and to my father's hurt feelings, I offer nothing further.

CLIPPINGS

Age: 13

I am sitting on top of a desk and I am chewing gum while Kenny Noyce is leaning against the blackboard with his arms crossed, staring up at David Traxler's chalk drawing of circles in a huddle and an H of a goalpost. Seventh graders I do not yet know are racing around the room. We're all heady with the knowledge that we have survived elementary school.

It is the first hour of the first day of class, and the door opens. Miss Lavender, whose eyebrows resemble two fuzzy caterpillars, whose wiry salt-and-pepper hair resembles an untrimmed hedge, and whose worn-off red lipstick and very fitted polyester pink pantsuit hint at a less forbidding side to her, issues a challenge in a loud and angry voice.

"I have been teaching for forty years. For God's sake, will one of you please, this year, surprise me?" she bellows. Everyone rushes to a seat, lest she start picking off individuals as targets. I slip into my chair. The gum I tuck into my cheek is my first rebellious act of seventh grade.

The room echoes with the sounds of scraping chairs, and she waits for it to grow silent. She waits so long that my throat starts to tickle, and someone quietly coughs in the back.

She passes out index cards. "Put your last name in the top left corner, comma, first name," Miss Lavender says. "Then the date, spelled out, no abbreviations, fully: September four, comma, one nine seven one. Please under that put your home phone number. I am certain I will never want to talk to any of you after school hours, but I might.

"This is the format I want you to use for every single thing you compose in this class. I will give anything that is not in this format a Zero, and it will be as if you did not complete the assignment.

"No talking, no eating, no candy, no chewing gum. If you are caught, you will get detention and a Zero for the day—as if you were not here.

"Number 2 pencils for rough drafts, blue Bic pens for final copies, loose leaf paper with holes, *never* torn out of the notebook. If you use a black pen, I will give it a Zero and it will be as if it has never happened.

"If you turn in an assignment on paper you have torn out of a notebook, I will give it a Zero, and it will be as if it never happened." She stops and walks to the back of the rows to take the leftover cards from the last person to receive them.

"This is English class, and I know what I plan to teach you to the day, the hour, and when it comes to pop quizzes, every second," Miss Lavender says. "Kindly tell me what you want to learn about this year. It *could be* 'stronger sentence structures.' Maybe you are the weirdo I've been waiting for my entire life who lives and dies to diagram sentences. There may be someone in here who is a gerund fiend. A prepositional wizard. Someone may send my soul singing by writing down 'topical paragraphs' or 'improved hyphenating of compound words.' I am ready to take all suggestions, and on Fridays in here we will concern ourselves with granting your wishes."

I almost swallow the gum. It's so clear that I have met the strictest teacher ever. I love her immediately.

In fact, I am shocked to realize that junior high school does not scare me. I have been living with Miss Essington's comments all summer. I took swimming lessons at the outdoor community pool over the summer, and the coach loved to shout, "Sink or strive!" through her megaphone. I don't want to sink.

It is while I am lost in this thinking that I start chewing the gum again, and don't even realize that Miss Lavender has come to a stop in front of my desk. She puts one hand open in front of my mouth, and with her other waves a tissue at me. *Surrender.*

"There's always one," she declares triumphantly. "See you after school." She tosses out my gum. I feel like a perfect idiot.

Despite this setback, I roam the halls with a sense of excitement. The hallway is papered with sign-up sheets, and when I see one for an autumn piano recital, I write down my name.

I'm looking at the lists of sports clubs, and think I might try volleyball, when my eye lands on something completely different. CREATIVE WRITING—THIS CLASS IS FOR AUDIT ONLY. THERE WILL BE NO GRADES.

I'm hooked. I have never audited a class. The hard part is that it's taught by Miss Lavender on Mondays after school. Maybe it will get me back on her good side.

After school I phone my mother about detention, then head into Miss Lavender's classroom, where she is at her desk. Without looking at me, she points to the blackboard, and says, "Take this down."

I pick up a piece of chalk, and stand ready.

A bald man in a tweed jacket leans into the classroom, and says, "Letitia?" and she snaps her hand at him, palm out, full stop. She does not lift her head and instead continues to mark the papers in front of her.

"Do you have just a moment?" he asks when she lowers her hand.

"No, I do not," she says. "Leave a note for me in my cubby."

"It will only take a minute," he says, half in desperation, half in disbelief.

"I'm with a student," she says brusquely, her head over the papers, and he shuffles out, tail between his legs.

"Not only is—" She looks over at me. "Write this on the *board*," she says with elaborate enunciation.

"'Not only is gum-chewing detrimental to my teeth, but the bovine countenance it presents is one of sheer stupidity.'"

I write as fast as I can to keep up, and she does not have to repeat the sentence. I wait for her next instruction.

"Sign your name."

I do. And drop my arm to my side. I find myself fully enthralled by Miss Lavender and her decisiveness, her attitude of *I don't have time for this*. I have never heard a woman address a man this way. Ever. *Full stop. Leave a note.*

"Do you know the meaning of the sentence?" Miss Lavender asks.

"Um, 'Gum is bad for you and you look like a dumb cow when you chew'?"

She snorts, glances up at me, and mimes chewing her cud. Then waves at my seat in the classroom. "Write that sentence one hundred times, with a blue Bic pen, and then you may go," she says. "If you make a mistake, draw a straight line through the mistake and start a new sentence below it. In the morning, your single sentence on the blackboard will serve to remind everyone not to chew gum in class."

It takes me one minute to write the sentence five times on a piece of loose-leaf paper. But I cannot keep up that pace, and it is an hour and a half before I silently leave the room, my hand cramping.

My mother comes to pick me up, without any sympathy for my punishment.

"So very pointless," she says, "to think the rules are not for *you*."

Over the next few days, and unlike almost every other kid swarming the halls, I find that I am an old hand when it comes to changing schools. Amy Grismer and others look as lost as I felt when I started Windsor, and this building is far larger. Carolyn Waters from Windsor comes up to say hello in the hallway, and Martin Schweigal gives me an expectant, very polite nod. When I discover Mary McCracken in gym class, where we get two days off a month for our periods, I feel more at home at Franklin on the first day than I ever felt anywhere else. And I've already had detention. There is almost nothing left to fear.

The first creative writing class with Miss Lavender is a repeat of what she told us in English. "It will be as if it never happened" is becoming one of my favorite threats. I can't wait to use it on someone else. When she takes attendance on the first day from the sign-up sheet, her eyes land on me for a moment before she moves to the next name.

Our first assignment is to tear out a newspaper clipping and bring it to class. I know exactly what clipping I'm going to use. I found it one week my parents were gone, and all the newspapers had piled up.

It was about the man who murdered Pamela Powers on Christmas Eve in 1968, and how he was serving life in prison. Miss Lavender's assignment is called "Point of View."

We are supposed to use the facts in the clipping and write from the perspective of someone in the story.

I will call it, "Inside the Mind of a Murderer."

Grandma Jenkins picks me up from school that evening, and I tell her about school, and the assignment. She has been at work all day at the hardware store. When we were little, she would let us design signs for the store: ALL YOUR NAIL NEEDS HERE, SOLD BY THE WEIGHT, and NO TWO-PARTY CHECKS, which, when I was six, seemed so sad. Two parties, gone.

My grandfather is in front of the television at our house. "Hey there, toots!" he calls, "Come in here!" I go upstairs to wash before dinner, pretending I haven't heard so I can avoid any demand for a kiss.

Grandparents are like salt-and-pepper shakers, to me. They go together, but they are not alike. Grandma Jenkins will stop whatever she is doing at any time of day if she sees one of us with a coloring book or a board game, or to play a game of cards or listen to questions. She is the best part of babysitting, because her food tastes like my mother's and she pays attention. When I try to help her with dishes after dinner, she tells me to work on my story. The mystery of why she is married to Grandpa Jenkins lingers. She once declared that he was dashing in his youth and had a great automobile. All I know is that he's mean to everyone except customers in the hardware store.

I sit at the kitchen table with the clipping in front of me. I try to imagine how a murderer would explain what he did and why, and as I reread the story, I know I'm still fuzzy on the details. I still don't know what, exactly, he did when he "sexually molested a seven-year-old" two years before he murdered Pamela. Despite the sex book at Amy Grismer's sleepover, I don't really know how a rape would go. How it happens.

I have my fresh lined paper in front of me. One sharp number 2 pencil. One Bic pen, color: blue. Miss Lavender has told us to draft out the story only, so I don't need the pen yet, but I keep all my tools in one place.

Grandpa Jenkins passes me, to freshen his drink, and on the way back, puts a hand on my shoulder. He leans over me and I worry that he is going to try to kiss or cuddle me, but he only picks up the clipping to read it.

"What's this for?" he asks. His breath smells of whiskey and Coke. "Why are you reading this garbage?" He reads over it again and waves it under my nose.

"It's for class," I say, editing the truth just a bit.

"Listen, sister, what kind of teacher would make you read this sick trash?" he says.

"A really good teacher, Grandpa," I say. *And it's the newspaper*, I think. *It's not sick trash.*

"Did she give you the goddamned thing?" he asks angrily. His nose is large and red with veins most of the time, but now his whole face is purple.

"No, I picked it," I say.

He puts the clipping in his pocket. "Pick something else," he says. "Those goddamned people at the paper just dump garbage into a person's home. Right into a person's kitchen. There should be a law against it." He goes back to the family room and back to the television, leaving me speechless with anger.

Grandma Jenkins comes around the counter and sits down next to me. "You probably have another idea, don't you, Kimmy?" She pats my hand, and fusses with the dish towel she's brought over, swiping at invisible crumbs.

That's not the point, I think, and look at her mouth, with all the hairline wrinkles fanning out from her lips. Her mother has those lines. So does mine. The Kendrick, Jenkins, and Castle women have such deep lines around their mouths—and I once thought it was from smoking. Now I know that it's from pursing their lips closed whenever one of their husbands, sons, uncles, nephews, grandfathers, insert-male-relative-here, starts spouting off about anything.

I am so mad that I don't say a word to her, just gather up my things and go upstairs to work in my room. I hate Grandpa Jenkins. I hate him. My brother comes out of his room and sees my face. He is building a plastic V-8 engine, and he's holding two parts together as if waiting for the glue to set. I love the scent of that glue.

"What's up?" he asks.

"I hate Grandpa Jenkins." It feels great to say it out loud.

"He's a trip, isn't he?" he said. "The guy has serious problems."

"Why? Why do you say that?" This was so unexpected. I thought I was being disloyal. Paul was agreeing?

"Well, listen to Sherry and Mom talk—Deo, too," Paul says.

"Wait, they talk around you?" I prod him. My mother and her sisters are notoriously buttoned-up when they talk in front of me.

He shrugs again. "You know, they don't pay attention to me."

I'm impressed. "What have you heard?"

He looks at the plastic parts in his hand. "Well, Sherry was really, really young when she married Gary, do you remember that?"

I did.

"And then, think about it. Only a couple of months later, she had Jeffy."

At the time, I thought that was a pretty good deal. Get married, have a baby.

"Sherry says she remembers him hitting her," Paul says. "And that she blacked out a lot of it. So they all talk about how she sort of escaped, by getting married. And that because she was pregnant—you know, the shame of it and all—Grandpa couldn't stop her."

There are so many questions exploding across my brain like fireworks, and my heart is feeling every single one. "Paul, you know things!"

"Sure. I know. What did Grandpa do just now?"

I tell him, and he smirks. "Yeah, once I was reading *Death Wish* at the lake, and Grandpa said kind of the same stuff. He made me read it out loud to them, you know, so Mom and Dad could hear all the curse words. Gross."

I had loved that book. It was about a vigilante, but for me it was a vocabulary lesson splashed in blood across city streets.

"Why did Mom and Dad go along with that?" I ask.

"I don't know. I guess because he's her dad."

"Oh, I hate *them!*" I said, shocking myself.

"Well, I'm probably not supposed to let you say that," he replies. But he's grinning.

"Now I don't have a clipping," I moan. "I have to go find the newspaper and figure out another one." I am a little distracted by Paul's access to information. I wonder if I can ask him the questions that my mother never answers.

"You just need a news story?" he asks. I follow him back into his room, where he places the joined parts on a square of wax paper. All the pieces of the model are carefully laid out on a grid. The rest of the room is messy, but his work tools are lined up as if for surgery.

He hands me a newspaper clipping, a bit faded, and I see the date in his handwriting on it. Not his handwriting now, but scratchier somehow. It's paper-clipped to his sixth grade class photo from that year, with all the kids' faces in stiff smiles, lined up on bleachers in the Cowles lunch room.

August 1968. That's when a girl from our neighborhood was electrocuted in the bathtub. I remember everything, then. The newspaper said the mother was napping, but we'd heard adults call her a drunk, and her father had been out of town. They divorced right after Jennifer died and then moved away.

"Does this help?" Paul asks. *It could not be more perfect*, I think. I don't really know how some man rapes and kills a child, but I do know about adults who drink, and business trips, and being ten years old.

Paul has saved this for three years. I wonder if he loved Jennifer, if he'd talked to her about all that was wrong in her family, too.

"It's great, Paul. I mean, really great. I'll take good care of it," I say. "Why do you still have this?"

He shrugs. "I don't know. I didn't like her or anything," he adds defensively.

"No, I know."

"I guess it was seeing someone's name in the paper that I knew. Actually sat next to. And then—she was gone." We are both silent. It's the way I could not figure out how Pammy Powers could be dead just from going to wash her hands.

I leave him and go to my room, where Nellie is already settled. Except for going to school, she barely moves from here when our parents are out of town. The overhead light is off, so it's dark, but she aimed a small circle of lamplight across the bed, where she is working. She doesn't look up as she cuts a shape out of a magazine. In the shadows, I could see the quilt littered with cutouts of the space capsule, waving astronauts, and pictures of Earth from the moon.

At my desk I turn on the small light. I sit still, remembering the day Mrs. LaPrad came over to tell us Jennifer had died, just as we were sitting down to dinner, and my father's open exasperation that someone had interrupted us. He was also mad that a distant dog's bark could be heard through our screens, that the pheasants in our backyard had woken him up at five that morning.

It's exhausting, just being around him. Recently, anything can set him off. And our mother just rolls her eyes at him but lets him rant, his frustrations raining down on us, making it hard to know if we can keep eating, or if we should remain quiet till our food is cold. He ruins so many dinners. And we're still expected to clean our plates.

I pull a small mirror from my desk drawer and look at my own lips for wrinkles. So far, so good.

There is a knock on the bedroom door, which startles me. From the shadows, Nellie sits up, and I can make out the whites of her eyes.

Grandpa Jenkins opens the door and starts to come in. "Wanted to check on you girls before bedtime," he says. "Kimmy, I hope I didn't come down too hard on your homework." He glances at Nellie, who has backed into her headboard.

"It's fine, Grandpa," I say dutifully as Paul comes in behind Grandpa. The darkened bedroom is getting awfully crowded. Nellie is tense and I want to calm her.

"Actually, they're going to sleep," Paul says, slipping in between Grandpa and Nellie's bed, and turning to face him. Even in the light, I can see Grandpa Jenkins's face is red with drink, and when he takes a step toward Paul, my brother does not back up or move.

"Well, then they can give their grandpa a kiss good night," he says, slurring the word "kiss."

But Paul blocks the path. "Grandpa," he says.

I come over to stand next to him, and Grandpa looks from Paul to me and back to Paul. Paul says "Grandpa" again, and it sounds like a warning.

I think of Ernie, and that long-ago boat ride, the last time Paul and I were on the same side. That time, it was a stranger. This time almost does not make sense to me. I'm supposed to be nice. He is my grandfather.

Grandpa tries to push past us, dividing us with his arms.

"Just get out of here," I say in a very quiet voice. "Get the *fuck* out."

He straightens up abruptly. He is shocked. And distracted.

"Oh, sister, I will tell your mother you used that language with me," he says. "You're in for it, girl, you're in trouble."

"You tell her." I don't care.

He looks ready to hit me, and I swear, I am so sick and tired of his demands, I will hit back. That girl died in a bathtub. Where the *fuck* were her parents? Pammy died at the YMCA? Where were the authorities? Where was God? Who is in charge here?

Grandma Jenkins is at the door then, her blue-gray hair in tight lines of pink foam rollers, and a face masked with cold cream. She switches on the overhead light.

"There you are, Frank, you look tired," she says. Her words are firm.

"I am, Mother," he says, sagging slightly, and allowing himself to be led away. All the fight just drains right out, and I don't know how it happens. Nellie slumps down into her covers and turns her back on me. There are still cutouts of Apollo 13 all over her bed, some safety scissors, and cellophane tape.

Jesus, I am in so much trouble.

"Holy cow," Paul says with a scoff in his voice. "Holy cow." His voice is shaky but he pats me on the shoulder, like a buddy. I know. Just another night in the Castle family.

"I know," I answer, and adrenaline leaves me.

He starts to shut our door, then pokes his head back in. "If anyone asks, I never heard a thing."

I shrug. "I don't care. If anyone asks, I still hate him." I felt as if I'd just run an entire race, or aced the monkey bars.

"Me, too," Nellie says, muffled, from somewhere under the covers.

I turn back to the desk.

I read over the clipping, again and again, looking for a word, or sentence, that would tell me anything at all about Jennifer. Paul is right. She sat next to him in class, and then she didn't.

All the warnings come back to me, that litany of horrors recited at us all our lives, about sticking bobby pins in electrical sockets, picking up broken glass with our bare hands, riding our bicycles in traffic, straying from the neighborhood after dark. There were dozens, if not hundreds, of rules governing us every hour of every day.

The question was no longer how did she die? How do the rest of us manage to stay alive?

She had been found in the bathtub, electrocuted. She was watching television and it fell into the water. I couldn't imagine being dead *and* naked, and that the medical people in the ambulance would find her that way. I try to figure out why she would have the TV in the bathroom at all. I try to picture everything—what program was that important, why her mother was sleeping, why she didn't just watch the television in the living room like everyone else. I write about how dozens of things had to happen, even accidentally, to add up to her dying right then.

Then I go straighten up Nellie's bed, carefully picking up the cutouts, and her tools, and putting them on her desk. I brush down the quilt very lightly, making sure I haven't left paper clips or scissors behind. She is in deep sleep when I finally turn off her bedside lamp.

I reread what I have, and hand it in on Monday, with the newspaper clipped to the left margin, as I'd been instructed. The following Monday we go over other people's stories, but not everyone's, and definitely not mine.

I had already thought about the other ways I could have written it. I could have been more careful about how I told it, and maybe left out the part where she was naked. Maybe I should not have been so angry at the father for going away that morning on the business trip. Or maybe I should not have mentioned that the mother was drinking, or anything else that I guessed at, instead of using facts.

Through my fretting, I miss part of the discussion. When I look at the clock, I see that creative writing is over for another week. But as I pass her desk, Miss Lavender raises her caterpillar brows at me quizzically, and hands me my paper. She doesn't say a word.

I'm in the hallway before I dare to look down, and there is only one comment.

"You can rewrite this in ink—exactly as it is."

BABYSITTING

Age: 14

In South St. Paul Presbyterian Church on a summer Sunday, Mrs. Gustafson gives me an appreciative look up and down. I am wearing a checked ensemble that my mom has sewn and which looks like a Mary Quant minidress straight out of Carnaby Street. I had read of such things in *Young Miss* magazine.

I have on white tights and Mary Janes, and have lined my eyes with a watercolor marker I found among the art supplies, wishing I had the confidence to add in tiny lines of drawn eyelashes like Twiggy did.

My mother had not wanted to hem the dress as short as I wanted it. "It makes you look too boxy—you need a longer line to slenderize you," she said.

I was four years old the first time the word "slenderizing" was uttered in front of me. I heard it, and I knew what it meant. My grandmother and mother were shopping for me, and their pick for my birthday dress, a jumper in dark purple instead of the mystical apricot color I loved, is what shows up in my kindergarten class picture that fall.

"It's just better on you," my grandmother Castle said.

"And it won't show the dirt," my mother chimed in. I was aware of something amiss in their arguments, that I could be dirty and we could hide it, and that I would still be fat, but no one would notice. When the saleswoman took the apricot-colored jumper, with perfect little embroidered flowers the colors of blue jays, away and brought back the plum-colored one with mustard embroidery, a size up so there was room for me to grow into it, all the excitement of shopping with them leeched out of me.

"How old are you?" Mrs. Gustafson asks. Turning to my mother even more eagerly, she rephrases the question. "Is she old enough to babysit?"

"She's going into eighth grade," my mother replies. "We're so happy we found this church in time for her to join the confirmation class." I am not as happy as my mother. I am desperately alienated by all my surroundings. We'd moved from Des Moines, Iowa, to Mendota Heights, Minnesota, over the summer.

My father is reborn amid the changes; Grandfather Castle retired and my father sold the company, the only place he'd ever worked, to a larger real estate company in downtown St. Paul. He has moved us into a bigger house, bought two new cars, and made several appointments with his New York tailor for fittings.

I am mystified. We are no longer in Iowa, where our name is known. I thought this was my father's currency. It's a new side of him, that maybe he didn't want to be yoked to that name anymore. It's a strange thought, that adults want to escape any part of their lives. They are the ones who have set them up, after all. Why is there anything to escape?

More, he and his father fought. The minute the papers were signed, my mother said, finalizing the terms of my grandfather Castle's retirement, my father sold the business.

I learn this as my mother sews us new school clothes, leaning over the sewing machine, pursing her lips in a tight grimace to hold in her mouth the pins she sticks and unsticks in the seams, muttering about the cost of his trips to New York and the suits themselves.

She sighs along with every snip of the thread, till I want to apologize for needing clothes.

I still haven't forgotten finding out, a few years back, that she doesn't like going up to the lake each summer, something that makes the rest of us so happy, we cannot sleep the night before we leave.

I always thought she made my dresses, the ones for which I received so many compliments, because she loved sewing, and because she loved me. This is the year I've learned that it's just another economy because of something that is mentioned more and more frequently—his suits, his new cars, expensive shoes. Grandfather Castle has retired to Arizona, and it's a plane trip to go see them. I have never been on a plane.

As my father grows happier with his new job, my mother has settled into a mild depression, a sadness that trails her wherever she is in the house. I take on the burden of cheering her up, and I try to make her laugh when we do chores together, but it's getting more difficult.

Finding out she despises sewing for me eats at me. When we go to a new fabric store, near our new house, I try to find patterns that will not be hard. I stop customizing my requests. I stop asking her for a jacket from this pattern, and pants from that one. I let her pick the fabric, I let her pick the styles. I hate the idea of being one more project for her, one more piece of homework.

That the layout of the new house is roughly the same as our old one in Des Moines makes this new knowledge about my mother, and the ongoing waves of homesickness, worse. I am desolate. I ride my bike two or three times a week to the nearest library, sweeping books off the shelf wholesale and immersing myself for days at a time.

"You need to get your nose out of the book and get fresh air," my mother says once or twice a day. "You'll never make new friends if you won't leave the house. Look at Paul!"

It's true. My brother, about to be a sophomore, was adopted at once by a lanky athlete named Scott who lives one street over. Scott is tied into a large group of garrulous teenage boys who love talking about hockey, hanging out, fixing cars in their massive driveways, and smoking pot in wood-paneled suburban basements. I haven't met anyone yet.

"Does she babysit?" Mrs. Gustafson asks again, talking about me while also looking at me. I want to flare my nostrils, like the cows at my great-grandparents' dairy when the veterinarian comes.

"She's taken care of her little sister," my mother says, gushing helpfully and pointing at Nellie. "Babysitting would be good for her. She hasn't made any friends since we moved here, so it would at least get her out of the house."

"Mom," I say. "I'm right here." This has no effect on my mother, but Mrs. Gustafson switches into full-on Minnesota nice.

"Of course, I'm Martha," she says. "You're Kim. Would you like to earn some money this summer before school starts? Be a mother's helper during the day?"

My mother's face shows excitement, but she is swallowing her words.

"Why doesn't your whole family come over for a cookout tonight? You'll meet the kids, and Sully—he's home with the baby today—and I'll show you the house. If you all get along, well then, you can tell me if you'd like the job."

And that seals it. My mother had been worried about moving to Minnesota, away from her mother, and sisters, and a lifetime of friends. I saw it in a flash, just as my great-grandfather Kendrick had predicted one day on the farm. "Your dad will meet people at the office. You kids will meet people at school. This move? I'm worried about your mama. She's a shy woman, and this is a big step."

As first jobs go, babysitting for the Gustafson family is like being transplanted into a magazine story about a perfect family. I love Martha, who is outdoorsy and given to bursts of great laughter when she is on the phone. She belongs to something called the Junior League. On evenings when I babysit, she leaves soda pop in the refrigerator and a bowl of buttered, salty popcorn in the oven, where it stays warm and crisp.

In the last few years, I have become known as a master teller of scary stories at campouts, up at the lake, and during sleepovers: a bowl of berries where a half-eaten strawberry reveals a half-eaten green worm; a playground near school where on rainy days you can glimpse a neighbor child who'd died, still twirling on the swings.

I feel adored when the children beg me to repeat particularly horrid tidbits, and I find I love to linger on the description of the plastic doll's shoe that floats in a playground puddle, or the hair ribbon tangled in the oak tree's branches in the days before the car is hauled away and the tree cut down.

The tales are never overtly gory. I have no stomach for blood and bones and gristle. The power of implication conjures scenes more vivid and terrifying than anything I could actually describe.

When I'm telling a story, I feel different than any other moment in my life, so it's easy to love the smiling, lively, and attentive Gustafson children—Janie, Katie, and Aaron. Two towheads, the little girls follow me around and beg me for stories, which I edit considerably and populate and act out with their dolls and stuffed animals. Baby Aaron, thumb in his mouth, just likes sitting in my lap, or his sisters', and listening with grave eyes under a mop of reddish hair like his father's.

The father, Sully. He works in my father's new office and was the one who told my father about our new church. He is over six feet tall and I have a crush on him the first time he shakes my hand and folds it into his own.

Long and loping, a young father who is only ten or eleven years older than I am, he doesn't talk down to any of us. He talks cars with Paul, asks Nellie about the science fiction she reads, and asks me about my writing.

Clearly one of my parents has mentioned it, and I do not know what has been said, and don't like to talk about it normally. But when Sully asks, I am not embarrassed. Behind thick lenses in horn-rimmed glasses, his eyes always look large and a little puzzled. But they are kind. I am comfortable with him because he seems to be what happens after gawky boys my age get a little more mileage on them. He is all I ever want as a date. Or for life.

The first time I babysit at night, he gives me a tour of his collection of comedy albums, housed in an entertainment console in the basement family room. He has George Carlin, and someone new to me, Lenny Bruce. He has *The 2,000 Year Old Man* by Mel Brooks, and a collection of energetic jazz recordings from the 1920s and 1930s with lyrics that make my groin tingle—"It ain't the meat, it's the motion," and "Take a young boy, ladies, and raise him to your hand."

That summer, I babysit three or four days a week. My jobs are to make simple lunches, clean up, let the kids run around in the backyard all day, and give them baths before Martha makes supper. I play house while Martha is free to come and go, and I have free time, too. When the kids nap in the afternoon, I read or watch television. And get paid to do it.

For an entire fall, Friday and Saturday nights at the Gustafson house are my escape from a junior high school I am not yet part of, and from football games I don't enjoy. I dress for my work with all the care of going on an actual date.

My mother drives me there, and Sully drives me home. He is often in a tuxedo, but with the bow tie loose, after he and Martha come back from "JL" balls and other galas. My mother loves the Gustafsons as much as I do. They widen her social circle and sponsor her initiation into old St. Paul organizations. Martha is younger and without family in the city, so my mother is happy to answer parenting and household questions, or discuss sewing projects. Missing Grandma Jenkins back in Des Moines, she slips into the role of wise, slightly older aunt. I am so relieved to see her laughing again, I feel as if I, too, can draw a breath.

I join the choir at school, chew gum with absolute alacrity in Señor Nonnemacher's Spanish class, and chart my week and my moods by how much time I'm scheduling with the Gustafsons. When I read "The New Babysitter's Checklist" in *Seventeen* magazine, I feel like I'm pretty close to normal.

Their basement family room is cool summer and winter, and after getting the children to bed, I always fall asleep on the couch under an old crocheted afghan that smells of Sully's pipe, either listening to comedy or watching the late, late movie. Martha is always the one to wake me up, just by turning off the television, or the stereo, and I stand up, sleepily, and report anything that has gone wrong, or right, or how many stories it took to get them to bed.

There are months, a short period, when Katie is having trouble sleeping and Martha asks me to lie down with Katie when I tuck her in, just till she falls asleep. There is another period when Aaron's tiny form, the bundle he makes of bulky diaper and blankets and clothes, fills me with so much love that I fairly ache with it. I do my homework and read in his room, and fall asleep in the wingback chair near the shuttered windows.

I adore this family. And they need me. Like my mother, I like being needed.

The minute I leave the house on those nights, though, and walk down the front path to the car with Sully, I am shaking, almost hyperventilating. I always lag behind him a little, trying to take slow steady breaths, but he waits for me to catch up, slipping one arm around my shoulders and hugging me lightly.

Time after time I relish that short walk, and I lean into it. With everything I have, I draw myself close to him. It is an affectionate hug, nothing more. But it feels so easy, and welcoming, like the smooth motion of a confident boyfriend holding me close, making us a couple. We are together.

Sully opens the car door for me, makes sure I am tucked in, and closes it shut. My father doesn't do that. My brother doesn't. No one is so tender with me. It wears me down a little, and makes me want more.

He always asks me about my night, taking the turns to our neighborhood slowly, his large slender hands gripping the steering wheel, keeping us safe on snowy night streets. He asks about school, and reminds me that I don't always have to work on weekends if I have something else to do.

My heart thuds a little, that he thinks I have other ac-
tivities, things that are more important than seeing him before he and Martha leave each night, and spending this time
with him once they return. I feel both wistful that he knows
so little of me, and hollow, too, about any hope, but I love
the picture he conjures up of me, a popular student with a
lot of friends and stuff going on, so different from my soli-
tary bookish self.

"And boys, right?" he asks one night, pulling into the
cul-de-sac where our house stands. "If you're going out, absolutely let us know. We don't want to come in the way of
that."

"You wouldn't," I reply. "I mean, you couldn't. There
isn't a boy, or boys." And then, so I don't look hopelessly
alone, I add, "We don't date, we all just go roller-skating, or
something. A big group meets."

He stops the car in the driveway and gets out. He comes
around the car and opens my door.

"No dates *yet*," he states as I climb out. He walks me to
the kitchen door, while I get my key ready. The topic has left
me blushing. I glance up, noticing his lips and kind smile. Is
it more than kind? I wish with some shame that it is.

He leans down to kiss my cheek, and gives me a quick
hug. "There is plenty of time for that, Kim." And then he is
gone, home to his family, and to his wife, whom I love, too.

If I could not picture the mechanics of sex before, I did
now. With him, I can envision it all. Now that I have his
face, and that tall, almost awkward body, I can figure it out.

I have a whole winter of those nights, punctuated with
choir practices and concerts, the rhythm of the holidays,
and slowly, new friends.

The clocks change in March, and the spring days in Minnesota grow a little lighter and a little warmer, and I become

happy. I have almost survived my first school year in a new city and I am strong and fit playing volleyball and ice-skating over the winter. All my clothes fit in a new way, and for the first time in my memory, getting dressed is a pleasure.

One May evening, the first long hot day that reminds all of us that school will be out soon, giving way to summer, I go over to the Gustafson house to babysit. In Minnesota, there is little need for air-conditioning any month but July, and so the house is somewhat warm in the waning light. Martha is dressed in a striped shift and low heels, while Sully is in a navy sport coat and jeans. Janie is playing with Aaron on their patio.

"Katie's napping upstairs," Martha says. "She had a little fever, and came home from school early. There's chicken soup in the cupboard, if she doesn't want pizza."

Martha and Sully scuttle out the front door in a hail of good-byes, and I go out to the patio. It's a beautiful evening, and I am young. I'll have the drive home with Sully, and it will be more than enough.

Aaron is walking, and becoming willful, on the way to turning two. We chase him around the yard till we are rosy with sweat and then go indoors for pop. The house feels still, after the shouts and chases outside, until Janie pulls over the high chair to corral active, struggling Aaron. The grating of the high chair's legs on the linoleum floor is deafening.

"Shush, now," I say in a low voice. "We don't want to wake up Katie." I put the French bread pizzas that we are having for supper on a cookie sheet and into the oven. "We'll get her up in time to eat."

We sit around the table, sipping Shasta orange pop, with the sounds of birds in the backyard to remind us of twilight slipping in.

211

Aaron is so sweet, and when he says he wants a story, it's easy to comply.

Janie says, "Make it about people we don't know."

"Like who?" I ask, not really understanding.

"Someone dead," she says, a little ghoul.

"There was a girl in my neighborhood named Jennifer," I begin.

"Ooh," Janie exclaims. "It's almost my name!"

"It is," I say, plotting how much I should say to them, and if Jennifer actually needs to die in this version. "This was a girl in my brother's class."

I continue. Aaron asks to be in my lap, so I pick him up to cuddle.

"You said 'was' in his class," Janie says delightedly. "What happened to her?"

The buzzer goes off, so I kiss Aaron's head and deposit him in his chair, then turn the oven to low. Aaron bangs his sippy cup in excitement, and I go upstairs to see if Katie is hungry.

I glance into the room she shares with Janie. I'd spent hours in there, telling stories, playing games, tidying up. One bed is neatly made and the other is rumpled but empty. I walk down the hall to the bathroom, but the door is open, the light off.

My pace quickens. "Katie," I call. I check Aaron's room—she's not there. She's not in her parents' room, a place that makes me anxious as I imagine what married couples do, what Sully and Martha do, in there. I open closet doors, laundry hampers, looking behind open doors, checking the bathtub behind the sliding door.

"Katie!" I shout. I cannot imagine what is happening. A little girl is missing. On my watch. While I was right here.

"Janie!" I call, but she is already at the bottom of the steps. "Is Katie down there—maybe in the basement?"

Janie, only seven, stares up at me with large, concerned eyes. "She's not up there?" she asks in a small voice. Her smallness, it's so familiar, as is her child's worry. She reminds me of Nellie, coming up the basement steps from the workshop.

"No, she's not." I run up and down the hallway, calling her name, then run down the steps. Rounding the corner on the way to the kitchen, I open the door to the basement and flip the light switch. Why do all basements smell the same, even when they are finished? A mustiness under paint, a wet scent within thick floor covers, the odor of fresh wood and rotten, mottled and falling away. The basement is a yawning black hole, and no one is down there.

"Stay with Aaron. Katie? Katie?" The basement is dark and quiet. I can feel how empty it is. The powder room, too.

Janie and I run outside, while Aaron thumps his feet happily on the high chair. "Katie?" I call, shredding my throat into ribbons from the effort. "Katie!" Janie joins me, and neighbors on either side of the house, outside on this first hot day, come into the yard. I run to them, relieved. Adults. And then I recoil: adults.

A short man, a little bald, pushes a baseball cap back on his head. "Katie—did you say you're looking for?" he asks.

Yes, yes, yes, I think, my heart tight with panic. I am so far down the road of terror, I can hardly process his calm. We are miles away from his question, his state of mind.

It's not his fault, this registers with me. It's a portal I'm stepping through—the wish to collapse into silence, stillness, next to the urgency of finding Katie.

"Yes," I say out loud, and my voice is calm. "She was napping and now she's gone."

"Was the front door locked?" he asks. "Someone could come right in the front door and you'd never know it from the kitchen." He glances in the sliding glass door where Aaron is still in the high chair.

That is not helpful, and I need to breathe. A woman jogs into the yard holding the hand of a toddler who is about Aaron's age, his small legs pumping to keep up.

"Katie's gone?" she asks. "Did you call the police?"

No, no no no.

More neighbors pour into the yard; in Minnesota, being outside in May after a long cold winter is a privilege no one wastes. A dozen people walk toward me. A couple of them are calling Katie's name.

It is chaos. It is nice. I want to say thank you. I want to cry. I want my mother.

"Janie, come inside," I say. I am the babysitter and I have lost one of my kids. I won't lose more. I call my mother, and the minute I hear her voice, the back of my raw throat, hoarse from calling, swells. Tears leak down my cheek. I wipe them away and tell her three words I hate saying out loud. "Katie is missing."

"I'll call the police," my mother says, spending no time on useless questions about what I've already done. She gives me exactly what I need.

I replace the receiver of the pale princess phone and turn back to Janie and Aaron, in the high chair. Outside, people are fanning out across the yards, front and back, and calling Katie's name. It's like a terrible game of hide-and-seek. *Ollie, Ollie, all come free.*

A neighbor knocks on the sliding door and peers in at us. "Did you call the police?" he asks through the glass.

"Yes!" I shout, anxious to confirm that something, anything has been done. "Yes, thank you!" The back of my blouse sticks to me, between the shoulder blades, and I am suddenly aware that I am drenched, clammy, and sick with worry.

In this moment, the moments before we know what has happened, she can be okay. She is not a body dumped in a ditch on Christmas Eve.

I hear the crunch of the tires before I see the police, in a standard black-and-white cruiser, pull in. My mother is right behind them in our station wagon. She is out of the car before they are, and runs to the door to hug me. Janie, at the sight of my mother, bursts into tears and reaches up for a hug, too. Aaron joins in with hearty wails.

The two police officers move with no urgency whatsoever toward me. "Did you search the house?" one asks.

I nod.

"Search it again," he says to the other one, who looks about my brother's age. He takes the steps upstairs two at a time.

The first one turns back to me, and over the sobs of Janie and Aaron, says, "Okay, let's get everyone into the backyard."

He cuts through the house and out the sliding glass doors and we all follow him. My mother hugs Janie close with one arm and holds Aaron in the other.

"Listen up, everyone. We're going to walk next to each other, in a row across all the yards. Some of you, take the front yards. Keep your eyeballs peeled. Please look left and right. Report anything you see. We're looking for Katie. We're calling her name. Do you all know what Katie looks like?"

"Of course we do, Officer!" says the woman with the toddler. "We've lived next door for years. Known Katie since she was a baby!"

"Great," he intones grimly. "Let's get out there."

We have already crossed two lawns when the younger policeman comes out of the Gustafson house, holding

Katie's hand. She is rubbing her eyes, clutching a blanket, blinking against the sunlight and stumbling a little, still heavy with sleep.

"Found her in the basement, sir."

"The basement?"

"It's a family room. Asleep on the couch."

"But I checked there!" I protest.

"It's okay," my mother says soothingly. "Hi, lovey," she says to Katie, feeling her forehead. "Are you better?" Katie nods, and pushes her thumb into her mouth. I haven't seen her suck her thumb all year.

As quickly as the neighbors have amassed, they leave, back to their grills, or homes, or children. The bald man who talked to me first makes a point of catching my eye.

"Glad it worked out. Remember what I said about locking the front doors," he says.

"Okay," the older police officer says. "We just need everyone's names—especially yours," he says, looking at me. He pulls out a pad of paper and begins scribbling. "Who's the mother?"

"I am," my mother answers, stepping forward. "Not of Katie, of Kim."

"I'm Kim," I fill in hastily. "My mom called you."

"That would make you—Connie Castle?" he asks, looking at his notes. She nods.

"Okay. Where's this little girl's mother?"

"I'm the babysitter," I say.

"That's right," my mother replies. He writes down another note.

"Sir?" the younger officer says. "Sir, the little girl's safe, and no one's hurt."

"Yeah," the older one answers. "Yeah, Miz Castle, this is—this is what we're going to do." He puts the notebook into his back pocket. "When are the parents getting back?" he asks my mother.

"Midnight or so, right, honey?"

"That's when they are usually home," I say.

"We're family friends, officer," my mother adds. "From church."

"Yeah, that's fine. Please just—well, first move your car so we can back out," he tells her. "Then if you'd just stay here with Kim—till the parents get back. I think we can leave it at that."

"Of course," my mom says. She picks up Katie and smooths her hair, then holds out her other hand—to me. I take it. Janie and Aaron, no longer crying, cluster around her.

Inside she settles us around the table and then leaves to move her car. When she returns, we eat dried-out, still-warm French bread pizza while she smokes a cigarette. I am silent with the relief of being a child again, not the one in charge. We pull out games and coloring books till bedtime. Katie's fever is gone, and she hardly seems aware that she's been missing.

I wash dishes, while my mother tucks them in upstairs. She returns, and says, "We have to tell Martha and Sully, you know."

"I know. I did check the basement," I repeat.

"The officer said she'd probably gone outside looking for you all, and came back in. He said it was normal. It's not your fault."

And I hear Pamela Powers's mother, "She just went to wash her hands."

Jennifer's mother: "I was just taking a nap."

My own parents, about Ernie, "He was just taking the children out for a boat ride."

My grandfather, showing Nellie the workshop.

Even though we don't live in Iowa anymore, we have not forgotten any of it. No one is to blame, and everyone is. We were just—we were looking there when we should have been looking here. It's sickening and I cannot see how I will heal from this. In my old book of broken things, where does this loss go?

I don't have the words for any of this, and without words, I can't explain it to myself or anyone else. It's somehow shaming. Local know-it-all actually knows *nothing*.

And I can't tell my mother how I took the babysitting job for the ten-minute ride home. That I had spent hours and days hoping someone would kiss me—someone who didn't belong to me. That I didn't even know I'd looked away, from my one task, to keep the children safe.

It is all my own shame, and it makes me cry, and my mother waits it out. She finds a tissue, and lights another cigarette, and seems to recognize that there is nothing to say that could ever make me feel worse than I already do.

We wait for the Gustafsons to get home, and my mother does all the talking, and I come off looking like a quick-thinking heroine.

Martha shrugs, and hugs me, and in all ways takes it really well. I can't look Sully in the eyes as we leave. I hold my mother's hand all the way to the station wagon, and open the door myself, then try to make myself small and invisible in the front seat. I want to be in her care, her utter care, and I want to be the passenger, perhaps, for the rest of my life.

"I think the Kopeskys are looking for a summertime mother's helper," she says as we pull into the driveway of our darkened garage. "They're right in the neighborhood, you know. They're close." She leaves me with some dignity, through her omission: She'd be nearby if anything happened.

I am silent as we go inside and turn off the outside light. Everyone else is in bed. "I think I'm done babysitting," I tell her. "At least for now."

She nods, too quickly. "Of course," she says. "I just meant if you—no, of course not."

Upstairs, she hugs me and says good night.

"Thank you, Mom," I say. She hugs me harder, lets go, shakes her head.

"Of course. Oh, Kimmy," she whispers. "Forgive yourself. You take things so hard. Please."

I go down the hall to my room. I am aware that I have been thinking of this moment all day—the moment when I find refuge here. It's not a new house anymore. It's home. It's a landing spot. And I probably need to talk to my parents, or to someone, about all the missing girls. The missing children. Who, like Nellie, can be right under our noses, but living through experiences we cannot fathom.

I am so tired. Just to make sure, I test the sore spot, and say Sully's name out loud. Abruptly, I am free of him. It doesn't hurt as much as I thought it would. And except in church and at occasional family outings, I never really see him again.

BONFIRE

Age: 15

Farm work is hard work, and Great-Grandmother Kendrick, approaching her nineties, is always in motion. That woman loves a party, everyone says so, and there is no bigger reason to celebrate than all the kin returning to her and her husband Ralph's farm in New Market, Iowa, for a summer family reunion. There is baking for days, and cooking early morning to after sunset, and then it's all stored in a large refrigerator and a deep freezer her children gave her a few years back. We arrive, the ones from Minnesota, and it's like we never left.

I've outgrown carsickness, but I've also outgrown reading the miles away. I travel with a steno notebook, with wire loops across the top, and it is so plain, and brown, that it's invisible to everyone but me. I can't bear to make a mark in all the blank books people have given me, frilly diaries, leather journals, locked books with little fake keys.

With the end of my carsickness, Paul takes his place next to me in the back seat. Sometimes my mother sits there, while my father takes the passenger seat up front so Paul can drive.

We are almost happy. On the farm, there is nothing to worry about. We will be fed. We will behave well around others. There will be a bonfire. Only Nellie, in the cargo section of the station wagon, remains quiet during the drive while my mother updates us on who will be there, and why they count as relatives.

It's so much coordination, making food for that many people, and there are going to be so many of us that my family arrives three days early. We stay at a motel with a strip of musty-smelling rooms, just outside of town. We make day trips to the farm, and return every night to air-conditioning, color television, and a swimming pool, fenced off from a nearby cornfield. My great-grandmother's house is already full of relatives from Arizona, California, and Missouri, including her older sister, Great-Aunt Katherine.

She's the one who scared me when I was a child because she comes apart. In the bathroom, at night, her rather large plastic breasts were in a polished wooden box on the back of the toilet, her teeth were in a glass by the sink, and in a little jewel box next to the teeth was one blue eye. I spent a lot of time studying her. She didn't talk much and kept to herself.

For years I had questions about adults falling apart, leaving pieces of themselves everywhere. Then I came across my mother and her sisters talking in low voices about Katherine's cancer and her operations, how she was a nurse in World War II, and how tough she was. Lucky to be alive, they said.

Walking in on adult conversations without interrupting is an art both my brother and I have at last mastered. It's where all the really important things are discussed, so I have learned to bring in a cup of coffee or an iced tea, hand it to anyone, and then just not leave. At the reunion, this is child's play. My mother and her sisters are so busy gossiping, chopping, and prepping giant bowls of vegetables from the garden that they hardly have time to smoke.

I mostly follow whatever Grandma Jenkins is doing. She dips all the carrots in a silver bowl of water, then uses a vegetable peeler back and forth to scrape off the outside. "Waste of vitamins," mutters my great-grandmother, her mother, and this is the soundtrack that accompanies peeling potatoes, de-ribbing celery, and cutting off spots on radishes. Making far less a fuss is Great-Aunt Katherine, sitting stooped on a kitchen stool, her legs swinging like a girl's, chopping up red peppers for corn pudding.

If I were a cat, my ears would be up. I've just heard the phrase "Don Hume's daughter," and, I don't know why, all the ladies lean in and talk about the last time anyone saw her, and what she was wearing. Don Hume is a second or third cousin, a calculation I do not know how to think about. He is as old as cats, Great-Aunt Katherine says, and wears a plaid sport coat on the hottest day, along with a porkpie straw hat.

Whenever someone uses that much spit and eye-rolling to talk about sequins and high-cut skirts, I can tell the subject is one I need to know more about. I wonder if they ever talk about my clothes: "Blue jeans with embroidered butterflies across the fanny?"

Or maybe that's just my mother as I'm leaving the house for school. I've abandoned all the dresses and tailored jackets she has sewn for me, for peasant blouses and denim jackets, ripped bell bottoms and hoop earrings. I stopped getting haircuts and curling my hair, preferring it to fall in long waves down my back.

"Are you going out like that?" Whenever she asks this, and it's becoming a daily refrain, I stop moving. My hand is on the doorknob. I have my schoolbooks, and the bus will be at the bottom of the street to pick us up in two minutes or less.

It is the most pointless of questions, and the most poisonous. In six words, every bit of confidence I have in my clothing choices, hair, and ability to cover up the acne that splays across my chin, cheeks, and forehead vanishes.

I don't have an answer. As far as I'm concerned, she should be grateful. I'm still wearing a bra even though many girls at school are not. Every morning, I ignore a classmate's offer of her vodka-laced orange juice in a thermos during homeroom. Every day, all day long, I smile as I pass the stoner kids, offering me free weed, via a clumsy blunt.

I sing in the choir at school and church, get good grades, belong to Job's Daughters, practice piano, watch television with the rest of the family, read in my room, go to sleep. Going out like *this?* I am a good kid, and I know it.

At the farm, my father and uncles and other male relatives are gathered in lawn chairs under the shadiest tree, drinking beer all day and swatting houseflies. My brother is turning eighteen in the fall, so he's allowed to drink with them; I seem to be the only one who knows that he has been drinking since we moved to Minnesota, two years before.

All around the yard, cousins cluster for games and scatter at regular intervals throughout the day to go explore the farm, armed with rules: Don't climb in the hayloft, stay away from rotting wood, watch out for yellow jacket nests. I always thought "drinking and operating farm equipment" needed to be on that list. On a farm, a man can go from whole to crippled in one swipe of the scythe. A dairy cow can panic and kick the brains right out of a farmer's head. The loamiest pile of compost includes a harvest of maggots. Horrors, lurking everywhere. Bucolic.

When I was younger, I waded into cornfields where the corn was just a little taller than I was, enjoying the disorienting feeling of not really knowing the path back to the farmhouse. A truck on the road, or my grandmother ringing the bell for dinner, or one of the tractors returning to the barn ruined the reverie, but I loved feeling lost, alone, and without. Without family, without direction, without worry.

At the motel each night of the family reunion, my mother and father have drinks by the pool, so she's a little looser with information than she would be around her mother and sisters by day. One evening, I recognize the opportunity. I wait till my dad goes to the room to shower, and I ask.

If I once peppered her with questions about words and their meaning, I now want to know about relationships, and why certain details matter—like what Don Hume's daughter wears, and why my mother is so hung up on it.

My mother is a bit stuck on this, unsure of the territory. She tries to explain. "It's just that she's kind of trashy, Kim," she finally says. "She's young to be dressed that way."

"Well, why can't her mother tell her that? Don Hume's wife."

My mother takes a drag on a cigarette, leaving coral lipstick on its paper, and stares at me thoughtfully, exhaling smoke. She nods her head to herself, and seems to make up her mind.

"We call her Don Hume's daughter, right?" she asks.

"Yes," I reply, wondering where this is going.

"Well, do you know Jerry Lee Lewis?"

"Of course I do! 'Chantilly Lace'!"

She takes another long draw. "You know how Jerry Lee Lewis married a fourteen-year-old? That's what Don Hume did. He is married to her."

"To his daughter—what?"

"No, no. Hm, he married a very young girl. We call her his daughter when we're talking about him around you, but she's really his wife."

"Ewww." Younger than I am, married to a man my grandparents' age—this makes me queasy.

"I know. And actually, because you're asking me all these things, it makes me think we shouldn't gossip like that." My mother stubs out the half-smoked cigarette in the ashtray.

"I mean, she is trashy, but you're right, no one has told her, and maybe she didn't even have a mother who could let her know that kind of thing. We really know nothing about her. I don't even know if it's legal for them to be married."

"And they have sex?" I ask.

My mother drops her pack of smokes into her handbag. "God, Kimmy. You really can't talk like that about these things."

"Actually, I think it's way worse that we *never* talk about these things," I answer.

My freshly shaven father finds us there, and offers my mother a nightcap at the motel bar. She is relieved that we're done talking. "Remember?" she says as she is led away, giggling like a teenager, by my father. "The other cousins. Don't gossip."

When we arrive at the farm the next day at noon, we see that twelve picnic tables have been set up like a circle of wagons in the field just west of the farmhouse, gathered from all over New Market, population 401. In the center is a smoking pit, burial site of a hog that gave its life for the celebration.

I want to love this, the laying of the hog over coals and fragrant wood the day before, and the men tending it through the night, too. It was one of Great-Grandfather's tired old sows, which he'd slain and drained over a large bloody basin the day before the fire was laid. I had watched that process only once, years before.

By midafternoon, my aunts and cousins and too many women to count are streaming out of the house with piles of baked breads, salads, roasts, casseroles, pots of boiled potatoes, and mountains of steamed corn, carrying them to the circle of tables. Cousins and children of cousins dare each other to leap over the smoke pit.

My grandparents and uncles and all boys with strong shoulders and ready arms are emerging from the ice house with chunks of ice, soda pops, beers, and giant tubs of lemonade, heavily sweetened with sugar and covered with clean white cheesecloth, to keep the horseflies out. Despite some skepticism I'm clinging to, I recognize that it's as close to a barn raising as my family will ever get, where all the hands available are in service to the feeding of us all.

The spectacle, with the tassels across cornfields stirring with the wind, and the scent of the feast filling the air, and populated with people I love—I give myself over to it then.

Nellie, in the long sleeves of a sweatshirt and full denim overalls, stays close to my parents and rarely speaks to anyone else during the feasting. In fact, this is nothing new; she stopped talking months ago, keeping to her own room next to mine and playing the *Star Wars* soundtrack over and over.

I have learned to leave Nellie alone; in fact, in the two years since we moved, I began thinking that I had imagined something happened with Frank. I made it up, just like my parents say I do. I'm being dramatic. I'm exaggerating.

It faded. Except for the five days when we're at this reunion. We skirt away from Grandpa Frank. Nellie, at twelve, knows how to dodge him. I certainly do. I haven't let him kiss me in years, and even when they came up from Des Moines at Christmas, I patted him on the arm or the shoulder to avoid the hugs.

The scent of the smoked hog permeates every corner of the orchard, and out back, there's a line of laundry drying in the sun, sheets and pillowcases blowing in the wind, with the chit-chit-garble of the hens pecking around the yard, and just beyond that, the family cemetery, and always, always, a drift of manure.

I can only smell it when we arrive, because within the hour it has soaked into our clothes and hair and I won't notice it again until I take off my outfit at the motel. And then I'll notice it again when I unpack at home, a pile of laundry and the scent of the farm, and memories of this day, already long past.

At the end of the reunion, near the end of that night, it is Great-Grandmother Kendrick who enthralls us around the bonfire, telling the story we often beg her for, about poor Raleigh, and his grandmother Margaret. I sit next to my mother and listen, lean on her a little, and I cannot count the generations I have to go back to know who this story is about.

Years ago, Uncle Thaddeus told it to us the first time, but it was a small audience of captive children, on a hot summer day. I don't remember knowing him after that. I sure didn't notice when he died. He was someone from when I was four, and then he just faded from view, perhaps in a puff of vanilla-scented smoke.

Tonight, against the fire, we are all together, rushing the storyteller along yet trying to make her stop, wanting to absorb it all, wanting the ending where a boy is ripped in two, the ending we already know.

It is told in a hush—there are always those who have not heard it yet, it is hands down the most horrible thing that has ever happened to any member of my family, and without the storytelling, we would not know about it.

Something so terrible, and the only thing to keep it alive is the oxygen of the words, in a certain order, with a certain cadence, repeated by one of us. Told in a way to make us listen, told so we always know what is true.

No one tells it the way our great-grandmother does, though, because she was one of the children there, when *it* happened, or maybe her mother was. That's what I mean about keeping families straight, but they have moving parts, like someone's son is someone else's father, and he's a brother, too, and then an uncle to somebody's children, somewhere. Kinship is a knitted piece, or maybe it's crochet. The one with the loops, I suppose.

"That's who the Castles were," she says, she always says at the end. "That's the story of who we were."

We all stand up with satisfied sighs and walk away. The women move toward long tables of chicken carcasses and stripped hog bones, or empty bowls and platters, of scraped-through egg salads, drying out on trays, wilted gelatin molds, and now slimy greens, turned to mush by time, temperature, and the acid of the dressings.

The stars disappear behind clouds and fireflies fade; the children's play is muted, as it would be indoors at church on a snowy evening, on the other side of the year.

My brother pokes a few sticks into the fire and watches them blaze up, lighting our faces for a moment. The other boys and men move toward the plastic coolers to pull cold bottles out of the rustle of melted ice, in water with dead bugs that flew too close, or twigs so lightweight that even the smallest breeze sent them toward the ground.

My sister, so awkward, looks at me, her eyes glistening in the light of the flames, her red curls dark and matted with sweat on her neck and around her face. I move closer to her, watching her take a great shuddering breath. She is not a child, with those eyes, and not a grown woman either. I feel her in-betweenness as I once felt my own, growing more into some pear shape in fourth grade before I got taller and my breasts and hips started to balance out. Her overalls fit her like a snowsuit gone small.

"The story of 'who we were,'" she repeats, her voice soft and stuttering, for my ears only. This is how she communicates now, stumbled whispers where once she had words, and usually only directed at me. I put my hand on her arm in kinship, but she yanks it away, as if in pain, and I see that stripes of rust—dried blood—have come through the fabric.

"Do you cut yourself?" I ask, alarmed.

"It doesn't matter," she says. What does she mean about the story? It always ends in the same way. Nellie puts her hands deep into her pockets, resting under her belly, which looks sort of like a beer drinker's paunch. No one is talking about her weight gain, in the way that no adult talks about anything important in front of us, still children by their measure, but things happen whether you give them words or not.

She is not even a teen, and yet she is as gruff as an old woman, and I can see she's swaying slightly, her face shiny, and she smells of warm beer. As if it's been splashed on her like a perfume. It's too hot for overalls and the long sleeves even in the cooler night air, when everyone else is dressed in tank tops and shorts and sandals and smelling of bug spray.

I really look at my sister for the first time in months, and I see what has been done to her. I don't wait for her to answer. I have answers. Not all of them. But what I have is descending at once. Like a flare exploding overhead, bringing the landscape into flickering but certain clarity. No more smoke. It settles on me like a weight.

All the adults are walking away. Why are the adults always walking away? The ladies move toward the kitchen. Inside are dishes, congealed food, silverware, and more, all to be washed, and dried, and put away. There are tablecloths to wash, counters to wipe down, a floor to mop. All my life I have been comforted by the ordinary gestures of daily upkeep.

Now, they are obscene.

"If you have something to say, you go ahead," I tell Nellie, and reach for her elbows, on either side of her swollen belly, to pull her close so she can see my face in the darkness. "You say it."

I don't know all of it, but the some that I know? It's deadly.

Her nod, defiance in the tilt of her chin, unknowable sadness in her eyes, makes my knees weak. It is the look in the horse's eyes before it's put down with a shot to its head. It knows what is about to happen, and for it, the terror is past.

For my sister, it's all over now. Whatever she has faced, she's not afraid. And I don't think she's the one going down.

In a lifetime of the great unspoken things, this one should not be hers to keep. I see her at age six, quietly shuffling up the steps from the basement workshop, with damp blood and whatever else on her underwear.

We tease her for the way she grunts at us and won't talk. We don't see the monster in the corner threatening her.

I move my palms from her elbows to lie flat on her stomach. She puts her hands over mine and guides me down the denim to a lump, a bump, a tiny foot that responds to my pressure with a feisty kick. Flesh and bone and pain, twisted up inside her.

The crackling of the bonfire is all I hear.

Her eyes travel over to the orchard, the branches strung with Christmas lights.

Her gaze lands on the men, hoisting beer cans under the leaves of the apple trees, and all of them are horrifying to me, in that queasy way when you've seen half a caterpillar in the salad, or a worm in an apple. You know it's all infested, it's all ruined, there is no way to unsee it.

"He always asks if I have my period yet," Nellie says as we watch Grandpa Jenkins show Paul how to knock off a beer lid by snapping the bottle against the bark of the tree.

I look at him, and I want to fly at him. I have known, in some tip-of-the-tongue kind of way, for years but these words turn the world inside out. I'm white hot with anger and too full of questions, as if answers could ever explain anything. "I'll kill him," I say.

She tugs at my arm. No. I bend over with my hands on my knees to clear some lightheadedness. I peer up at her eyes, red-rimmed and fringed by rusty lashes.

"Why?" I say. "Why didn't you tell someone?"

"Because." She scoffs. I suddenly feel like the younger one.

"No, come on. Why didn't you just tell Mom and Dad. Or me?"

Her jaw is shaking, her teeth are chattering. Her hushed words, from those beautiful rosebud lips, rush at me like the shuddering steam of something about to explode.

"He said he'll hurt you if I tell."

I am dizzy from the heft and force of it, and of what she has done for me. Does for me.

"I'm sorry," I whisper, and those words dissolve, without meaning, because they are that useless.

"It's okay," she answers softly. "I feel, maybe, strong. It's bad, what he does, but I make sure it isn't worse." Her eyes brighten, the firelight reflecting in her deep brown irises. "I like protecting you. It's what I think of."

"Mom!" I shout. I am seeing black gnats, like spots. "Mom!" I stand up straight, keeping my eyes locked on Nellie.

My father jerks around, away from the men. Never known for being acute about his children, my father at this moment is utterly tuned in and striding toward us. Our parents are at their best when they sense impending doom, anxious not to miss whatever emergency we are about to declare.

The alarm quickly spreads to any other mothers within earshot. If you need help, yell "Mom!" into a crowd. Someone will answer.

The women come out from the kitchen, wiping their hands on towels, peering at us in the distance, in the dark. All of them begin coming toward us, as if gathering for another family story they can't wait to hear.

They are circling the fire, and I put Nellie in front of me, and wrap her shoulders in my arms, and put my lips near her ears. She is trembling, her breathing almost hiccups, and she is such a narrow thing, despite the bulk around her waist. Her cheeks are scarlet, and her neck is moist from the heat of her clothing, or maybe the Iowa humidity, not yet dried off by the evening breeze. It's too close, the air. Like a storm is coming.

My mother turns at my call, stopping before she can light a cigarette, snapping her lighter closed and taking us in. Her eyes grow wide, and she gasps. Maybe it's the bonfire or me next to Nellie creating some measurable normal, but everyone sees her as if for the first time.

My mother is unsteady as she approaches us. But Nellie's own shaking quiets, I can feel it, as soon she is next to my mother.

"Grandpa Jenkins," Nellie begins. "He—he put me on his, on his lap, when I was six." My mother has gone still, so still, absorbing the words. "He always wants to know if I have my monthlies," Nellie adds, and her voice is loud and sure. Grandma Jenkins is the only other person who has ever used that phrase about menstruation.

Grandpa Jenkins draws off a swig of beer as he walks toward us, and the sight of the skin under his chin waggling as he swallows sickens me. He is absolutely unaware of his own evil.

Grandma Jenkins sways a bit, then stiffens. "You stopped! You promised!" she shouts at Frank. "Goddammit, Frank! Goddammit!" and she never swears and her children are surprised and I heard my brother's nervous giggle. She is flushed, with her fists clenched up by her chest, and looks ready to pummel him. And then instantly backs away when he angrily grabs her sleeve. It's the most violent thing I've ever seen. I am stunned that Grandma knew. I am repulsed by them both.

"Hold on there, sister," he says, all but sneering. "That little girl has got nothing to say. Nothing."

My father approaches from behind them, grappling with a switch of applewood that has come into his hand, and raises it high over his head.

I can feel the intake of breath of every spectator there, hoping for easy violence to cure this awful despair. And why not?

I want to kill Grandpa. I want to will him into oblivion, and wipe away all he has done, I want to wrap up the little girls and little boys in bunting and whisper stories into their ears, that bogeymen aren't real, and fairness prevails, and nightmares may hover around their sleep pillows, but never crush their days. But those are the lies I've been told, and a breeze like a whisper tells of the brewing storm, and something more.

This is my heaven, right here, with you.

No more than a few seconds pass, but I feel the air pressing on me like an airplane at takeoff, and my ears are aching.

"Dad," I call, moving past Grandpa Jenkins. "Dad, not this. Don't." I approach him and grab the applewood from his hand. His eyes are wide and curious, watching me already on to the next thing.

I have never been in charge of anything, but I know what to do.

No one moves. No one breathes. Amid all the fear hissing and sparking in the bonfire, where was the simple homely love that Margaret Castle brought from over Memory Way when the boy Raleigh breathed his last? Why couldn't that be a salve, the salvation, and why is all the anger just leeching out of me? I, for one, am tired of being tossed on the ever-changing waves created by adults who, it turns out, have no clue what they are doing, and are just making it worse.

I pull myself up church straight, and move toward my grandpa. My legs feel as heavy as in any dream. It is like swimming through humidity. And he—he ignores me because, by his measure, I can't do a thing about him.

I kick his shin as hard as I can. "Get yourself out of here, you old fuck," I say as he yelps.

He pulls back his fist, and I can't even grasp how angry he is, at *me*. "Now listen, sister," he sputters, indignant. I am calm. I put up my own hand, right in front of his blue-veined nose and angry raisin eyes.

"Yes, you! Get out now!" I stand there until he moves, switch in hand. He grumbles, and then turns in the direction of Grandma Jenkins, who starts to follow him.

"Grandma!" I say warningly.

"Mom," my mother says in almost the same breath, holding Nellie's hand and reaching for her own mother.

"Phyllis Kendrick Jenkins!" my great-grandmother snorts. "I am sick with shame that I ever let you go with that man all those years ago. You stay here. Enough is enough."

"Mom," my mother says again, grabbing her mother's arm with urgency, and something like begging in her voice. Grandma Jenkins is my favorite of all the grandparents, the one I love the most no matter how unfair it is. I'd said so, back when I took them to show and tell. Back when I was five. But she knew about him. She did. That changes things.

My mother fixes herself into the ground. "If you go now, Mom, you don't have any of us left. Not one. You don't. Please don't."

"Connie, I—" Grandma Jenkins says, shivering with the meaning of my mother's words. She covers her face, and begins to low like an old cow. It turns into some kind of gasping, then blossoms into crying, the only kind of crying that counts.

We are startled by the honk of the Buick's horn. And at that, Nellie acts. She drops my mother's hand to wrap Grandma Jenkins in her arms, to keep her close, to marry her to the rest of us. Nellie, who always leaned in when she was little, tucks Grandma into her bulky form till the moment passes.

Great-Aunt Katherine bursts out of the screen door, a wraith in a long white nightgown, her arms flapping like a choirmaster's. For the first time ever, I witness her without her prosthetics. Her swaying bosom is gone, and she is as flat and flailing, a one-eyed child and twice as compelling.

"I don't like any of this, none of it!" she screeches. "Where's that old devil?" She practically gallops to the driver's window of his car and pounds on it till I think it has to break. It inspires Grandpa Jenkins to throw the car in reverse and send up all kinds of white gravel as he speeds out of the driveway.

"Good riddance. He gives rubbish a bad name." Great-Aunt Katherine finds her way to Nellie's side, separating her from Grandma Jenkins, and looks upon her gravely.

"Look here!" she exclaims. "Oh, my God, child! Where does it hurt?"

Nellie is sweating from the top of her head, her face puckered up in pain. "She's poorly, Milt. Will you give me a hand?" says Great-Aunt Katherine.

Nellie abruptly vomits into the ground. My father wipes her mouth with his bare hand, then wipes that hand on his pants. My immaculately tidy father. He lifts her into his arms, just as he did when her appendix had to come out. He kisses her forehead, her stink, her sweat, and begins walking rapidly toward the farmhouse.

There is a hush that happens in the five minutes before the rain comes. And in that time, before anyone hears a plop of rain, sending up the scent of growth and decay, no one remembers to breathe. The universe does not stop, but its sigh is beyond our ears, and it's sacred. Then one drop of rain hits the ground and you start counting. One. Two. Ten. You count faster. But there's a hundred, and then the downpour. And in trying to keep count, you don't notice that something as big as a bonfire has gone out, melting into a damp and smoky heap.

Nellie and my father disappear into the kitchen with Great-Aunt Katherine, followed by Great-Grandmother Kendrick. I want to go inside, to bright lights, and soap. My mother, standing with me in new streams of mud, seems unaware that we are soaked. I pull her along with me. Grandma Jenkins looks at me, beseechingly, and I cock my head toward the house.

Somehow, I am still in charge. And they come along with me.

Paul is watchful, sipping on a beer, holding back. At the kitchen door, he glances back in the direction of the driveway.

"Jesus," he says to me. "Jesus. Grandpa."

"I know." I push my mother inside.

"Did you know?" he says. "Did Mom and Dad?"

"Like a piece of a dream, or a sound in the wall," I answer. "We thought—I thought—it wasn't real." We push open the screen door.

"I thought Dad was going to cream him," he says, almost admiringly.

In the glare of the kitchen, Great-Grandmother Kendrick, who has birthed calves, babies, and sheep alike, times out Nellie's cramping, and determines warm milk is the answer for this turn of events. Great-Aunt Katherine has located an old cot to put in the keeping room off the kitchen, more of a pantry, and Nellie is laid out and coddled while they wash her arms with Ivory soap, and the cuts dyed with iodine. I am comforted by this, that her wounds are attended to, the ones we can see.

When her moans get louder and more terrible, we're all asked to step out to the screened porch, my father, Paul, and me.

I don't go.

I know where the bowl is and I fill it with soapy water, and carry it like the elements of communion to the keeping room.

I'm not my sister, but I will stay with her in this moment, the best I can do, and plan how to lift her away, to give her a glimpse of it like a mountain in a rearview mirror. She will survive Grandpa Jenkins.

That feeling of never being able to hold on to things—I think I already see my family in my past. Right now. Smaller, smaller, smaller, till they are out of sight. *Heaven is right here, with you. It fills me up.*

On a farm, there is blood everywhere, and no child is very alarmed by it.

On a farm, births and deaths mark time better than a calendar or seasons. Sometimes a birth and a death happen in the same moment, and that's what happens with Nellie's little boy. There are bloody rags in a basin and his still form is wrapped lightly in clean white dish towels. Everyone is crying, and Nellie, too, more exhausted than any child should be.

On a farm, some seeds take, and others don't. Transplants take, and quicken, or they droop. A calf comes out whole and giddy, or still as stone. A baby dying because it's too young to be born—that's as natural to the heartbeat of a farm as the sun rising and falling each day.

On a farm you pray for rain when it's dry, sun when it's been too wet to run machinery on mud, clouds on the days you're plowing, wind in the spring to carry pollen across the crops. It's a very practical kind of praying, and now, though I don't know what they are thinking, no one says God, no one says sin, and in one way or another, they indicate through shrug and glance that this is all for the best.

And then, in the morning twilight, while most of the relatives sleep off the bonfire and let a few hours and rain soften the evening's sharp edges, my great-grandmother Kendrick locates a beautiful dress, long and trailing as widow's weeds, a buttery white from a hundred years of baptisms, heartbreakingly tiny in the shoulders, sewn for a baby.

In the morning twilight, ladies like murmuring doves surround the basin. Great-Grandma Kendrick tests the water on her wrist even though it doesn't matter, and then washes tiny fingernails, and ears like silk blossoms, and she fits out the little boy. Great-Aunt Katherine donates the fine old wooden box her false bosoms rest in at night, and lines it with a scrap from the quilting bin, crushed velvet the dusty color of a faded rose.

Fingers of light spread over the fields in the east, and the night is scrubbed clean, leaving a properly contrite group, tending to our dead. In this, they know what to do and I am learning. When they close up the box, over soft sighs, I reckon the baby has given us grace.

In the parlor, the room my great-grandmother never uses, we find a pile of blankets and pillows contributed by every other guest in the house. It's growing light, but no one is ready to leave this moment. In time, I hear my father snoring, as his mother does, as I probably will one day, and Paul is nestled in a corner, limp from beer and the night. I listen to the very early morning tick away with the help of an old clock on the mantle.

It's not too long before I give up all rest and go to find my mother in the keeping room, where she is watching Nellie sleep. She has lines under her red and swollen eyes, moving like an old lady as she stands up to kiss me. She's in someone's faded old nightgown and her feet are bare. I sit cross-legged on the ground, my eyes almost level with the cot.

She puts the back of her hand on Nellie's forehead, and my sister, startled awake, sits up on her elbows. My mother cups my sister's jaw, tracing her chin with a trembling thumb.

"Oh, my girl," she says.

My mother probably won't sleep for the rest of her life, but the way she looks at Nellie tells me she sees us. It is all I need, and I lean back against a pantry shelf and feel at home. In a childhood of presents and parties, gifts and big gestures, vacations we couldn't pay for and new cars in the driveway that make dinners silent and tense, and in the dresses she sews for us while my father orders bespoke suits with the Castle monogram sewn into the silk lining, perhaps this is our happy ending.

My mother rustles around and locates the pack of cigarettes she has tucked into a pocket of the nightgown, and smokes till the sun is high in the sky.

Acknowledgments

In a classroom of my ten-year-old's dreams, there would be my kindred spirit and literary agent, Mary Krienke; Samia Fakih, who puts up with me when things get messy; Mike, who was always more than just a neighbor to our family and Jennifer Campbell Brown and Sandra Jordan, who wanted the horror stories; Amy Grantham, the gremlin who will see us all through the apocalypse; and Jan, the very best version of a human being and who I want to be when I grow up. They all understand me at the molecular level and I thank them. It's rare.

ABOUT THE AUTHOR

Born in Iowa and raised in Minnesota, Kimberly Olson Fakih first glimpsed New York in black-and-white movies on the late, late show and moved there when she was twenty-one. It was there, against a backdrop of limestone and brownstone, amid tall buildings and shadowed canyons, while she went to work in children's book publishing at Harper & Row, and married, and had a child, and became a freelance writer and then the editor of *Kirkus Reviews*, that she began to hear the whispers from the fields, farms, and lakes where she grew up and began to piece together family half-truths and memories. She has written several books for children, but *Little Miseries* is her adult debut.

She writes at a 250-year-old pine desk she inherited from her late husband in a sunny apartment near the East River in Manhattan.